PRAISE FOR PAUL LEVINE

BUM LUCK

"A one-sit, must-read novel full of memorable characters and unforgettable vignettes. Levine's pacing is perfect as always, and the pages just fly by, even as he juggles multiple plots with his own unique aplomb. Put *Bum Luck* at the top of your reading list."
—Bookreporter.com

"A gripping and often quite an amusing thriller with a surprising climax, all of which is built around an intriguing cast of characters as it achieves an almost flawless rhythm."
—BookPleasures.com

"Paul Levine continues his trademark brisk pacing with timely storytelling and well-placed humor. *Bum Luck* is elevated further by teaming Jake with Steve Solomon and Victoria Lord. The trio make an unstoppable team—concerned about the law, but even more about people."
—*South Florida Sun-Sentinel*

BUM RAP

"The pages fly by and the laughs keep coming in this irresistible South Florida crime romp. A delicious mix of thriller and comic crime novel."
—*Booklist* (starred review)

"Levine effectively blends a puzzling crime, intelligent sleuthing, adroit courtroom maneuvering, and a surprising attraction between Victoria and Jake in this welcome addition to both series."
—*Publishers Weekly*

"Ebulliently seamless melding of Levine's two legal-eagles series."
—*Kirkus Reviews*

TO SPEAK FOR THE DEAD

"Move over Scott Turow. *To Speak for the Dead* is courtroom drama at its very best."
—Larry King

"An assured and exciting piece of work. Jake Lassiter is Travis McGee with a law degree . . . One of the best mysteries of the year."
—*Los Angeles Times*

"Paul Levine is guilty of master storytelling in the first degree. *To Speak for the Dead* is a fast, wry, and thoroughly engrossing thriller."
—Carl Hiaasen

NIGHT VISION

"Levine's fiendish ability to create twenty patterns from the same set of clues will have you waiting impatiently for his next novel."
—*Kirkus Reviews*

"Sparkles with wit and subtlety."
—*Toronto Star*

"Breathlessly exciting."
—*Cleveland Plain Dealer*

FALSE DAWN

"Realistic, gritty, fun."
—*New York Times Book Review*

"A highly entertaining yarn filled with wry humor."
—*Detroit Free Press*

"A dazzler, extremely well-written and featuring so many quotable passages you'll want someone handy to read them aloud to."
—*Ellery Queen's Mystery Magazine*

MORTAL SIN

"Take one part John Grisham, two parts Carl Hiaasen, throw in a dash of John D. MacDonald, and voila! You've got *Mortal Sin*."
—*Tulsa World*

"Recalling the work of Carl Hiaasen, this thriller races to a smashing climax."
—*Library Journal*

"Wonderfully funny, sexy, and terrifying."
—Dave Barry

RIPTIDE

"A thriller as fast as the wind. A bracing rush, as breathtaking as hitting the Gulf waters on a chill December morning."
—*Tampa Tribune*

"Filled with smart writing and smart remarks. Jake is well on his way to becoming a star in the field of detective fiction."
—*Dallas Morning News*

"A well-focused plot that stresses in-depth characterization and action that is more psychological than macho. The author keeps the suspense high with innovative twists."
—*Atlanta Journal Constitution*

LASSITER

"Since Robert Parker is no longer with us, I'm nominating Levine for an award as best writer of dialogue in the grit-lit genre."
—*San Jose Mercury News*

"Lassiter is back after fourteen long years—and better than ever. Moving fast, cracking wise, butting heads, he's the lawyer we all want on our side—and on the page."
—Lee Child

"Few writers can deliver tales about sex and drugs in South Florida better than Levine."
—*Booklist*

SOLOMON VS. LORD

"A funny, fast-paced legal thriller. The barbed dialogue makes for some genuine laugh-out-loud moments. Fans of Carl Hiaasen and Dave Barry will enjoy this humorous Florida crime romp."
—*Publishers Weekly*

"The writing makes me think of Janet Evanovich out to dinner with John Grisham."
—Mysterylovers.com

"Hiaasen meets Grisham in the court of last retort. A sexy, wacky, wonderful thriller with humor and heart."
—Harlan Coben

THE DEEP BLUE ALIBI

"An entertaining, witty comedy caper with legal implications . . . sparkles with promise, humor, and more than a dash of suspense."
—Blogcritics.com

"A cross between *Moonlighting* and *Night Court* . . . courtroom drama has never been this much fun."
—Freshfiction.com

"As hilarious as *The Deep Blue Alibi* is, it is almost possible between the cleverly molded characters and sharp dialogue to overlook that the novel contains a terrific mystery, one that will keep you guessing."
—Bookreporter.com

KILL ALL THE LAWYERS

"A clever, colorful thriller . . . with characters drawn with a fine hand, making them feel more like friends than figments of the author's imagination. Levine ratchets up the tension with each development but never neglects the heart of the story—his characters."
—*Publishers Weekly* (starred review)

"Levine skillfully blends humor, a view of Miami, and the legal system into tidy plots."
—*South Florida Sun-Sentinel*

"Another successful fast-moving, highly entertaining mystery. Irreverent to juveniles, judges, and the judicial system, but does it all with a wink. Encore . . . encore."
—*ReviewingTheEvidence.com*

HABEAS PORPOISE

"Steve Solomon and Victoria Lord are smart and funny and sexy in a way that Hollywood movies were before comedies became crass and teen-oriented."
—*Connecticut Post*

"A *Moonlighting* crime novel. Great fun."
—*Lansing State Journal*

"Entertaining and witty with lots of laughs."
—*MysteriousReviews.com*

IMPACT

"A breakout book, highly readable and fun with an irresistible momentum, helped along by Levine's knowledge of the Supreme Court and how it works."
—*USA TODAY*

"Sizzles the Supreme Court as it has never been sizzled before, even by Grisham."
—F. Lee Bailey

"A masterfully written thriller, coiled spring tight. The plot is
relentless. I loved it!"
—Michael Palmer

BALLISTIC

"*Ballistic* is *Die Hard* in a missile silo. Terrific!"
—Stephen J. Cannell

"It's easy to compare Levine to Tom Clancy but I think he's better
for two simple reasons—he's a better storyteller and his characters are
more believable, good guys and bad guys alike."
—Ed Gorman

ILLEGAL

"Levine is one of the few thriller authors who can craft a plot filled
with suspense while still making the readers smile at the characters'
antics."
—*Chicago Sun-Times*

"The seamy side of smuggling human cargo is deftly exposed by the
clear and concise writing of the Edgar Award–nominated author.
Illegal is highly recommended."
—*Midwest Book Review*

"Timely, tumultuous, and in a word, terrific."
—*Providence Journal*

BUM
DEAL

BOOKS BY PAUL LEVINE

THE JAKE LASSITER SERIES

To Speak for the Dead

Night Vision

False Dawn

Mortal Sin

Riptide

Fool Me Twice

Flesh & Bones

Lassiter

Last Chance Lassiter

State vs. Lassiter

THE SOLOMON & LORD SERIES

Solomon vs. Lord

The Deep Blue Alibi

Kill All the Lawyers

Habeas Porpoise

LASSITER, SOLOMON & LORD SERIES

Bum Rap

Bum Luck

Bum Deal

Stand-Alone Thrillers

Impact

Ballistic

Illegal

Paydirt

BUM DEAL

PAUL LEVINE

THOMAS & MERCER

Text copyright © 2018 by Nittany Valley Productions, Inc.
All rights reserved.

Published by Thomas & Mercer, Seattle

www.apub.com

Amazon, the Amazon logo, and Thomas & Mercer are trademarks of Amazon.com, Inc., or its affiliates.

ISBN-13: 9781503951716
ISBN-10: 1503951715

Cover design by Ray Lundgren

Printed in the United States of America

For Stuart Grossman,
trial lawyer extraordinaire and the brother I never had.

"I'm not moldering. My paint's not peeling off. I'm good for years!"
　　—Henry II *in The Lion in Winter by James Goldman*

"The young man knows the rules, but the old man knows the exceptions."
　　　　　　　　　　—Oliver Wendell Holmes Sr.

-1-

Bedroom Games

The surgeon laced his fingers and cracked his knuckles, a concert pianist preparing to tackle Tchaikovsky. "I could strangle you with one hand, sweetheart." His voice soft and seductive.

"You're pathetic." She spat out the words. "Worms have more backbone."

He wrapped his right hand around her neck, just below the chin. "I'll shatter your hyoid bone, watch your eyes pop."

"Worm!"

A low growl came from his throat. "I'll laugh as your tongue shoots out of your filthy mouth. You'll look like a dead raccoon. Roadkill!"

"How many men have I screwed since we've been married? Take a guess, Dr. Worm."

Puzzled, he studied her. Same pouty lips, same dark eyes glistening like hot lava. But the insults? This was something new.

"Or just count them on your fingers," she taunted him. "Whoops! You'll need your toes, too."

He blinked. "What's this? A twist in the game?"

"Every man better than you."

PAUL LEVINE

His fingers found her carotid artery. He tightened his grip, and a wet noise like the growl of a small dog caught in her throat. His left hand shot forward, and now both hands encircled her neck.

"Getting excited, worm? Going to . . . ?" A guttural sound choked off the words.

He was becoming aroused, as he figured she wanted. He eased the pressure, let her grab a greedy breath, then squeezed again. Pink streaks colored her cheeks like a sunset over the Gulf.

"You look lovely, sweetheart," he said. "No need for blush today."

A gurgle came from her throat.

"Are you ready?" he asked.

She didn't answer. Couldn't answer.

Three more times, he squeezed and released. The fourth time, he squeezed and didn't release.

She lost consciousness, her eyes rolling back in her head.

It had happened once before. He had used simple CPR—chest compressions and mouth-to-mouth—to revive her. Afterward, her ribs were sore, and bruises the color of eggplants kept her from nude sunbathing for a week.

He scooped her up and tossed her onto the bed. A 107-pound rag doll. What was that crap about other men? She'd never said anything like that before. It broke the rules—wasn't part of the game. Why was she trying to provoke him?

He examined her neck. Red-and-purple striations. She would be furious tomorrow.

If tomorrow ever came.

-2-

The Sunny Side of Justice

When my cell phone rang, I figured someone was dead. Nah, I don't have ESP. I have caller ID.

State Attorney Raymond Pincher on the line. That could mean several things, many involving a corpse. Maybe a client of mine, out on bail, was machine-gunning tourists in the Fontainebleau lobby. That's one of my recurring nightmares.

Civilians think that criminal defense lawyers are cold-blooded mercenaries, carrying our spears into battle for killers, con men, and crooks of every stripe. But we get the night sweats over the consequences of our actions. Or at least I do.

"Jake Lassiter, you damn fool!" Pincher greeted me. "What the hell's wrong with you?"

"Where oh where should I begin, Ray?"

We'd been friendly antagonists for years, sparring in court and in the boxing ring at the Riverfront Athletic Club. But no more fisticuffs for me. For the last year, I've been under doctors' orders to avoid blows to the head. Too many concussions going back to my playing days at Penn State, where I was a starting linebacker, and with the Miami

Dolphins, where I was an unguided missile on the suicide squads when I wasn't warming the bench.

"Phil Flury intends to file a Bar complaint against you," Pincher said.

"Aw, let him, the little weasel."

I leaned back in my chair and admired the view of a placid Biscayne Bay in the fading light. I was drinking solo on the patio at the Red Fish Grill at Matheson Hammock, a couple miles south of my Coconut Grove home. An easterly breeze kicked up sand from the beach and ruffled the palm trees a few feet from my table.

I was sipping tequila, Don Julio 1942, and I could feel the warm Mexican sun in my belly, but Pincher was fast becoming Mr. Buzzkill.

"You punched Flury!" he thundered. "You can't strike an assistant state attorney, Jake. It's a felony."

"I only poked him with my index finger to make a point."

"He's got a bruise on his chest."

"Dainty little thing, isn't he?"

My pals Steve Solomon and Victoria Lord were supposed to join me for dinner but, as usual, were late. They had something important to tell me, had even offered to treat me to pan-fried snapper. I assumed the deal also included some top-shelf tequila.

"Flury thinks you're psychotic," Pincher said.

"He withheld a witness statement favorable to my client."

"He denies it."

"Lying prick!" I must have raised my voice, because an elderly couple at a nearby table shot me dirty looks. "Flury violated *Brady versus Maryland*. Ever hear of it, Ray?"

At the other end of the line, Pincher sighed, then said, "You still undergoing treatment?"

"Injections of God-knows-what. Plus, hyperbaric oxygen therapy."

"So how's your . . . ?"

4

He left it hanging, so I said, "Drain bamage. All gone. I'm tip-top. A-OK. Ready to ride, got a glide in my stride."

Deflect and evade. So much simpler than describing all those medical tests and illnesses with unpronounceable names.

"I never thought you had brain damage," Pincher said.

"Excellent news. I'll fire my doctors and cancel my therapy."

"Those symptoms of yours. Irritability. Irrational behavior. Unprovoked anger. That's not CTE. You're burned-out—that's all. You need a change of scenery."

I sipped at the tequila. Rich and smooth, liquid gold. Maybe a hint of licorice in the agave. "Burned-out, sure. I've been toting my briefcase from courtroom to courtroom for more than twenty years. Who wouldn't be a little scorched around the edges?"

"Only because you've been on the wrong side too long."

"Not my fault most of my clients are guilty."

"That sad old song of the defense bar."

"If our clients knew our real winning percentage, they'd jump bail and flee to Argentina."

"Maybe it's time to do something about it."

"What? Only represent innocent clients? I'd starve. Sure, I'd prefer a cause that's just, a client I like, and a check that doesn't bounce. But these days, I'm happy with a client who doesn't steal the potted ferns in my waiting room."

Strands of miniature white lights wrapped around the palm trees blinked on. The sun was setting behind me, the horizon tinted the reddish gold of a ripe peach.

"Tell me something, Jake," Pincher said. "Is there any defendant you won't represent?"

"Only those my granny calls bottom-feeding gutter rats. Men who abuse children or women."

"In those cases, you'd rather be on the sunny side of justice—wouldn't you, Jake?"

"Sorry to break it to you, Ray, but the criminal justice system is nothing but dark nights and dangerous alleys."

"Not on my side of the street. I represent the people of the great state of Florida."

"Good for you, pal."

"You may not realize it, Jake, but you're a natural-born prosecutor."

I laughed and nearly spilled my drink. "The hell I am. My heart's with the little guy, not the behemoth of the state."

"Really?" He chuckled at the other end of the line. "Do you believe in the fundamental goodness of humanity?"

"After serving purgatory in the so-called Justice Building, how could I?"

"Exactly! You know the evil that lurks in men's hearts. You've seen it, as I have. You know how many nights I've sat at my desk with a bottle of bourbon and a stack of murder scene photos?"

"Who are we talking about here, Ray? You or me?"

"Both of us, but you're the one perched on the precipice. One faulty step, you'll plunge into the abyss."

"Not following you."

"I'm offering you wings to fly away."

"Meaning what? When you called, I thought someone was dead."

"Someone is. A woman."

"Yeah?"

"I want you to prosecute her husband."

-3-

Los Tres Amigos

Roughly ninety seconds after I hung up with the State Attorney, Steve Solomon and Victoria Lord—spilling apologies—hustled onto the restaurant patio. I stood and kissed Victoria on the cheek and clopped Solomon on the shoulder. Hard. He clopped me back. Harder. We're guys. It's what we do.

"Sorry, sorry, sorry," Solomon said. "But it's Vic's fault."

"Motion to suppress in federal court ran late," Victoria pleaded in her own defense. "We'll win if Judge Sachs follows the law."

"I give you a twenty percent chance," I said.

Solomon plopped into his chair, and Victoria elegantly swiveled into hers. The server immediately delivered a Moscow Mule—vodka, ginger beer, and lime—in a copper mug for Victoria and a Funky Buddha beer for Solomon. I had placed their order in advance, and Solomon saluted me with the bottle.

"Jake, my man, you remembered." He sniffed the brew, so dark it was nearly ebony, and smacked his lips. "I do appreciate the Buddha's maple-syrup aroma with that hint of bacon and coffee."

"That's not a beer," I said. "It's a smorgasbord."

He gave me the sideways smile that always preceded a dig. "It occurs to me, Jake, that we have virtually nothing in common, except we both love Victoria."

"You love Victoria. I simply like Victoria. A lot."

"And you and I, Jake, are best friends." He took a hearty swig of his beer.

"You're a pest and a nuisance. You're the aggravating friend I am most likely to kill."

"Boys, please," Victoria said. "Jake, how are you feeling?"

"Why does everyone keep asking?"

Solomon shrugged. "I dunno. Maybe because you're brain damaged."

"I'm fine."

No way would I whine about my condition and get buried by two tons of sympathy like sand from a dump truck.

"Are you still seeing those bursts of light?" Victoria asked.

"Perfectly normal. They're UFOs."

"Jake . . ." Her tone schoolmarmish.

"Let him alone, Vic." Solomon rose to my defense. "Jake's old-school. A man's man. Never complains. Doesn't run to a shrink to find out why his daddy never came to his Little League games."

"He was dead. Knifed in a bar fight in Islamorada."

"I know, pal. Just a figure of speech. All I'm saying, you're a throwback."

"A brew-and-burger guy in a pâté-and-chardonnay world," Victoria agreed.

"Jake still helps little old ladies across the street," Solomon pitched in.

"And tall young ones." Victoria chuckled.

"I'm happy you two kids find me so amusing. But I'm not ashamed to have old habits and old values."

"And old clothes." Solomon gestured with his beer. "Your suits are so out-of-date they're practically back in style."

"So sue me, Solomon. Then have your kale salad and meditate an hour before your Pilates class."

This was our usual patter. I'm the third wheel on the tricycle. Sometimes I wonder why Solomon and Lord hang out with me. They're in their midthirties, and I'm fifty. Middle-aged, if I make it to an even 100 or 102, which seems increasingly unlikely with every doctor's appointment. We're all criminal defense lawyers, or at least I was, until ten minutes ago when I was offered a job as a specially appointed prosecutor for one case. I told Pincher I would give him my answer in the morning. Oh, how Solomon will roast me if I take that gig.

Victoria Lord was an Ivy Leaguer with cool smarts. Tall and blonde, the word *regal* sometimes came to mind. She likes rosé and ballet. Dark-haired and wiry, Solomon is in constant motion. He favors beef jerky and ridiculous beers. In court, Victoria plays by the book, and Solomon burns the book. Despite their differences—or perhaps because of them—they make a powerful trial team.

I've taught them a few of my moves in front of the bench. I've told Solomon a hundred times to stop jitterbugging across the well of the courtroom.

"Plant your legs shoulder-width apart, and stand there, motionless, solid as an oak. Force the judge and jury to hear your words, not watch your dance moves."

Victoria was easier to coach because she was a natural advocate. Smart and focused. In the beginning, like a lot of young women lawyers, she erred on the side of caution.

"Don't be timid or obsequious, Victoria. Don't let judges intimidate you, and on cross-examination, go for the jugular and spill blood."

A quick study, Victoria began wielding a saber at government witnesses, and the ones she didn't bloody, she drew into the quicksand of their own contradictory statements.

Maybe Solomon and Lord liked me around for the wisdom that comes with experience. Or maybe it's more than that. Who's to say why we choose our friends? Just as with lovers, there's a certain mystery to the chemistry of friendship. Whatever the reason, as Solomon likes to say, we're *Los Tres Amigos*.

Once we ordered—sea bass for Victoria, hanger steak for Solomon, calamari in a chili-banana sauce for me—I asked what was the big news that brought us out on this balmy evening.

"We're getting married, pal," Solomon answered, beaming.

"Of course you are," I said. "You've been engaged for what—almost three years?"

"No, I mean, we're *really* doing it. Right, Vic?"

"Our trial schedule has eased up, so, yes, perhaps we can squeeze it in around Labor Day."

"How romantic," I said.

"Oh, you know Vic," Solomon said. "Work. Work. Work."

"One presumably innocent dirtbag after another, preyed upon by vindictive law enforcement," I agreed.

"The ceremony will be at Vizcaya," Victoria said, referring to the hundred-year-old mansion on the bay between Coconut Grove and downtown.

"And you're my best man," Solomon said. "So start working on your toast for the reception."

"I'm moved, Solomon. Our friendship means a lot to me."

"You're not being sarcastic, Jake?"

"No way. This is real."

It was the truth, but I didn't want to get all weepy about it. I lowered my voice into stentorian tones suitable for appellate courts and Episcopal weddings, lifted my glass in toasting mode, and said, "As even Steve Solomon's best friends can agree, Victoria deserves better."

Solomon barked a laugh, and we toasted each other, glad to be pals, glad to be here, glad the sun was down. It had been another soggy, sweaty, buggy day. The morning's mashed-potato clouds, white and fluffy, had been replaced by a threatening sky the color of a gray flannel suit. Then came the usual late-afternoon twelve-minute thunderstorm, lightning creasing the darkened sky, a gale driving the rain sideways as if shot from firemen's hoses. Later it cleared, and steam rose from slick pavement.

Welcome to Hades-on-the-Bay.

At dusk, with the temperature falling to a manageable eighty-two, with the breeze tasting of salt and jasmine, with a glass of tequila at hand and my friends nearby, life was not half-bad. Just then, Victoria's cell rang. She looked at the caller ID, wrinkled her brow, and answered.

"Clark, is that really you?"

Solomon and I had no choice but to listen to her half of the conversation.

"Yes, it has been a long time."

A pause and then, "Oh, that's frightening. Do you know where she's gone?"

Solomon and I exchanged puzzled looks.

"Of course you didn't, Clark. Why would the police think that?"

At the word *police*, I put down my tequila.

"Please don't make any more statements to law enforcement. Tell the detective to speak to me. What you're calling a missing-persons case, the police obviously think is a homicide."

The word *homicide* made Solomon lick his lips, and the hair stood up on the back of my neck. We were pretty much tigers catching the scent of zebras.

"No, Clark. Do not give them permission to search your home." Another pause, and she said, "Oh, you already did? Yes, I understand. Everyone wants to appear cooperative with the police. But what if Sofia cut her leg shaving, and there are traces of blood in the bathtub? What if an overzealous cop plants evidence or the State Attorney suborns perjury?"

As a possible newbie prosecutor, I resented that last remark.

She listened a moment, then said, "Are the police gone now?" Another pause. "Good. I'll be at your house at eight o'clock in the morning. I want you to walk me through everything on the last day you saw her."

She clicked off, and Solomon said, "Who's Clark, and who'd he kill?"

"He didn't kill anyone. He's a surgeon." She took a breath and exhaled. "And an ex-boyfriend of mine."

"What? When? Why haven't I heard of him?"

"Long time ago. I was an undergrad at Princeton. A freshman, really. He had finished his residency and two fellowships and was working at University Hospital in New Brunswick."

"You saying he's a lot older? Almost Jake's age?"

"Not quite. But older, sure."

"It's a wonder he can still walk," I said, "much less kill anyone."

"He didn't kill anyone," Victoria reminded us.

"I always assume my clients are guilty," I said. "It saves time."

"I never pictured you with an old guy," Solomon said. "So who *didn't* he kill?"

"His wife. Sofia. She disappeared three weeks ago."

"Wait!" I said. "Not another word."

Victoria turned toward me. "What is it, Jake?"

"This Clark. Your ex. He's an orthopedic surgeon, right?"

"Yes."

"Is his last name Calvert?"

She nodded. "Dr. Clark Calvert. How did you know?"

"Ray Pincher says the doc killed his wife."

"The State Attorney told you this?" Victoria's blue eyes went wide.

"Why would Pincher even talk to you about it?" Solomon asked.

"Because he asked me to—"

"Clark didn't kill her!" Victoria interrupted. "They had an argument, and she took off. He looked for her all day. When she didn't come home that night, he reported her missing the next morning. He isn't hiding anything."

"Fine. If that's what the evidence shows, I won't even take the case to the grand jury. No indictment, and you can invite the doc to your wedding. Plus one, if his wife shows up."

Solomon gestured toward me with his fork. "What do you mean *you* won't take it to the grand jury?"

"That's what I've been trying to tell you. Pincher asked me to put my hand on a Bible and promise to support, defend, and protect the Constitution from the likes of you. If I say yes, you're looking at a specially appointed assistant state attorney."

"I don't believe it, Jake," Victoria said. "This is one of your practical jokes."

"Nope. But like I said, if I'm handling the case and there's insufficient evidence, everybody goes home. On the other hand, there might be a homicide case to try with you two kids on one side of the courtroom and me on the other. Oh, the tricks you will learn."

They exchanged worried looks. "He's not joking," Victoria whispered.

"He could be delusional," Solomon whispered back.

"I can hear you guys, so you might as well speak up."

"We're just worried that with your . . . ah . . . illness and . . . ah . . . treatments . . ." she fumbled along.

"Maybe you think Pincher appointed you to prosecute," Solomon pitched in, "but it really didn't happen."

"I'm not delusional," I said. "I'm not brain damaged. And you two are starting to piss me off. What did you say your names were again?"

-4-

Little Gold Handcuffs

S olomon spent the next ten minutes busting my chops while Victoria studied me, a quizzical look on her face.

"Forget it, Jake. It's Chinatown."

"What are you talking about, Solomon?"

"The Justice Building. The downtown power establishment. Corruption. Dirty deals. Secrets and payoffs. You'll step into a sinkhole, and we'll never see you again."

"Isn't that a tad melodramatic?"

"Okay, try this. You can't prosecute because it's not in you."

"Why not?"

"Prosecutors have no heart. No soul. No empathy. They're automatons, tools of the state."

I swatted away a gnat that was dive-bombing my ears and sipped at the Don Julio, the fourth one just as mellow as the first. A motor yacht in the thirty-five-foot range churned through the channel from the nearby marina.

"Good prosecutors stand for justice," I said. "They don't coach cops to lie or bury exculpatory evidence. I admire them, and maybe I ought to be one, at least for a while."

I was just repeating Pincher's sales pitch, but strangely enough, I was beginning to believe it. I didn't mention Pincher also agreed to forget about my bruising Phil Flury's delicate torso if I switched sides.

"No way, Jake," Solomon said. "You're a rebel, a rule breaker."

"*You're* the rule breaker. I just believe in the vigorous defense of individual rights."

"Precisely! The individual, not the great gray monolith."

"Victims are individuals, too."

"Irrelevant! You're antiestablishment, and prosecutors are the embodiment of the establishment."

Victoria reached across the table and took my free hand, the one not wrapped around the tumbler of tequila. "Are you ready for this kind of change in your life, Jake?"

"Not really. I'll have to buy a new suit. Gray with a starched white shirt and a tie the color of blood."

Victoria kept after me in that soft, persuasive voice she used with juries. "I'm not sure you understand the magnitude of what you're doing. It's not like getting traded to the Patriots and the next week you just put on a different uniform."

"I wasn't traded. The Dolphins cut me from the roster. The Saskatchewan Roughriders offered me a contract, but I'd have to drive a cab three days a week and wash my own uniform."

"I'm not speaking literally, Jake. I just want you to think strategically. What's your goal? What's your long-term plan?"

"Victoria, you sound like an insurance agent peddling annuities."

"Your entire being is grounded in your identity as a defense lawyer. You fight against superior forces who have unlimited resources, and you never yield, never give up. You compel the state to prove its case, just as the Constitution demands."

"Dude, it's in your blood," Solomon said.

I hate it when Solomon calls me "dude." The only one who's earned that nickname is Jeff Bridges in *The Big Lebowski.*

"Let's say you want to build a house," Solomon said. "Do you hire a carpenter or a vandal?"

"Is this a trick question?" I asked.

"You hire a carpenter to saw a sure cut and to hammer the nails straight. Nothing fancy. No razzle, no dazzle. That's a prosecutor. But you're the punk who comes along at night and spray-paints graffiti on the walls and rips down the two-by-fours."

"I'm a vandal?"

"We all are, dude! We tear down the prosecutor's house. It's our job."

"Maybe it's time I try to build something. I told Pincher I'd give him my answer in the morning."

"There's still time." Solomon turned to Victoria. "Help me out here, babe."

"Did the State Attorney say why he needs you to prosecute?" Victoria asked.

"He has a conflict that knocks his whole office out of the case. He's gonna fill me in tomorrow."

Victoria gave that a moment of thought, and I looked across the bay. The moon was rising over the water, creamy beams of light dancing on the light chop. Just three weeks ago, the moon had passed the closest to the earth in several decades, and we'd had a King Tide. The very patio where we dined was under two feet of water. In another couple of decades, if the scientists are right, knee-deep flooding will be a weekly occurrence, and Miami will begin its inevitable descent back into the sea. Tourist brochures will have to be rewritten to include the word *Atlantis*.

Victoria said, "The usual procedure would be for the governor to assign a prosecutor from another circuit or someone from the Attorney General's office in Tallahassee. So why you?"

"According to Pincher, the governor has a conflict, and so does the AG."

Victoria's cell rang again. She checked the caller ID and shot me a look, accompanied by a shake of the head that said, "Scram."

I stayed put.

"Yes, Clark," she said.

"Cover your ears, Jake," Solomon said.

My ears stayed uncovered in the soft evening breeze.

"Of course you didn't intend to kill her cat, Clark," Victoria said.

I whispered to Solomon, "Killing your wife is one thing, but the cat? Abominable."

"I can't talk right now," Victoria said, looking straight at me. "I'll be there in the morning. Please try to get some sleep."

She clicked off, and Solomon said, "You mean *we*."

"What?" she asked.

"You told our new client, 'I'll be there.' Didn't you mean 'we'?"

Ah, trouble in paradise, I thought. Already, Solomon and Lord were on different pages. A prosecutor could use that, even a prosecutor who loved them like younger siblings.

"Sure, Steve. We'll go together," Victoria said. "If you think that's the way to proceed, that's fine."

"We're partners! Why wouldn't you want me there?"

"I was thinking that maybe Clark would be forthcoming on a first meeting with me alone."

"Why? Because you used to sleep with him?"

"Uncalled for, Steve," she said.

"Oh, I don't know," I said. "Psychologically speaking, Steve might have a point."

"Really?" Victoria glared at me as if I were the cockroach in the potato salad. "And this is based on what, Jake? Your knowledge of relationships gained from a lifetime of dating Dolphins cheerleaders and outcall masseuses?"

"Your fiancé asked a legitimate question. Solomon can bring an objective analysis to your ex-sweetie's case. Why would you shut him out?"

"Jake, you know how much I adore you," she said.

I heard a *but* coming.

"But I know you. You're a very cagey lawyer, and you're a lot smarter than you look."

"Thank you," I said, choosing to take that as a compliment.

"And you're not going to sow dissension between Steve and me. As for Clark, I've known him since I was eighteen. We spent nearly three years together."

"Three years?" Solomon shook his head. "It lasted that long?"

I loved this. Confusion to the enemy, even if they're my best pals. Before long, they'd be Sparta and Athens, stalwart allies during the Greco-Persian Wars, then chopping each other to pieces during the Peloponnesian War. Hey, I got a B-plus in Ancient History at Penn State, thanks to sitting next to a brainy girl with excellent handwriting.

"All I'm saying, Steve," Victoria continued, "I know the man."

"Three years, I guess you do," I said, tossing petrol on Solomon's slow burn.

Victoria ignored me and said, "Clark would never kill anyone."

I raised my eyebrows, one of which had nearly been ripped off by a New York Jets lineman known for his dirty play. "Victoria, you remind me of those neighbors of serial killers. 'He always kept his lawn mowed.'"

"Clark's a brilliant man. His IQ is off the charts. He speaks five languages. He plays classical piano. He flies his own plane. He was the chief resident in orthopedics, had two prized fellowships, and from what I've heard, is a wonderful surgeon."

"Sounds like a catch," I said agreeably. "Seems to me you're marrying the wrong guy, though I doubt Solomon would ever kill your cat."

Victoria kept her voice even, but her blue eyes had turned ice-cold. "If you prosecute Clark, it will be the biggest mistake of your life."

"Bigger than a holding penalty on a kickoff return that negated a touchdown against the Colts?"

"I'm going to defend Clark, and I'm going to beat you," she said firmly.

"She means 'we're' going to beat you," Solomon said.

"And when *we're* done with you," she continued, "your reputation will be in shreds. You'll be humiliated. Pincher will dump you, and when you resume your practice, no clients will hire you. You'll be the guy who couldn't cut it as a prosecutor."

"Wow," I said. Thinking Victoria didn't need any more lessons in assertiveness.

"Wow," Solomon repeated. "That's pretty brutal, Vic. Jake's our bestie."

"In my opinion, Victoria," I said, "you can't represent Clark Calvert."

"Why on earth not?"

"A surgeon doesn't operate on a loved one. Same goes for lawyers."

"I don't love Clark."

"But you once did, right?"

She was quiet a moment. What could she say? I nearly felt guilty for picking on her, but she was so damn competitive. Truth be told, so was I. God, I hate to lose.

"I take your silence as a yes," I said. "Of course you loved him once."

"I was a kid, Jake. I was infatuated with Clark. Maybe even overwhelmed that he cared for me. But what does it matter now?"

"Emotions cloud our judgment, and judgment is our stock-in-trade."

"Thanks for the advice, oh wise one."

I glanced toward Solomon. "Have you ever seen your fiancée like this?"

He shook his head.

"Me, either. If I were you, Solomon, I'd look into those three years with Clark Calvert she never told you about. And I'd ask just what bond still exists between them."

19

"Damn it, Jake!" Victoria's fine porcelain complexion was turning sunset pink. "There's no bond, just distant memories."

"How distant when he has your cell phone number?" I turned to Solomon. "If she were my fiancée, I might ask a few questions, starting with 'When's the last time you saw each other?'"

"Steve, don't listen to him. He's just trying to drive a wedge between us to gain an advantage in the case."

"I'm not listening," Solomon said, a lie so bald-faced it wouldn't have to shave in the morning.

-5-

Who Is This Guy?

Victoria Lord . . .

Riding shotgun, Victoria considered grabbing the steering wheel and yanking it hard right, sending the car over the curb, through a fence, down an embankment, and into the Coral Gables Waterway.

That's how much her fiancé was aggravating her, and it had been only five minutes since they had left the Red Fish Grill. They were heading north on Old Cutler Road in Steve's torch-red Corvette with the personalized license plate, "I-OBJECT." Victoria disliked the sports car's low-slung seats that were difficult to get into with her long legs. Now that she thought of it, she despised the car, hated the license plate, and—at this moment—wasn't terribly fond of the driver.

Steve had Clark Calvert on his brain and couldn't let it go. She tried to divert his attention by talking about their upcoming wedding. They had to pick a date. It cost $12,500 to rent Vizcaya Gardens on a Friday or Saturday night and only $7,500 during the week. And that's before the food, the band, the flowers, the valet parkers, and a bunch of other expenses that would undoubtedly pop up. But did she really want a Wednesday-night wedding?

Steve couldn't be distracted. He was fixated on the man in her past. "It doesn't compute," he said. "You and this doctor. Were you ever engaged to him?"

"No! Of course not. I was a kid."

"You were engaged to Bruce Bigby, the avocado king, when we met."

"And I broke it off when I fell in love with you. Why are you acting so threatened?"

"You broke off one engagement. Maybe you'll break off another."

"Oh, please!"

"Why didn't you ever mention this guy? Haven't I told you about all my relationships?"

"Multiple times," she said, "and in exhausting detail."

"So why were you holding out on me?"

"I tried to tell you about Clark very shortly after we met. But you kept changing the subject to your athletic triumphs and romantic conquests."

The Corvette was about to navigate LeJeune Circle when she pondered the steering wheel and weighed the merits of crashing through the guardrail and into the waterway. The night was warm and moist, and with the top down, the air was heavy with jasmine, which grew wild in Coconut Grove.

"I honestly don't remember you ever mentioning Calvert," Steve said.

"It was our third date. I told you about being with a doctor when I was an undergrad, but you interrupted with a story about hitting a home run to win a game in the College World Series."

"The Regionals, not the World Series. And it was an infield hit. In the series, I was picked off third base in the bottom of the ninth of the championship game."

"Oh, right. Bad call, you told me."

"The pitcher balked! I should have scored. Instead, the series ended with me being tagged out."

"Life's so unfair."

"Don't be sarcastic, Vic. That was a very traumatic moment for me. Still is."

Honestly, she thought. *Men and their games. Baseball, football, hockey. All the time and energy they waste.* Okay, baseball at the University of Miami was Steve's game. He'd played. That she could understand. But sitting in front the television, yelling his brains out for some professional team just because they're from his city . . . well, that was incomprehensible. Every time Steve took her to a Marlins game, she thought, *Here go three hours I'll never get back.*

"Another time, I told you I had lived with a man when I was young," she said. "That was Clark, of course, but you didn't express much interest, didn't ask any questions. As I recall, you immediately launched into a story about a flight attendant for Qatar Airways who bunked with you when she had layovers in Miami. *Bunked* was your exact verb, by the way."

"How do you remember this stuff?" he asked.

She shrugged. "It's a feminine thing. We remember when our mates are acting like thick-skulled knuckle draggers."

Steve turned right onto Loquat, faster than necessary. The Corvette hugged the road with nary a squealing tire. "Your cell. How did this long-lost love have your number?"

"Five or six years ago, before you and I met, Clark moved to Miami to relocate his practice. He looked me up."

"Ha!" He shot a triumphant look at her, as if he'd scored a major point on cross-examination. "Did you start dating again?"

She shook her head. "Clark was already involved with Sofia and was thinking about asking her to marry him. We had lunch, and he basically asked for my advice."

Steve eased the 'Vette left onto Kumquat. Two blocks from home.

"He told me they were very different," she continued. "Clark has always been introverted, the way a lot of intellectuals are. Sofia was outgoing, very social, lots of friends. But also very mercurial and given to mood swings and depression. She told him she'd attempted suicide as a teenager, but he wasn't sure she was telling the truth."

Steve processed this, his defense-lawyer brain taking over from his jealous-fiancé brain. "Suicide is a helluva good defense to murder." He shot her a look. "Did you advise your old boyfriend to marry this drama queen?"

"I told him to follow his heart."

"Oh, jeez. I never understood what that means."

She smiled to herself. "Oh, yes, you do."

"Did you ever consider that he was giving you the right of last refusal?"

"To marry him?"

"Sure. He comes to you, hoping you'll say, 'Oh no, Clark. I made such a mistake dumping you back in the day.'"

"I never said I dumped him." She exhaled a long breath. "But . . ."

"But you did, right?"

"By the time I graduated from college, I realized that Clark had been a passage in my development, so yes, I'm the one who suggested we each go our separate ways but remain friends."

They pulled into the brick driveway of their Grove bungalow, and Steve said, with more certainty than the evidence would allow, "He wanted you. Maybe he still does."

"I doubt that."

Steve killed the engine, and they sat there in the darkness. It was quiet, except for a peacock screeching from a neighbor's yard.

"Was he ever abusive to you?" he asked.

"No, never."

"Any acts of violence toward anyone?"

"None."

Steve thought a moment, then asked, "Is there anything you're not telling me?"

For a lawyer, Victoria was a terrible liar, so she was glad Steve could not make out her features in the dark. "Of course not," she said. "Like you said, you and I are lovers and law partners. We're going to marry. We can't have secrets. We can't tell lies."

Except little ones, Victoria thought.

-6-

The Beast in All of Us

Victoria Lord . . .

Sitting in Steve's Corvette, Victoria considered the difference between "facts" and the "truth."

She had told Steve the facts, things that actually happened.

But were her answers the truth, the whole truth, and nothing but the truth?

No, because she had omitted and edited. She had pruned the branches of the unsightly leaves that would cast the truth in a harsher light.

She had not told Steve about Clark's hair-trigger temper. How he could explode at the slightest provocation or none at all. A waiter who delivered lukewarm soup, a cabdriver who missed a turn, a hotel desk clerk slow delivering the room key. And occasionally—not often, to be sure—he could lash out at her.

But he was not violent. Not in actions. Therefore, she'd told the truth when she said that Clark had never abused her, had never acted violently.

But the whole truth was complex. She tried now to remember the precise notion she had so long ago when breaking up with Clark. Ah, there it was.

Clark intellectualizes violence.

The concept of violence intrigues him.

He thinks about violent acts but would never commit them.

She remembered their last week together and the terrifying incident that ended their relationship. A vacation in California. They drove north along the Pacific Coast Highway from Los Angeles to San Francisco. Clark had been even more withdrawn than usual, his quiet spells occasionally interrupted by bizarre musings. None weirder than on a chilly day on an ocean-side cliff near Big Sur, where the wind whipped strands of fog across the shoreline.

Far below, waves pounded at jagged rock formations and foamed into tidal pools. They stopped at a lookout point, their shoes just inches from the precipice. A steel-gray sky above, a steel-gray sea below. An unspoiled spot. No barrier or fence. No one else around. Clark spoke softly, and she leaned close to hear him over the cacophony of wind and waves.

"Ever wonder what it would be like?" he said. "How easy it would be?"

"What?"

"To kill someone." He moved a step behind her and gripped her shoulder with his right hand, a surgeon's hand that sawed through bones. "What would it take, twenty pounds of force? Maybe less if the leverage were right?"

"That's just the mechanics, Clark." She made no move to twist away. "It doesn't account for the person. Most of us—you, me, the people we know—would never do that. Only a beast would take another's life."

He raised his dark eyebrows and smiled. "We're all beasts. In the right time and place, we're king of the beasts."

Letting go of her shoulder, he roared like a lusty lion and laughed at his own joke.

"I don't have such a cynical view of human nature," she said.

"No?"

He shoved her hard in the back. Her knees buckled, and she stumbled forward, her head and shoulders over the cliff's edge, her arms flailing in space.

His left hand shot forward and caught her just above the elbow a split second before she would have tumbled over the cliff.

"Clark! What the hell! Are you insane?"

She was shaking, birds flapping their wings inside her rib cage. He was laughing, oblivious to her fear and rage. His failing, she realized then, was an inability to empathize. He had no idea how terror had just clutched at her heart. He was a man of contradictions. On the surface, he was caring and kind, sensitive to her needs. But underneath, there was a coldness that killed her feelings for him.

"Relax, Victoria," he said. "I just wanted to change your view of human nature to something more realistic." He roared with laughter again, the king of the beasts, then turned and walked back toward the car, leaving her there, shivering in the wind.

She broke up with him the next day.

The Pursuit of Happiness

Jake Lassiter . . .

I was smoking weed and feeling groovy. On doctor's instructions. More or less.

Dr. Gold, carrying a grocery bag, approached the park bench where I'd been planted like a fern for the past hour. I was in South Pointe Park at the tip of Miami Beach. A hundred yards away, a cruise ship flying the Norwegian flag plowed out of Government Cut, headed toward the Caribbean with three thousand fun seekers aboard. If a couple hundred contracted norovirus and spent their vacation pooping out their guts, maybe I could pick up a PI case or two against the cruise line. A hundred yards in the other direction was the beach, which ended at a jetty that formed a barrier to the Cut. A biplane flew along the beach trailing a sign advertising suntan oil. No mention was made of skin cancer.

"Hey, good-looking!" I called out. "What's cooking?"

"Jake, are you high?" Melissa demanded. She was tall, long-legged, and loose-limbed, with reddish-brown hair and light-green eyes.

I exhaled a long, slow, pungent puff from my vape pen. It looks like one of those silvery cigarette holders an effete villain would be waving around in an old movie. Claude Rains in *Notorious*, maybe.

"Jake! Answer me."

"I'm invoking my Fifth Amendment right to remain silent."

"Damn it."

"Also, my right to life, liberty, and the pursuit of happiness, as guaranteed by Benjamin Franklin and perhaps Timothy Leary."

Looking exasperated, she settled onto the bench next to me, hoisting the grocery bag between us. I leaned across the paper sack and gave her a brush kiss that doubtless carried the faint scent of a vaporized weed called "Krazy Kush."

Did I mention that my doctor and I were lovers? No?

About ten months ago, Melissa moved here to take part in a research program devoted to chronic traumatic encephalopathy. And to be with me.

CTE is to the National Football League what black lung is to coal mining, the inescapable industrial disease that keeps on giving, and I might be one of its victims. "Might be" because only an autopsy can yield a definitive diagnosis.

"Seriously, Jake, are you stoned?"

"I have a prescription."

"No, you don't. Not for psychoactive marijuana with THC."

"A legal technicality," I protested.

"Your prescription is for cannabis edibles with CBD and nothing else. There's no need to get high."

"Why deprive me of the joy of eating two bags of Fritos at midnight?"

"Where are those CBD cookies I gave you?"

"In the dumpster. They taste like chocolate-coated cardboard."

Melissa reached in her grocery bags for our sandwiches. A white heron landed in the grass near our bench, considered panhandling, then high-stepped it toward the beach.

Melissa said, "How are you feeling, Jake?"

"Why does everyone keep asking that? I could do a triathlon."

"I don't believe you."

"Sure, I could. Drinks, dinner, sex."

"Let's get through lunch first and take it from there." Melissa handed me a big, juicy sub sandwich, then took one for herself. Salami, turkey, and ham with Muenster cheese, onions, and tomatoes, the baguette slathered with mayo and drizzled with Italian dressing. For a slender, fit woman, Melissa had a hearty appetite. I liked that.

"Getting stoned will not stop the strands of tau protein from hardening in your brain," she said. "It's the cannabidiol, the CBD, that's neuroprotective."

"Hey, regular weed has that, too. Why can't I get a buzz at the same time I get therapy?"

The question stumped her, and that's not easy to do. The woman has a bachelor's degree from Columbia, a master's in neuroscience and a PhD in molecular science from Yale, a medical degree from Duke, and she's board certified in neurology and neuropathology.

Me? After the NFL decided it could sell oceans of beer without me, I went to night law school at the University of Miami and proudly graduated in the top half of the bottom third of my class. In truth, I've hit more blocking sleds than law books.

"Just don't overdo it," she said. "It's not healthy to go through life stoned." With that, she bit into her sandwich, and a tomato squirted juice over her lower lip. I also like a woman who isn't dainty at the table, on a park bench, or in bed.

A twentysomething bare-chested guy in surfer shorts skateboarded past us on the path. He had a tattoo of Chinese symbols running up one arm and around his neck. It probably translated into some wise philosophical saying, which I imagined to be, "Confucius says I am dumb as dirt for getting this tattoo."

"Do you mind if I ask you the questions for this month's university study?"

"Fire away."

"How's your impulse control?"

"Excellent. Yesterday, I repressed my impulse to wash and wax the car."

"Are you having any suicidal ideations?" she asked between bites.

"Suicidal, never. Homicidal, frequently."

"Do you find your mind wandering?"

"I do. And may I be perfectly honest?"

"Please."

"My mind wanders to you, Melissa. How thankful I am to have you in my life, and not just sticking needles in my butt. I care for you very deeply."

She raised an eyebrow. "Jake Lassiter. Getting real. So much better than Jake the Jokester."

"Truth is, you make me want to be a better man."

She cocked her head and appraised me. "Didn't Jack Nicholson say that to Helen Hunt in a movie?"

"Maybe, but if he did, he stole it from me. Point is, I care for you."

It's true, damn it. It's just never been easy for me to say.

"And I care deeply for you, Jake."

"Which brings us to where we are and where we're going. We care deeply for each other, but . . ."

The *but* hung there a second. Maybe thinking about Solomon and Lord getting married had triggered something in me. But where to go with it? I immediately regretted what I'd just said. I felt like I was prancing through the high-step agility drill on the practice field, trying not to stumble on the grid of intersecting ropes. One misstep and I'd plunge facedown into the web, while my teammates hooted and hollered.

"But *what*, Jake?"

"But nothing. I was being stupid."

But with the vague diagnosis of my medical condition, how can we make any plans?

That's what I wanted to say but didn't. I would save my concerns for another day. She didn't press me for an answer. Didn't badger me. Gave me my own space to fret. I liked that about Melissa, too.

Dr. Melissa Gold was a neuropathologist at UCLA. A little more than a year ago, she'd been an expert witness in a case of mine involving a female martial arts fighter who had committed suicide. Based on a brain autopsy, Dr. Gold determined that the young woman had been suffering with CTE. Yeah, just like all those former NFL players who descended into dementia and death.

In California I had taken Dr. Gold out to dinner, where I performed the charming stunt of fainting, facedown, into a platter of smoked pork bellies with roasted blackberries. This came after several weeks of piercing headaches and a few episodes of confused behavior and short-term memory snafus.

My symptoms were consistent with several very scary illnesses. Senile dementia, Alzheimer's disease, frontotemporal dementia, and, of course, CTE. They're pretty much first cousins of each other. Nasty, homicidal cousins.

My first brain scans were "murky," to use Dr. Gold's word. I had misshapen strands of tau protein, but not the stiffened tangles of sludge that indicate full-blown, fatal CTE. She called my condition a "precursor" to the disease. I took this to mean that the Grim Reaper had been spotted in my neighborhood but hadn't yet rung my doorbell.

Could the disease be stopped? Could the tangled tau strands be untangled? Melissa didn't know. We began experimental injections of protein antibodies, but so far the results have been inconclusive.

In the meantime, studies on rats showed that marijuana—specifically its compound CBD—helped brain tissue recover from injury. Like the rats, I smoke weed, just as I did decades ago after every football game that left me with bumps, bruises . . . and the occasional concussion.

"If you're done with the interrogation," I said between bites, "what did yesterday's scan show?"

"We're getting to that. Are you having any feelings of aggression?"

"Only when someone I care about is being evasive. What did the scan show?"

"In a minute. Feelings of depression?"

"Considering the state of the world, who wouldn't be?"

I watched a second cruise ship follow the first one out to sea. It was a big, blocky, ugly vessel that took on the appearance of a twenty-story office building toppled onto its side. I don't like having dinner with three strangers, much less three thousand, so I'm not a good candidate for a Caribbean cruise.

"The scan," I repeated. "Give it to me straight."

"The technology has improved dramatically in the last year," she said. "The ligand, the molecules we injected with radioactive atoms, were specifically chosen because they bind onto the tau protein. It gives us a much clearer picture."

"And what did the picture show?"

She let out a long breath. "More misshapen tau protein than a year ago."

"Damn!"

"But we can't tell if that's because of a worsening condition or just a more highly defined picture of your brain tissue. All we can say for certain is that the disease—or precursor to the disease—hasn't reversed. And . . ."

"It may have progressed."

At the mouth of Government Cut, the giant cruise ship sounded its horn—a loud, elephantine bleat, disturbing the peace of the park.

"Yes, that's possible. I wish I had better news. You must think this is such a bum deal."

"I'm not gonna whimper about it. What's your pal at UM say about the scan?"

"Dr. Hoch believes it's a fifty-fifty proposition that you're a step closer to full-blown encephalopathy. But that's just another way of saying he doesn't know. He wants you to increase your intake of cannabinoids."

"More weed. That's fine."

"He's also considering adding another experimental drug. He'll get back to me on that later today, and I'll let you know at once."

"You're not telling me to get my affairs in order?"

"Not at all. But I'd like to add meditation and mindfulness to your drug therapies. I could teach you."

"Might as well try teaching Pilates to a rhinoceros."

"The body-mind connection, Jake. What's the very first thing I learned about you when we met?"

"That I was both irresistible and modest."

"That you suffered from cognitive dissonance. You'd won a murder trial for a man you were sure was guilty, and it ate you up inside."

"And you said I should do something that sounded like pneumonia."

"Eudaimonia. A philosophy of Aristotle's."

"Didn't he believe the sun revolved around the earth?"

"Virtue ethics, a method of living a fulfilled and contented life. Meditation can help."

I thought about it a moment, determined to be earnest and not a wisecracking fool. "What about doing good deeds?"

"That, too, of course."

"Ray Pincher wants me to switch teams and prosecute a case. The sunny side of justice, he calls it."

"How do you feel about that?"

"At first I was skeptical."

"Skepticism is your default mode."

"But the more I think about it . . ."

"Go on, Jake."

"I hate to sound so damn earnest, but maybe I could contribute to society in a way I've never done."

She smiled warmly at me. "Change can be very therapeutic, Jake. Especially good deeds."

In the distance, a siren wailed. An ambulance maybe. What they used to call a Miami Beach Limousine, back in the day when the little island was God's Waiting Room for senior citizens. Maybe one day soon, the limo would come for me. That realization, too, pushed me toward switching teams.

"I'm gonna do it," I said. "Represent the people of the great state of Florida. Virtue. Ethics. Good deeds. Maybe I'll find the key to that contented life you're always talking about."

-8-

Well and Faithfully Perform

Judge Melvia Duckworth eyed me a bit suspiciously, or was that my imagination?

"Put your left hand on the Bible, and raise your right hand," Her Honor said.

I did as I was told, and the judge spent a moment examining the back of my left hand.

"Is there a problem, Your Honor? Is smoke rising from the Good Book when I touch it?"

She gave me a faint smile. "I just want to give you a moment to consider the ramifications of what you're doing today."

It was just the two of us in her chambers in the Justice Building. Dark wood and leather volumes and the quiet we associate with scholarly pursuits. Melvia Duckworth, a retired army captain, had served in the Judge Advocate Corps. She was a calm and strong presence in court and had always treated me fairly, even when my rambunctiousness would have rankled her more uptight brethren. A petite African-American woman close to sixty, she wore her black robes with a pink filigreed jabot at her neck and stylish eyeglasses with orange frames. The woman liked splashes of color, maybe to offset the austere robes.

"What's your concern, Judge?"

"News travels pretty fast in God's little acre of the civic center," she said.

"News, Your Honor?"

"Everybody knows about your medical situation, Jake. All those concussions and then your bizarre behavior. Is it true you punched out ASA Flury the other day?"

"No way, Your Honor. Just a little love tap to get his attention." I wiggled my right hand's harmless index finger, which was bent at the knuckle, having once gotten stuck in a lineman's face mask and broken into three pieces.

She shook her head, a bit sadly. "Conduct unbecoming an officer and a gentleman, Jake. Rumor mill says you've got brain damage."

"A *precursor* to brain damage, Judge."

"What in the name of General Patton is that?"

"Some misshapen protein that hasn't hardened into the tangles that indicate full-blown CTE. Really, I'm fine."

She pulled the Bible from beneath my hand and examined me with a judicial gaze. Judge Duckworth had stared into the eyes of murderers and bank robbers and check forgers, as well as the rarest of birds, the innocent man. What did she see now?

"No symptoms, then, Jake?"

"An occasional headache."

But what *occasions* they were. A jackhammer inside my skull, eviscerating bone and tissue, working its way toward my optic nerve, ready to puncture my eyes from the inside out. At least that's how it felt. All accompanied by an explosive flash of searing bright light that seemed to radiate heat.

She tilted her head, still evaluating me. "What about memory loss?"

"Nothing anyone else my age hasn't encountered. Sometimes I open the refrigerator and can't remember if I wanted milk or a tangerine. Usually, I settle for beer."

If the judge found this amusing, she didn't show it. I chose not to tell her about the occasions I took the wrong exit off I-95 and found myself lost, even though I've lived in Miami for most of my wastrel life.

"I'm doing really well," I said, without my nose growing or lightning striking me. "I'm undergoing some treatments that'll slow the growth of those nasty proteins, maybe even stop them in their tracks."

"That's good to hear."

I still had one hand extended, as if I were expecting a manicure. My other hand pointed toward the ceiling, where the air-conditioning vent exhaled chilled air and likely asbestos pores, too.

"Are you worried I'm gonna screw the pooch if I have to prosecute a murder case?"

She gave me a rueful smile. "I surely wouldn't want you brought up on dereliction-of-duty charges. I just keep wondering why Ray Pincher talked you into enlisting."

"When we're done here, I'm gonna walk across the street and find out."

"He's a slippery one, Jake."

I liked her calling me by my given name. Judges only do that if they're fond of you.

"He's the county's first African-American state attorney," she continued, "and I've always been afraid he'll do something to set back our cause."

"If Ray screws up, that's on him. Not you or anyone else in the community."

She chuckled. "Only a white man would think that, but that's okay, Jake. Your heart is in the right place." She slid the Bible back under my extended hand. "Just one thing. If you change your mind, if you think Pincher is leading you into some ambush in Fallujah, hurry yourself back in here, and I'll let you resign your commission."

"Aye, aye, Captain."

"I was army, Jake. Not navy."

"Be all you can be, Judge."

"One caveat, soldier. Should you want out, you gotta ask before an indictment is handed up. If you're walking point, I won't have you throwing down your rifle and jumping into the bushes just as you're about to engage the enemy."

"Understood, ma'am."

"Okay, let's do this."

I didn't need a cue card or a repeat-after-me. I've done four-hour closing arguments in homicide cases without a note or a break to pee. With the gravity that the words demanded, I said, "I do solemnly swear that I will support, protect, and defend the Constitution and government of the United States and the state of Florida, that I am duly qualified to hold office under the constitution of the state, and that I will well and faithfully perform the duties of Special Appointed State Attorney, the position upon which I am now about to enter. So help me God."

"Yes, indeed," the judge said, looking toward the heavens. "May God help you."

-9-

Into the Light

"The Jakester!" Ray Pincher greeted me, as usual. "The lawyer who put the *fog* into *pettifogger* and took the *shy* out of *shyster*."

"Stow that, Ray," I said. "I'm here to help you out, and you play that sorry old tune."

Ray Pincher retreated behind his desk, a slab of mahogany the size of an aircraft carrier's flight deck. On his walls were his merit badges from the Kiwanis, the Friends of the Everglades, the National Association of Persecutors—excuse me, Prosecutors. Plus, several dozen photos of the Honorable State Attorney himself shaking hands with various politicians, bankers, and real estate developers who hadn't yet been indicted.

"Just welcoming you from the dark side into the light," Pincher said. "Let me tell you what we've got on the surgeon."

"First tell me why you're conflicted out."

Pincher swiveled his high-back leather chair and opened a cherrywood humidor on the credenza behind his desk. He pulled out a big, fat Cohiba. "Want to indulge?" he asked.

I shook my head. The state office building is smoke-free, and especially Cuban cigar smoke–free. Some stogie suckers seem to believe there's a constitutional right to stand their ground and fire away in any place at any time. Just another one of my beefs about the coarseness of modern life.

I waited while Pincher used a miniature guillotine to snip a hole in the head of the cigar. Then he put it in his mouth and inhaled the cold stogie. Withdrew the fat cigar, examined it, and struck a long wooden match, which he placed not on the tobacco but on the wrapper underneath the open end. Then he rotated the cigar between thumb and forefinger.

"How long's this ritual gonna last, Ray? Do I have time to take a piss?"

"Just toasting the filler leaves to dry them out."

"Your conflict of interest in the Calvert case. What is it?"

"You know the name Pedro Suarez? His friends call him Pepe."

The outer leaves of the cigar were glowing red, but the tobacco was still unlit, and he shook the match until the flame died.

"Big Sugar," I said. "The Suarez family owns about a zillion acres of sugarcane. They've been in the news for years for Pepe's charitable giving, his political contributions, and his polluting Lake Okeechobee."

"That's the man. Lives large. Built a medieval castle on a lake near Orlando. Even has a moat with alligators."

"I saw him on TV. *Lives of the Rich and Disgusting*. What's his connection to the case?"

"Pepe Suarez is Sofia Calvert's father. He's pushing hard to indict his son-in-law."

"Who cares what he wants?"

"Just listen a second, Jake. Suarez claims he warned his daughter against marrying Calvert, that he sensed the guy was a psychopath."

"I'm not hearing anything that sounds like admissible evidence. But I'm sensing that Mr. Moneybags contributes to the political campaigns of Sugar Ray Pincher."

"True enough." Pincher struck another match and this time lit the damn cigar, rotating it until the entire foot glowed deep orange. "Pepe has been heard to say that there's a mansion in Tallahassee that I might find comfortable."

"*Governor* Pincher. So why not prosecute the case yourself? Carry Pepe's sword into battle. Be his champion."

Pincher sipped at the cigar as if it were a fine wine. He exhaled a whiff of white smoke and said, "Why do you think?"

"Because the case is a loser. You've got no evidence, and you need a fall guy. Someone to blame. Maybe a guy who might have a meltdown in court due to his medical condition."

"To the contrary, Jake. I think you can use your dementia to your advantage."

"I don't have dementia."

"Whatever it is. A judge cuts off a certain line of questioning, but you'll just keep going."

"I've always done that when I believe in my case. That's why I've been held in contempt so many times."

"Sure, in the past you've been sanctioned. But now, with your condition, the Americans with Disabilities Act protects you. Jake, my boy, you can get away with murder."

My allegedly addled brain tried to process that. Clouds of smoke encircled me, as if from the volcanoes of hell. "Tell me if I've got this right, Ray. You have a shitty case, but a deranged prosecutor who violates courtroom procedures might be able to win it. If he loses, who can blame you?"

"Not entirely right. You're a helluva trial lawyer, deranged or sane. I hope you win. But should the case go south, sure, you're the buffer between my office and ignominious defeat."

I got out of my chair and walked to the window. Directly across the street was the jail with its enclosed bridge into the Justice Building. Shackled prisoners made the trip each day for arraignments, hearings, and trials. Three hundred yards to the left were the elevated spans of the Dolphin Expressway. Named for the team that played in the Orange Bowl, less than a mile from the courtrooms where I now toil. The Bowl was torn down years ago, replaced—at taxpayer expense—by the billionaire owner of the city's Major League Baseball team. Money talks in Miami. Hell, it was talking right now.

"All right, Ray, tell me about the evidence. Or better yet, show me the file."

"I haven't seen the file. As I said, I'm conflicted out. We've erected the proverbial Chinese wall in the office, so you'll have to talk to ASA Flury and Detective Barrios. They're waiting in the war room down the hall. I can tell you that Flury is quite convinced Calvert killed his wife."

"Flury thinks everyone is guilty. He's also one of the most irritating people on the planet, the skinny version of Chris Christie."

"I've ordered him to get you up to speed on the file, then bow out. And I'm ordering you not to slug him. Which leaves Detective Barrios."

"George is a good man. I can work with him."

Pincher placed the cigar in a black onyx ashtray and lowered his voice to a conspiratorial tone. "Barrios has an explosive piece of evidence, the likes of which you have never seen."

"I thought you didn't know anything about the case, Ray."

"Oh, come on, Jake. That's my public posture. Between you and me and the deep-blue sea, I think you're gonna get a conviction. I'm an optimist, buddy. I think you're gonna beat this medical problem and be back in the ring, sparring with me at the club."

"Not without headgear for my brain and a cup for my balls."

"And just maybe, Jake, old pal, when I'm governor, Pepe Suarez will support you for state attorney. What do you think of that?"

"What I think, old pal, is that you're peeing on my leg and calling it champagne."

-10-
The Flop-Sweat Stink of Guilt

I marched thirty paces down the hall from Ray Pincher's office to the war room, as the pugnacious State Attorney likes to call the windowless dungeon filled with investigative files, ancient corkboards plastered with photos of corpses, and trash cans overflowing with takeout lunch containers.

Detective George Barrios and Assistant State Attorney Phil Flury were sitting at a long oak table stained by a million cups of coffee. Half a dozen file folders were spread in front of them.

"You smell like a brush fire in the Glades," Flury said as I entered the room.

"Blame your boss. He's violating the Cuban Embargo Act and the Clean Air Act, not to mention his cardiologist's instructions."

"For the record, I object to my office associating with you, Mr. Lassiter," Flury said.

"For the record, there is no record," I replied. "And it's not your office. Ray Pincher is the duly elected state attorney. He's the captain of the team, and you're the water boy."

Flury smirked at me and said, "They say you have brain damage. That would explain a lot."

"Yo, Jake," Barrios said, interrupting our fun. "You don't look half-bad for a guy with Alzheimer's."

"I don't have Alzheimer's, George."

"If you did, how would you know?"

That set both of them to laughing. I didn't mind Barrios, a veteran cop and an honest guy. He was already past retirement age but couldn't give up a lifetime of weaving together patches of evidence into the quilts of murder investigations. A small, wiry man, he had a shaved head suntanned the color of chestnuts, and he wore a pale-yellow guayabera.

Flury, on the other hand, was a noodle-necked weasel in a pin-striped suit trying to oil his way up the ladder in the slippery world of the Miami-Dade judicial system.

"Before we begin," Flury said as I eased into a chair, "Mr. Pincher says you have to apologize to me for your unprovoked battery upon my person."

"If I'd battered you, Flu Bug, your person would be in traction."

Barrios sipped at his coffee, enjoying our byplay.

"If you're ridiculing my name," Flury said, "I'll file a report with the county Human Rights Commission."

"What the hell for?"

"Based on my German heritage, your remark is, at the least, insensitive and, at worst, a hate crime."

Barrios put down his coffee. "Jake, why not just apologize for whatever the hell you did so we can do some work before it's time to drink lunch?"

I appreciate commonsense advice, so I took it. "Okay, Flury. I'm sorry if I poked you in the chest the other day and also for my insensitive mocking of your name, which was not intended to ridicule your ancestors but merely yourself."

"I graciously accept." Flury adjusted the nosepiece on his wire-rimmed spectacles. He was in his midthirties, with thinning straw-blond hair and a permanent smirk. He'd never done any manual labor, and I doubted he could bench-press a single volume of *Corpus Juris Secundum*, the ancient legal encyclopedia.

"What do you have on Dr. Clark Calvert?" I asked. "Pincher told me there's something explosive."

"A hundred-megaton warhead," Flury said.

"Do you agree, George? I trust you more than the rookie prosecutor with the Phi Beta Kappa key."

Barrios ran a hand over his bald, tanned dome. "I'd say it was the most unusual and inflammatory piece of evidence I've seen in three decades of sniffing around homicides."

"Tell me."

"In due time, Jake. Let's start logically with Calvert's 9-1-1 call and move forward from there."

"Okay, it's your story. Tell it your way."

Barrios opened a file and slid an eight-by-ten color photo across the table. It was Dr. Clark Calvert in a conservative blue suit and burgundy tie. He looked to be in his late forties. Dark hair, expensive cut, a little more forehead showing than likely a few years earlier. Tight little smile, thin lips, and eyes so dark they looked like polished obsidian. There was something stern and humorless about the guy, but that didn't mean anything. A lot of people freeze when posing for a head shot. I tried to imagine Victoria with the guy all those years ago when she was a college freshman and he was a young doctor. It didn't quite compute.

"You notice Calvert's eyes?" Barrios said.

"He's got two. And they're dark. I noticed that."

"Maybe it doesn't show that well in the picture. I spent three hours with him before he clammed up, and trust me—he's got this weird stare."

"Weird how?"

"Intense and yet distant."

"That makes no sense, George."

"Like his eyes are boring right through you. I've questioned enough killers to recognize a sociopath's eyes."

"Aw, c'mon. Where's your evidence?"

"I'm getting there. Twenty-two days ago, Dr. Clark Calvert called 9-1-1 to report his wife missing. A uniformed officer went to his home and took a statement."

Barrios handed me a folder containing the officer's report, a hand-written statement by the doctor, and a half-inch wad of other documents. I started reading.

The account was straightforward. Calvert told the uniformed cop that he'd quarreled with his wife, Sofia, the morning she went missing. That's the word he used. *Quarreled.* Sofia stormed out of their home wearing yoga pants and a sports bra in a bright-turquoise print.

Calvert told the officer that their arguments had been increasing in frequency. This wasn't the first time his wife had left in a blizzard of angry words only to return a few hours later. Makeup sex was part of the equation. Not this time. Sofia didn't come home that night. At 7:00 a.m. the next day, he called police to report her missing.

She had not been seen or heard from in the three weeks and one day since she went missing. Not by her husband, her parents, or her friends. Also, not a beep from her cell phone. All calls to her number went to voice mail. Police could find no pings of outgoing calls.

Something else in the file caught my attention. An earlier 9-1-1 call. Three months before the disappearance, Calvert sought assistance when Sofia had blacked out. When paramedics arrived, they found her bleary but conscious, with red marks around her neck.

"Consensual asphyxiation during sex," Dr. Calvert told the rescue crew. Sofia confirmed it. The doc had revived her with CPR while the medics were on their way. They administered oxygen for half an hour and left, with Calvert apologizing for the "needless inconvenience."

And now the disappearance. For ten days it had been nothing but a missing-persons case. Then Sofia's well-connected father, Pepe Suarez, called Pincher, who called Barrios. The veteran homicide detective dropped whatever drive-by shooting he was investigating and scooped up the file like a cornerback grabbing a fumble skittering across a frozen field. Oh yes, the rich and powerful can pull the levers of government pretty much at will.

Suarez told Barrios it had been a stormy marriage and that his son-in-law, Dr. Calvert, was *un loco de manicomio*, which I took to mean a major nutjob. Barrios interviewed Calvert, who was cooperative at first. He allowed crime scene techs to scour his house with their luminol and poke into corners with their miniature brushes, flashlights, and cameras. But their evidence bags remained empty. No blood, no fibers of any interest, no signs of a struggle or a room cleaned with bleach. The cadaver dog had remained as silent as the watchdog in *The Hound of the Baskervilles*.

Finally, Calvert wondered aloud why he was talking to a homicide detective.

"Do you think my wife is dead?"

"I have no idea."

"But if she's dead, you think I killed her."

"Why would I think that?"

"I watch television. Cops always think the husband did it."

"Did you?"

"You should leave now, Detective."

Barrios came away with nothing, other than his cop antenna picking up the flop-sweat stink of guilt. The doctor lawyered up—enter Solomon and Lord—and there would be no more interviews.

I closed the file just as the sound of a police siren came up from the street below. We were right around the corner from the county jail. "From what I see, George, you've got nothing. Where's the nuclear weapon you've been teasing me with?"

"We're getting there," Flury said.

"Four days ago," Barrios said, "I get a call from a guy named Billy Burnside. Tennis instructor at Campo Sano, which happens to be the Calverts' country club."

"I see this coming," I said. "Is Billy handsome and fit with a suntan he didn't get out of a bottle?"

"Yeah, Billy ironed out the kinks in Sofia's backhand and wrinkled her sheets."

"Banged her twice a week," Flury said, in case I didn't get it.

"Tennis instructor," I said. "What a cliché. I guess her personal trainer was busy."

"Motive!" Flury piped up. "Now we have the motive for Calvert killing her."

"Not unless you can prove he knew of the affair," I said. "And it wouldn't hurt if you had a body, a murder weapon and, oh, I don't know, some fingerprints or DNA. I hope Billy Burnside isn't the nuclear weapon that's been giving you a boner."

"Just a step in the ladder," Barrios said. "Burnside told me that the Calverts saw a psychiatrist for marriage counseling. Guy's name is Freudenstein."

"You're kidding."

"Harold Freudenstein. Full-fledged shrink with credentials. Used to be on staff at Mount Sinai. Then he started prescribing marijuana and peyote for everything from depression to psoriasis. Hospital tossed him, and he's had a private practice for the last dozen years or so."

"Freud-en-stein," I said melodiously. "A combination of Freud and Frankenstein." I turned toward Flury. "I'm not insulting Austrians or monsters, so don't report me to the Human Rights Commission, Flu Bug."

Barrios continued, "The shrink sees the couple together, and afterward, he writes them a letter." He pulled a thin folder from the file. Skidded it across the table to me. "Take a look."

It was a single page on the stationery of "Harold G. Freudenstein, MD." I read it once and then a second time to make sure I had it right.

"This is real?" I asked.

"*Verdad,*" Barrios said.

"Holy shit. When can I meet Dr. Frankenstein?"

Barrios checked his watch. "Thirty minutes. He's expecting you."

-11-

The Prescription

Dear Dr. Calvert and Mrs. Calvert:
You are to be commended for seeking professional advice concerning your personal and marital difficulties. However, your cases, when considered together, present a dilemma I have never encountered in nearly fifty years of study, research, and clinical practice.

Mrs. Calvert, it is my considered medical opinion that you are in danger of great bodily harm or death if you continue to reside with your husband. I urge you to immediately separate and refrain from all personal contact.

Dr. Calvert, I fear you are not aware of your own propensity for violence. I strongly urge you to obtain treatment for anger management and try to do something about what you admit is your domineering, controlling personality, your jealousy, and your communication skills. At the current time, it is my further medical opinion that you constitute a clear and present danger to your wife's safety and indeed her life.

Ignore this advice at your own peril. I shall not be liable for the consequences of your actions or inactions.

Sincerely,

Harrold G. Freudenstein, MD

·12·

The Chickee Hut Shrink

My ancient Caddy had been parked in the sun, meaning the steering wheel was too hot to touch. I put the top down, fired up the engine, wrapped an old Dolphins T-shirt around the wheel, and headed across the Rickenbacker Causeway toward Key Biscayne, the ritzy island where Dr. Freudenstein lived and allegedly practiced psychiatry. The V-8 was throbbing with a comforting roar as I climbed the steep ascent on the bridge, then powered down the other side. An insistent wind stirred up a light chop on the bay, the whitecaps sparkling like diamonds as I squinted behind my Ray-Bans.

My car, a cream-colored 1984 Biarritz Eldorado, had red velour upholstery that would have felt at home in a New Orleans brothel. The Eldo was my fee in a possession-with-intent-to-distribute case in the Florida Keys. Two hundred pounds of marijuana. My client went free on an illegal search claim, and I got the car, which had a suspicious aroma similar to pine trees and fresh-mowed lawns coming from the trunk.

Dr. Freudenstein's home was a two-room cottage at the rear of an estate on Harbor Point, a small peninsula of mansions on the Biscayne Bay side of the Key. This one was a three-story behemoth, Mediterranean

Revival with iron balcony railings, an orange barrel-tile roof, and lots of archways and loggias and gardens of blooming birds-of-paradise and red bougainvillea. It had a dock roughly the length of a football field.

The shrink's cottage probably had been a caretaker's place. Now, according to Detective Barrios, the elderly widow who owned the mansion provided shelter to the shrink to guarantee his 24-7 availability for therapy and late-night conversation.

I found Freudenstein in an open-air chickee hut set back from the seawall and close to the fifty-meter swimming pool. He was sitting cross-legged and barefoot on a bamboo mat in the center of the hut. The skin of his cheeks shined as if buffed with wax and a chamois, the sure sign of a face-lift and probably injections of various fillers. His hair, the color of storm clouds, was pulled back into a ponytail. He wore a colorful African dashiki over khaki cargo shorts. I didn't have a clue as to his age, but if I had to guess, seventy was in his rearview mirror.

His eyes were closed as I approached, and I figured he might have been meditating. Or possibly dead. But he must have heard me, because he waved a bony index finger toward a fluorescent-orange beanbag chair and said, "Welcome, Counselor."

"Is this your office?" I surveyed the pool deck and the bay beyond.

"Restful, don't you think? Aids in contemplation and meditation."

Just then two teen boys on Jet Skis roared past the seawall, kicking up a wake and scattering seabirds.

"Please sit." Freudenstein opened his eyes and smiled, revealing two rows of perfect white crowns any game-show host would have been proud to show off.

I eased downward into the beanbag without dislocating any vertebrae. The only sound was the tinkle of new age music and the *whompety-whomp* of a paddle fan overhead. Hanging from wooden beams that supported the palm-frond roof were half a dozen white origami birds, their wings flapping in the breeze.

"Tell me about Clark and Sofia Calvert," I said.

"No time for reflection in your world, eh, Counselor? You're saying, 'Cut to the chase,' aren't you?"

"More like 'Cut the crap.'"

A calm smile, perhaps with a bit of condescension. "Fascinating couple, the Calverts. Most dysfunctional I've ever met. And I've treated some doozies."

Doozies being a technical medical term, I figured.

"Tell me, Doctor."

"In a nutshell, Sofia has classic borderline personality disorder. Wholly unstable. Lives in constant fear of abandonment by her partner, yet engages in reckless, impulsive behavior calculated to force him away."

"Her infidelity," I said.

"A serial adulteress. But it's not just the promiscuity. As a teenager, she was a cutter, a self-mutilator, and there was a suicide attempt. As an adult, she's extremely needy and anxious. Yearns for security, yet does everything that threatens stability in her life once she obtains it."

"And her husband?"

Dr. Freudenstein paused as if to choose the right words. Above my head, the origami birds kept flying without getting anywhere.

"A narcissist," he said. "An oversize ego. Not only does he think he's the smartest guy in every room, he needs to prove it. Talking to him is like sparring. He has to land the last punch. He has an inflated sense of his own importance, an unquenchable need for the admiration of others, and yet a total inability to feel empathy for others. Calvert also has a penchant for getting lap dances at strip clubs. Sofia complained about it, and he admitted it."

"None of which makes him necessarily dangerous," I said. "And yet, your *Tarasoff* letter."

He closed his eyes, his expression pained. "Yes, poor Tatiana Tarasoff. A tragic case that haunts every therapist. When does the duty to warn outweigh the doctor-patient privilege?"

These days, all shrinks knew of the famous case from four decades ago; the court ruled that a therapist was liable for not warning the police of his patient's murderous intentions.

"You covered your ass by writing the *Tarasoff* letter."

"It was my moral and legal duty. I didn't want Sofia to end up dead, like Tatiana Tarasoff."

"Did Dr. Calvert take your advice regarding therapy?"

"I'm sure he didn't, not that it would make a difference. The man is a psycho-sociopathic criminal. He can't be cured."

"Whoa! When did you arrive at that conclusion?"

"Almost immediately."

The doc had a quick trigger finger, I thought. If his testimony could ever come into evidence, a defense lawyer would slice him up like a sushi chef with a piece of juicy ahi.

"Was Calvert having delusions or hallucinations?" I asked.

"Not that I know of."

"Showing signs of paranoia?"

"No."

"Did you give him any of the personality tests that point to psychosis?"

"Not the ones you're probably thinking of. But I did give him the HTP test. Are you familiar with it?"

"House, tree, person drawings. Supposedly, people's personalities are expressed through their art."

"No *supposedly* about it, Counselor. The drawings are revealing if analyzed properly, and I consider myself an expert at the task."

"What did Calvert draw?"

"It's not 'what' so much as 'how.' First, he's an excellent artist with great attention to detail. He drew one picture with his right hand and another with his left."

"What did you deduce from that?"

"His need to show off. It's in the details that he revealed himself. He drew a house with bars on the windows, obviously an indication that he stores secrets inside. He drew a man with extremely large hands. Dangerous hands. You don't have to be trained to figure that out when we now suspect him of strangling his wife, do you?"

"Isn't that a little simplistic, Doctor?"

"Let me finish. He drew a sky with a sun partially obscured by clouds, creating both a shadowed and sunny landscape, indicating a fragmented personality. Tree trunks split in half as if struck by lightning, as if his brain itself had been cleaved. Gnarled branches unveiling his own twisted self, the tree dying, indicative of his own emptiness and hopelessness."

This isn't a medical diagnosis, I thought. *It's an afternoon soap opera.* I felt a headache coming on. *Tap-tap-tap* inside my skull, the opening percussion notes of the overture. The booming tympani would soon follow.

"There are two Clark Calverts," Freudenstein continued. "The shiny marble he presents to the world and the nasty piece of work he reveals through violence and now, apparently, murder."

"Dr. Freudenstein, did it occur to you that Calvert was playing you?"

"How so?"

"He knows the HTP test. Hell, I know it because I've had clients take it, hoping they'd come back with schizophrenia and give me a defense. Calvert purposely drew the figures he knew would set off alarms. And he did it with both hands to show you he could outsmart you, whichever direction you turned. He was just having fun, toying with you."

The shrink snickered at me in a most condescending way. "I'm the expert here, Mr. Lassiter. I've been doing this a long time, and I know when someone is fudging."

As expected, my headache was gaining steam, the pressure building inside my skull.

"Were you stoned when you talked to Calvert and administered the test?" I asked.

"My mental acuity on psychoactive drugs is sharper than most people's—including yours—stone-cold sober. No offense."

I could picture him saying that under Victoria's cross-examination, alienating the jury, if they hadn't already laughed him out of court.

"I'd like to have copies of those drawings so I can give them to another expert."

"Happily, except I didn't keep them. He wasn't my patient, and I have no file. Everything, however, is stored in my hard drive." He pointed to his temple.

I exhaled a long breath and rubbed my eyes. When I opened them, the shrink was still there. This wasn't a bad dream. My headache throbbed in time with my heartbeats.

"What are you thinking, Counselor?" Dr. Freudenstein asked.

"Just that I'm jealous of Victoria Solomon, Calvert's lawyer. If you testify for the state, she will have the profound pleasure of cross-examining the bluster right out of you. No offense."

"None taken. I realize I'm a little unorthodox. But trust me, Counselor. After one hour, I had no doubt that Clark Calvert was fully capable of killing Sofia and of having no remorse for doing so."

"And you don't think your quick diagnosis is, at the very least, premature and, at the worst, reckless and wrong?"

"I'm quite confident in all my diagnoses over the years. My track record is impeccable."

Reckless and arrogant, I thought.

The shrink kept at it for a few more minutes, telling me about Calvert's domineering and controlling nature. I had no reason to doubt that Freudenstein was correct in identifying all the bullet points of Calvert's personality. But what is the sum of those parts? Add them up, and you have an unsavory man, but certainly not proof that he's a murderer. Then there was the evidentiary problem.

"Unless I come up with a fancy legal argument," I said, "your letter will be inadmissible, as will be your conclusions about Calvert's mental state."

"I don't see why, Counselor."

"First, you've got the doctor-patient testimonial privilege."

"Technically only Sofia was my patient. She brought her husband along for marriage counseling."

"Victoria Lord will argue persuasively that Calvert was protected by the privilege the moment he walked into your office, or your chickee hut, as the case may be."

Dr. Freudenstein seemed to consider that. Over by the pool, two men in khaki shorts and blue polo shirts began the task of scrubbing the sides to keep the algae in check. I could feel the wind shift from the ocean to the west. Soon the breeze would come from the Everglades, where storms were forming. Inside my skull, the headache swelled to a category five hurricane, snapping tree trunks, toppling power lines, and swamping the dinghy I clung to with all my might.

"And how will the judge rule?" he asked.

I squinted against the furious pain. "No way to tell. Judges are only human—or almost human—and they don't want to be reversed. The state can't appeal an acquittal, so most judges rule for the defendant in close cases, just to cover their asses."

He unfolded his crossed legs and stretched his back this way and that. "Wasn't it Dickens who said that the law is an ass?"

-13-

You Are the Cat

I spent the next twenty minutes looking for a nugget of gold in a pile of elephant turds. I did so while fending off a spike-through-the-eye headache and the clanging percussion of a Bahamian Junkanoo band in my brain.

"Dr. Freudenstein, what I need to prosecute Calvert is hard evidence."

"Such as?"

"Preferably a photo of Calvert standing over his dead wife's body. Lacking that, some admissions he might have made, even inadvertently."

"What kind of admissions?" the shrink asked.

"Did he ever threaten Sofia?"

"Not in my presence."

"Even indirectly? 'Sometimes I wish she was gone.' Anything like that?"

"Would it help your case if I said he did?"

"It would help the justice system if you told the truth."

"Jus-tice," he sang out. "It's such a slippery notion."

"Even without K-Y Jelly," I agreed. "But one thing is certain. Justice requires witnesses who tell the truth. Not to mention judges who know the law, and jurors who stay awake."

"How's that working, Counselor? Do most witnesses tell the truth in court?"

"Strangely enough, most do. In my experience, more lies are told in bedrooms than courtrooms."

The shrink nodded and continued, "Truth is, Dr. Calvert never said anything that could be construed as a threat, directly or indirectly. I gleaned my conclusions about his propensity for violence not from his words but from what I intuited based on my training and expertise and, of course, the HTP test."

The wind kicked up, whistling through the chickee hut. Fat, fluffy clouds were turning angry, taking on the gray pallor of a dead man. The afternoon storms would be early today.

"Anything else about Clark Calvert I should know?"

He thought a moment and said, "He liked to strangle Sofia during sex."

"I heard."

"His story is that she liked it. Enhanced her orgasms. More likely it got his rocks off. But he didn't confine choking to bedroom games. He used it to punish her."

That, I didn't know.

"Punish her for what?"

"If he caught her smoking. Or eating ice cream. She'd slip some Chunky Monkey into the back of the freezer. He's a health nut. Always railing about sugar and fat and carbs. Smoking drove him batshit. She'd sneak a cigarette outside the house by the seawall, and he'd go out at night with a flashlight and tweezers, looking for butts that she neglected to toss into the water. If he caught her violating his rules, he'd choke her until she reached twilight unconsciousness."

Dr. Freudenstein waited for my reaction. I didn't give him one, so he continued, "Do you know about her cat?"

I had eavesdropped on Victoria's first conversation with Calvert when he denied having harmed his wife's feline.

"Tell me about it," I said.

"Escapar, by name. Sofia claimed Clark strangled it because the cat didn't show enough gratitude for his cleaning the litter box. He said it was an accident. But Sofia was telling the truth."

"How do you know?"

"When she prevaricates, she blushes, her eyes blink, she turns away. Makes it easier to know when she's telling the truth, which she was. Clark's denial was very revealing to me. Understand that he admitted to all sorts of untoward behavior. The strip clubs. His controlling nature, his jealousy, his problems with anger."

"But not the cat?"

"Clark Calvert is incredibly bright, his IQ off the charts. And he took some psychiatry in med school. Intentionally killing his wife's cat? He knew what it would mean to me."

"I'm sorry, Doc, but I don't get it. I took phys ed at Penn State, with some theater thrown in because that's where the girls were. To me, there's a big difference between killing a cat and killing your wife."

"No, there's not! Not if you lack empathy for living things. That's what I explained to Sofia. That's why I wrote the letter. I told her, 'You are the cat, Sofia, and the cat is you.'"

-14-

Marching Orders

After leaving Dr. Freudenstein, my head throbbing, I aimed the Caddy toward the mainland and took inventory as I crossed the causeway into the teeth of the coming storm. The shrink had added one more opinion to the side of the ledger that read "guilty."

Yeah, opinion.

Not facts. Not evidence. Gut feelings.

Just like Detective Barrios, who knows a helluva lot about homicide, and whose judgment I trust. And ASA Flury, who needs two hands to unzip his fly, but whose opinion I didn't totally discard. And Pepe Suarez, Sofia's father, who had basically promised to buy Ray Pincher the governor's mansion if he convicted Calvert of murder.

So, too, Dr. Freudenstein *believed* Clark Calvert killed his wife. Sure, he dressed up his opinion in some medical jargon. He even patted himself on the back for predicting spousicide in his *Tarasoff* letter. But there was little chance of that testimony sneaking into evidence.

And what do I have in my trial bag?

As the proprietor of the Lassiter Five & Dime Homicide Store, just what products did I have to sell to shoppers, i.e., the jurors?

Opinions!

As wispy as clouds.

Consider what I didn't have on my store shelves: a corpse, for starters. If you're going to prosecute someone for murder, it's best to prove, as a starting point, that someone else is dead. What else did I lack? Physical evidence linking Calvert thereto, plus time and manner of death, and something indicating that the defendant was in the same zip code when all this happened.

My cell rang while I was brooding. State Attorney Pincher on the line.

"Jake, I've been calling you. How close are you to an indictment?"

"C'mon, Ray. I just got into this today. Cut me some slack."

"No slack, Jack! Get on the bus, Gus!"

"Jeez, and they say I'm punch-drunk."

"Where the hell are you, anyway, Jake?"

"On the Key. Just left the shrink."

"And . . . ?"

"He's colorful. Theatrical. Flamboyant."

"What the hell does that mean? Does he know his stuff?"

"He's either brilliant or a total whack job. He diagnosed Calvert with a psychosis pretty much after saying hello. Even if I can get his testimony into evidence, Victoria Lord will carve him into little pieces on cross."

I was on the causeway now, fat raindrops pelting my canvas top, *rat-a-tat-tat*, like machine-gun fire. The wind ripped across the pavement, and my two tons of metal swayed toward the rocky shoreline.

"That's disappointing, Jake."

"That's life, Ray. Aren't you the one who told me how many times you wished you could prosecute but didn't have the evidence?"

"Jeez, don't sound so defeatist. Don't make me regret appointing you."

"I don't work for you, Ray. I work for the people of the great state of Florida. Official motto, 'If you step on my lawn, I will stand my ground and shoot you.'"

"Damn it, Jake! Are you stoned?"

"I have a prescription. But, no, I am not, at this precise moment in time, stoned."

"Buckle down, buddy."

"Aw, chill, Ray. I'm coming back from Key Biscayne in a driving thunderstorm. The sky and the bay are the same gunmetal gray, and I'm clenching my teeth against the son of a whore of all headaches."

"You are stoned!"

"I swear I'm not. I'm just trying to live my life Aristotle's way. Something that rhymes with *pneumonia* and stands for contentment and fulfillment. In other words, I'm not going to have a stroke if we can't indict Clark Calvert."

"Lousy attitude. You sound like a real loser."

"I'm not giving up, Ray. Who knows? Maybe the cops can find a body so I don't have to waltz into the grand-jury room with an empty briefcase."

"No time for that. Pressure is mounting." He bit off his words, tension seeming to tighten his vocal cords.

"Hey, Ray. I can picture your legs bouncing up and down. Is that Pepe Suarez I see behind the curtain pulling your strings?"

"Screw you, Jake, and your stupid old Caddy, too."

The stupid old Caddy passed the old Seaquarium to my left. To my right was Virginia Key Beach, where I windsurfed so long ago.

"Jake, you don't understand life on this side of the fence. Sometimes you have to throw deep even if your instincts are to run off tackle."

"Thanks for putting it in terms I can understand. Do prosecutors ever call for a quick kick or maybe the old Statue of Liberty play?"

"Clark Calvert just booked a flight to Saigon, smart guy. He's leaving Saturday, unless you have him in cuffs by Friday night."

"Relax, Ray. He's not fleeing. He told Barrios he was going to Vietnam. He's in one of those groups like Doctors Without Borders. Last year it was Mexico. Year before, El Salvador. I think he flew his own plane, brought his own nurses and medication at his expense. Barrios made some calls, and his stories checked out. Our murderer is a hero in remote villages where he performs surgeries for free."

"What's the difference between Mexico and Vietnam, Jake?"

"Wild guess. Tequila versus rice wine?"

"We have no extradition treaty with Vietnam. Calvert booked a one-way ticket. I don't care how you do it. Just get him indicted and booked by Friday night."

·15·

On a Clear Day, You Can See Bimini

Pincher hung up on me, and I considered my options. No way would I ask the grand jurors—twenty-one solid citizens who pretty much believe whatever a prosecutor says—to return a murder indictment based on a diaphanous cloud of opinion, conjecture, and wishful thinking.

I needed to press matters—and quickly. I had two choices. I could either gather evidence that a murder had been committed and Calvert had committed it. Or bail out. Announce we had nothing, resign my appointment, and encourage the police to continue investigating in due course, without deadline pressure.

I imagined what I would say to the press: "Murder has no statute of limitations, so this matter is not concluded. I trust that lead detective Barrios will continue exhausting every avenue concerning the disappearance of Sofia Calvert."

Disappearance.

Which is what it was.

Not homicide.

Not yet, anyway.

Pincher would want to tar, feather, and disbar me. But he'd be in a bind. Appointing me was his idea. His judgment would be questioned if he took any shots at me.

To get to that point—indict or resign—I needed Victoria Lord's cooperation. I needed to ask her to do something she would initially resist.

The rain squall passed as suddenly as it had appeared. Peering now toward downtown, I could make out what used to be my office, four floors from the top of the fifty-two-story skyscraper. That was the home of Harman and Fox, a deep-carpet, high-rise collection of over-paid, overfed paper-shuffling establishment lawyers. They had hired me because I could handle a jury trial without peeing my pants. But I fit into the place the way a Brahman bull fits into high tea. No matter which way I turned, I'd break some china.

I squinted to get a better look at the high-rise where I had toiled before getting fired for insubordination and where, on a clear day, you could see Bimini.

See it. Floating there, a mirage on the horizon.

Seeing Bimini, of course, was not *being* in Bimini.

Fishing, sailing, drinking . . . screwing. None of that if you're keeping time sheets, renting out your life by the quarter hour.

I picked up my cell phone, intending to call Victoria with my idea that could either jump-start the Calvert investigation or end it. I was halfway through dialing the number when my phone rang.

Ah, the other woman in my life. Dr. Melissa Gold.

"Jake, how are you feeling?"

"Fine, really."

"No headaches?"

"Only a couple of bongo drums, not the full band." The truth, I long ago concluded, was sometimes overrated. Just what good would it do to complain? I would stick with the obsolete—and underrated—manly and stoic approach. "When will I see you?"

"I'm coming over. You remember, right?"

It occurred to me that Melissa was worried about my short-term memory. What did she know that I didn't? Or that I'd forgotten?

"Of course I remember. That was my way of confirming."

"I talked to Dr. Hoch, as I told you I would."

"About a new medication." I wanted to prove I had the memory of a pachyderm, or at the very least, of a *Jeopardy!* contestant.

"We've been cleared to do experimental treatments with lithium."

"That's a pretty serious drug."

"You're familiar with it?"

"I had a client on death row who kept trying to commit suicide. The state forced him to take lithium. They couldn't stand it if he died before they could execute him."

"It also has neuroprotective qualities that might stop the creation of tau proteins."

A fierce sun came hard on the heels of the passing storm, and patches of steam rose from the pavement. It felt as if the Caddy were rolling through a fog bank.

"Side effects?" I asked.

"Hand tremors in some people."

"There goes my knitting."

"Dry mouth and loss of appetite are common."

"That's a positive. I can drink beer and still lose weight."

"Some people experience loss of sex drive and impotence."

"Forget it. I'll take dementia."

"No, you won't."

"Hey, c'mon. I'm only thinking of you, Melissa."

"We'll draw blood tomorrow morning to establish baselines, and you'll begin the lithium immediately afterward. Understand?"

I always liked powerful women, so what choice did I have?

"Yes, ma'am," I said.

"I have a faculty meeting. See you later."

She hung up, and as I passed a Chevy Suburban hauling a three-hulled trimaran sailboat on a trailer, I dialed Victoria's cell phone.

"Hello, Jake." Her voice crisp and businesslike.

"Hey, where are you?"

"None of your business, Mr. Assistant State Attorney."

"Meaning you're at Dr. Calvert's house. Great. I'm just getting off the Rickenbacker, catching the flyover to I-95. I can swing across the Julia Tuttle and be there in twenty-five minutes."

"If you set one foot on the property, I'll have you arrested for trespassing."

"That's all you've got?"

"And disbarred for prosecutorial misconduct."

"Now we're talking. But hear me out, Victoria."

"You've got ninety seconds. I'm working with my client."

"I'll be honest with you. The state's case is a little thin."

"Thin? If you fed it a dozen Krispy Kremes a day for a year, your case would still be anorexic."

"I have a psychiatrist who'll swear your client is a psychopath."

"Oh, please, please, call Dr. Freudenstein. Jurors so seldom get a chance to laugh out loud in the courtroom."

"Fair enough. But I'm under pressure from Ray Pincher, and he's—"

"Under Pepe Suarez's left boot. I'm well aware of the politics. Go ahead, Jake. Indict Clark Calvert if you must. I'd welcome the chance to drop-kick your butt out of court."

"Wow! That was good. Just what I would have said."

"I've heard you say it. *Drop-kick* is a little antiquated, but I decided to stick with it. Anyway, go ahead and indict. You know what will happen."

"You'll get an easy acquittal, maybe even a directed verdict. Two days later, a crew from Florida Power and Light will be digging a hole in Calvert's backyard and discover Sofia's skull with an axe in it and your client's fingerprints on the handle. The state can't file . . ."

"Because of double jeopardy . . ."

"Calvert gets away with murder, and I look like a horse's ass."

"Not my problem, Jake. Do you remember what I said the other night at the Red Fish?"

"Don't overcook the sea bass."

"I warned you. 'If you prosecute Clark, it will be the biggest mistake of your life.'"

"Jeez, okay, already."

I was on I-95 now, heading north through downtown. The skyline was so thick with skyscrapers, even from the elevated expressway, there was no view of the bay. The new Miami had clogged streets, lousy parking, and dirty air. But lots of tall, shiny buildings. The condo builders and office developers would continue to borrow cheap money and build on spec until a bubble would burst, as it always had.

"Jake, not only do you have a stinker for a case," Victoria said, "but frankly, you don't have the makings of a good prosecutor."

"Why the hell not? It's easy. You put the cops on the stand and hope they tell a reasonable facsimile of the truth."

"For a prosecutor, you're fatally flawed. You have empathy and warmth and a generous spirit."

"The hell I do!"

"Sure, you hide all that under a tough bark, but really, you have a tender heart."

"Shows what you know. I'm a mean ass and a grim reaper, and don't you forget it."

Her laugh was the jangle of wind chimes. "Okay, tough guy. Why would I ever let my client talk to you?"

"Because of the ground rules. You'll be present. You can instruct him not to answer any question that ruffles your petticoats."

"Jake, your age is showing."

"Wrinkles your pantyhose?"

"Still way out of it."

A silver Porsche convertible cut across the lanes in front of me at the exit for American Airlines Arena. The driver was a young woman with red hair flying in the wind. The Porsche had one of those "Save the Manatee" license plates. I'm all for that, and also for not causing fatal crashes on the expressway.

"Calvert can refuse to answer any question," I said to Victoria. "There'll be no court reporter, no recording, and I won't take notes. He's not under oath and can't be charged with perjury. With no record, nothing he says can be used to impeach him, should he be indicted and choose to testify. Basically, he and I will have a conversation that never took place."

"What's in it for Clark? Why tell you anything?"

"Because if I finish the interview and have insufficient evidence for an indictment, much less a conviction, I'll quit. I'll make a public statement that Dr. Calvert cooperated with authorities, and there's no evidence that he committed a homicide. We all go home."

"And the flip side? What's in it for the state of Florida?"

"It's a long shot. Calvert tells me A, which by itself is meaningless. But it leads me to B, which is intriguing, and that leads to C, which stands for conviction."

"Clark says he is one hundred percent innocent."

"Then there won't be a B or a C. He's got no worries."

"You sound like the cop in the station house telling the suspect, 'Hey, kid, if someone thought I committed a crime, I'd sure want to tell my side of the story.'"

"Trust me, Victoria. There's something in this for everybody. You don't want a trial. Even if you win, your client's reputation will be shattered. He's way better off with me clearing him."

She was quiet a moment, and at her end of the line, I heard a piano. Something classical. Maybe it was Tchaikovsky's piano concerto number one or Rachmaninoff's number two. All those Russians sound alike to me. Didn't Victoria say Calvert was a classical pianist, besides being the world's greatest surgeon, brightest mind, airplane pilot, and ahem . . . former lover?

"I'll ask Clark and call you right back," she said. "It's his decision."

"Deal."

I swung right onto the exit for the Julia Tuttle Causeway to take me across the bay. I was heading to Miami Beach filled with optimism. I figured Dr. Clark Calvert would agree to talk. Basically, Dr. Freudenstein told me so.

"Not only does he think he's the smartest guy in every room, he needs to prove it. Talking to him is sparring. He has to land the last punch."

Calvert would take one look at me—a bent-nosed ex-jock with a couple too many concussions—and hop into the ring. Like Muhammed Ali, he'd showboat with a little dance and maybe a rope-a-dope before counterpunching. He'd want to show his ex-girlfriend that she made a mistake dumping him all those years ago. He'd talk more than was necessary. And maybe, just maybe, he would say too much.

My cell beeped with a text message from Victoria.

Clark says he'd love to talk to you.

I stomped on the accelerator and let the old V-8 roar to life. I intended to bring down Clark Calvert and prove Victoria wrong.

Damn it, Victoria! I don't have a tender heart!

-16-

Bloody Hands

I pulled the Eldo into a brick circular driveway in front of Calvert's house on North Bay Road, which, as the name suggests, is on the Biscayne Bay side of Miami Beach. The city is a skinny little island shaped much like the state of Florida, and here on the western side, it's about a mile due east to the ocean.

A row of towering royal palms formed a border along the driveway and gave the impression of sentinels guarding the place. There was a shiny red Ferrari 575 Superamerica parked closest to the house with a personalized license plate, "SAWBONES." My powers of reasoning immediately concluded this was Dr. Calvert's car. Perfect. A twelve-cylinder rocket that shouted money and speed and status. The retractable roof was tucked away, giving me a nice view of the tan leather interior, soft as a baby's ass. A limited edition, the car was in the half-million-dollar range.

Wearing a summery blue suit without a tie, Solomon leaned against the driver's side door, his arms crossed in front of his chest.

I slid out of the Eldo. "They start the party without you?"

He shrugged. "They're around back on the patio, which Calvert calls the 'terrazzo.' That's between the main house, which he calls the 'villa,' and the guesthouse, the 'casita.'"

"Outside? I assumed we'd be in your client's study, sitting in leather reading chairs."

"That's what Victoria figured you'd want."

"Why?"

"So you could ask to take a pee, then snoop around the house, rummaging through closets and peeking inside the medicine chests."

"Your fiancée is a damn suspicious woman."

"She just knows your tricks, Jake. Mine, too."

"What's going on, pal? You look troubled."

"You know how women feel about their first lovers?" he asked.

"Usually regretful."

"Wrong! They feel wistful and nostalgic. Dreaming of what might have been."

"What might have been, Victoria goes missing without a trace."

"I'm afraid you were right when you said she could still have a thing for him."

"I didn't mean that. I was just pulling your chain."

He shot a look at Calvert's Ferrari that said, *I'd like to drag a key the length of the car and then take a dump on those soft leather seats.*

"Do you have enough to indict him?" Solomon asked.

I decided to tell the truth, which I seldom do with opposing counsel. But Solomon was a friend, even if his principal avocation was irritating me. "Not even close to an indictment. More like a general suspicion without a hard scrap of proof."

He glanced toward the house, which would probably be called neoclassical, with its portico supported by sturdy white columns, a gabled roof, and a triangular pediment over the entrance. The place looked new, meaning Calvert might have knocked down an earlier neoclassical house to build this neo-neo one.

Solomon lowered his voice and said, "If I had anything inculpatory, I'd give it to you."

"Whoa, Nellie! I'm gonna pretend I didn't hear that."

"I mean it, Jake. The guy gives me the creeps, and Victoria just seems entranced by him."

"Solomon, you're overreacting, to say nothing of making an unethical suggestion. If you're gonna cheat, do it to win."

He shook his head wordlessly. Usually Solomon was an upbeat, self-confident guy. Now he looked shaken.

"Don't show any jealousy," I advised. "Victoria will perceive it as weakness."

He mulled that over. "Thanks. You're better at this than I am."

"You're doing fine. When's the wedding, anyway?"

"It was going to be September, but with this case, Victoria says we have to move it to late October."

"Not a college-football Saturday, Solomon."

"Not my call, Jake. Jeez, don't put me under any pressure."

He sulked a moment, then said, "Vic was engaged once before. Bruce Bigby. You know him?"

"Not personally, but I see his signs on the turnpike extension. Gentleman farmer and real estate developer with a couple thousand acres of avocados down in Homestead."

"Yeah. Mr. Guacamole. President of the Kiwanis. A Dudley Do-Right."

"What's your point?"

"They had a wedding date. Invitations sent out. Church of the Little Flower in Coral Gables. Then she broke it off."

"Yeah, because she met you!"

"I know, I know. It's just that . . . Calvert's got me a little unnerved."

"Solomon, you gotta toughen up. Victoria loves you. God knows why, but she does."

He smacked me on the shoulder a second time, and we started along a flagstone path that ran around the house. I stopped next to a stand of birds-of-paradise and looked into a large bay window. Sidestepping through the plants, I pressed my face to the glass.

"Hey, Jake. What the hell are you doing?"

"Snooping. Nice piano."

"It's Calvert's music room."

"Was that him playing when I was on the phone with Victoria?"

"Yeah, classical stuff, then some show tunes. Do you know *Phantom of the Opera*?"

"Sure. I had a girlfriend who dragged me to the Miami Beach production three times."

"Calvert was playing the piano and singing 'Music of the Night' just before you got here."

My eyes were adjusting to the change of light inside the music room. I spotted some photographs on a set of shelves. "Singing to Victoria?"

"I guess. He was looking at her as he sang."

"You know, that's how the Phantom seduces the young soprano. Puts her in a trance. She faints right into his bed."

"Aw, jeez, Jake. Stop."

I was squinting now, trying to make out the photos on the shelves. "Are those pictures of Calvert with his wife?"

"Yeah. Sofia."

There were at least a dozen photos of the couple in formal wear. Opera, theater, charity galas, I figured. Sofia Suarez Calvert was a brunette, petite and shapely. Smiled a lot.

"The one on the top shelf, left side," I said. "Is Calvert sitting in the cockpit of a plane?"

"A Marchetti acrobatic plane. Oh, wait. Calvert insists on calling it an 'aerobatic' plane. I guess that he doesn't have enough hobbies, so he picked up flying. Apparently, traveling to the Bahamas isn't exciting enough without doing some barrel rolls."

"Sofia's not in the picture. Does she go with him?"

"Only when he promises not to do tricks. But with or without her, he says he flies nearly every weekend."

I scanned the rest of the room. Tasteful midcentury furniture. Leather sofa and chairs, a painting on one wall of a fisherman in a small dinghy looking apprehensively toward stormy skies. It might have been a Winslow Homer. On a facing wall was a life-size portrait of the man himself, Clark Calvert, in green scrubs, his mask dangling around his neck, his surgical gloves bloody.

Bloody hands, I thought.

Who does that? Who would want it in a portrait?

"You're looking at the painting of the great man," Solomon said. "What's it say to you?"

"He likes to shock people. They come into the music room expecting harpsichord music and petits fours, and see their host with blood on his hands."

"Why do it?" Solomon asked. Clearly, my pal was trying to figure out his own client, but not for the case. For personal reasons.

"Maybe Calvert wants his guests to know that he's capable of things they're not," I ventured.

"Healing the lame?"

"Or killing the healthy," I said.

"I hadn't thought of that." Solomon motioned me away from the window. "C'mon, dude. They're waiting out back."

I stepped out of the bushes, and we continued along the path. We passed a bocce-ball court, a croquet lawn, a red-clay tennis court, and a full-size basketball court. The swimming pool was a no-nonsense twenty-five meters divided into four lanes.

I spotted Victoria and Calvert sitting at a glass table on the patio—or *terrazzo*—under what appeared to be a high-pitched silk tent, waving in the breeze. She wore a turquoise sleeveless dress. He wore white linen slacks, no shoes, and a short-sleeve blue cotton shirt with red stripes and a pair of tigers embroidered on the chest. Next to his bare feet lay a soft leather briefcase the color of melted butter.

"Is Calvert wearing a bowling shirt?" I said.

"I asked him the same thing," Solomon said. "It's a Gucci. Twelve hundred bucks. He said it's a sardonic commentary on a bowling shirt. Do you know what that means?"

"Only that he's a jerk. This is gonna be fun, pal."

"You won't get anything out of him."

"Unless his wife's body floats by in the bay, I don't expect to. Between you and me, I'm just going through the motions before bailing."

Solomon stopped in his tracks, forcing me to also. "The *emmis*?" he asked. "You being straight with me?"

"Yeah, Judge Duckworth said she'd let me out if I think Pincher is using me for political purposes."

"Do you?"

"I don't know, but I've got no hard evidence, and Pincher is giving me an unreasonable deadline."

"Before you bail, could you cut Calvert down a couple notches in Victoria's eyes?" he asked hopefully.

"For you, pal, it would be my pleasure."

-17-

The Doctor and His Verbs

Victoria made the introductions, and I said howdy to Dr. Clark Calvert, who stood and greeted me. "Pleased to meet you, Mr. Lassiter. I've heard so much about you from Victoria."

"Whereas she won't tell me a thing about you," I replied.

He was a shade under six feet tall, dark hair, expensively trimmed, receding a bit in front. His thin lips disappeared when he flashed me a smile, or rather, he showed some teeth without any pleasure in those dark, lifeless lizard's eyes. I held his gaze as we shook hands.

Well, I shook. He gripped. And having closed the pliers handle first, he got the better of me. My busted-up knuckles ground against each other until I crunched back. I've got the bigger paw, and I tip the scale at 235, and in a matter of seconds, I had him stalemated. Then, dipping my shoulder to get a little more leverage, I squeezed harder. He grimaced but didn't beg for mercy.

"What's the prize?" I asked.

"What?"

"Does the winner get to take Victoria to the prom?"

"Boys! Please sit down." Victoria the schoolmarm looked ready to whack both of us with a ruler.

"Hey, he started it," I said in my best sixth-grader whine.

I released the doc from my death grip. He wouldn't give me the satisfaction of rubbing his wounded mitt. Instead, he said, "I could beat you left-handed. I can use a bone cutter with either hand. Completely ambidextrous."

"Would that be a useful skill for masturbation?" I asked.

He started to say something, then realized I wasn't really looking for an answer, so he forced a chuckle that sounded like a frog burping.

"During my residency," he said, "I squeezed a tennis ball every night. Three hundred times, each hand. I still do it."

"Lifting the liter bottle of Jack Daniel's works for me," I replied. "As the night goes on, the bottle gets lighter, if you catch my drift."

We settled into sling patio chairs and stared at each other across the table. Victoria was to my right, a legal pad in front of her, a pen in her hand. Solomon was to my left, padless and penless, his eyes darting from Calvert to me. My pal looked out of sorts. He didn't seem to know what to do with his hands. After a moment, he pulled a pack of chewing gum from his inside suit pocket, unwrapped a piece, and popped it into his mouth. I caught the distinctive aroma of Juicy Fruit.

I let the silence play out and looked toward the smooth bay. Calvert's property had more than a hundred feet of seawall. A Bertram Sport Fisherman in the sixty-foot range sat in the quiet water at the dock.

"Well, then, Mr. Lassiter," Calvert said, "what would you like to know?"

"What's the meaning of life? Is there more to it than just this?" I spread my arms, as if to take in his bay-front estate.

"You'd like to discuss existential philosophies?"

"Maybe later. Let's start with this. Which of those strong hands did you use to strangle your wife?"

"Ha!" He exhaled a burst of a laugh, but his eyes were not amused. "That's not the way it's done, Mr. Lassiter. You're supposed to toss some softballs, lull me into a sense of security, then trap me with my inconsistencies."

"I'm not much for softballs."

"What makes you think I strangled Sofia? Why not drowning in the bathtub, Mr. Lassiter? Or poison in her egg-white omelet?"

"I'm just following the evidence. You told the paramedics about choking her during sex. You told Dr. Freudenstein, too."

"That quack! I'm going to sue him for violation of doctor-patient privilege and defamation. I'll see to it his ticket is pulled."

"He's not a big fan of yours, either. Thinks you're psychotic."

"Based on what? An hour's chat? If a patient comes to me complaining of knee pain, I don't tell him, 'That's awful. We have to amputate your leg.' Dr. *Fraud*-en-stein is the most incompetent shrink in Miami, and believe me, that's saying a lot."

"Maybe we'll just leave it up to judge and jury to evaluate his qualifications."

I wanted that to sound threatening. As if I were ready to tighten the knot on my necktie, stand at attention, point an accusatory finger at the defense table, and announce, "Ladies and gentlemen of the jury, this man, Clark Calvert, is a murderer."

Calvert didn't break out in a cold sweat or curl up in a fetal position. He just snorted an indifferent laugh and said, "Oh, how I would love to see my Victoria cross-examine that pompous gasbag."

My Victoria.

I shot a glance at Solomon, who squirmed in his patio chair and chewed his gum so hard I could hear his jawbones clacking. I felt for the guy. And I was starting to despise Clark Calvert. I didn't want Solomon's unethical help in prosecuting the arrogant prick. But I wouldn't mind making Calvert's life miserable for a while. Right now he was having too damn much fun. There's a lot of gamesmanship—strategy and tactics—in interrogation, and so far, Calvert was winning.

"Dr. Freudenstein might surprise you in court," I said. "Jurors like experts with strong opinions." It was a lame counterpunch—a weak, looping roundhouse that hit nothing but air.

"If, as that quack claims, I were psychotic . . ." Calvert cocked his head and gave me his thin-lipped smile. "Is that the right verb, Mr. Lassiter? Is it *were* or *was*?"

"Depends. If you're not psychotic, it's *were*. If you are psychotic, it's *was*."

"Bravo! You know your subjunctive form, Counselor."

"If I *were* you," I said in my best smart-alecky voice, "I wouldn't be enjoying this. But you are. This is a game to you, isn't it?"

"I'll admit that verbal sparring relieves the tedium."

"How nice for you. Your wife is missing and presumed dead, and you play around with verbs and make jokes about her manner of death." I imitated his supercilious tone. "Why not drowning in the bathtub, Mr. Lassiter? Or poison in her egg-white omelet?"

He stayed quiet, appraising me. I held his gaze. I could hear Victoria tapping her pen against the glass tabletop. Either she was nervous, which I doubted, or this was a trick I'd taught her, a prearranged signal to her client: *Stay quiet.* Across from her, Solomon cleared his throat. That could be a signal, too, but more likely it was postnasal drip.

Calvert followed Victoria's cue and didn't say a word.

"I interrupted you, Doctor. You started to say, 'If I were psychotic . . .'"

"I wouldn't have spent the better part of five years trying to help Sofia with her many problems. Additionally, as to my sardonic manner, which may be off-putting to you, I disagree with your major premise. I'm not making light of Sofia's death, because I don't for a moment think she's dead. This is just one of her histrionic games, her pathetic attempts to garner sympathy and to be the center of attention. She ran away from home as a teenager several times. Or didn't my dear father-in-law tell you that?"

"Pepe Suarez says Sofia would always call home within twenty-four hours of hitting the road. Didn't want her parents to worry. This time, radio silence."

"If you ask me, the little drama queen is on the beach in Buenos Aires or perhaps Maui. With a boyfriend. Or maybe just looking for one."

That perked me up. "You suspect she's been unfaithful?"

Solomon, who'd been quiet, stirred and said, "Jake, that's not an area we're comfortable with."

Calvert brushed him off with a theatrical wave of the hand. "Nonsense, Stephen. I'm not embarrassed to have been a world-class cuckold."

"It isn't that. It's that the state will use—"

"Please, Stephen!" Calvert's dark eyes looked toward Victoria for support.

She hesitated a moment, then shrugged. "Steve, it's okay. Go ahead, Clark."

Solomon looked deflated, as if his fiancée had just dumped him for another man, and maybe she had. In a normal case, where my opponents weren't my pals, I would exploit the situation. I'd let Calvert drive a spike between Solomon and Lord, then give it a couple hammer blows myself. That's what we do. Search for any weakness in the opposition, like an infantry commander probing for the soft spot in the enemy's front line. But I felt empathy for Solomon. Aggravating as he could be, he was still a friend. As for Victoria, bless her saintly heart, it's difficult for me to play shyster tricks on her.

"To answer your question," Calvert said, "I didn't suspect Sofia of being unfaithful. I *knew* she was. So what?"

"Motive," I said. "That gives you the motive to kill your wife."

Solomon grimaced. Of course, he knew that's where I was headed, and that's why he didn't want Calvert to answer. Victoria knew, too, but she was letting Calvert call the shots. Probably just as she did when they were dating so long ago and he was the sage older man.

"How *bourgeois*," Calvert said. "Jealousy as a motive for murder."

"Human nature, Doctor. Jealousy over the betrayal. Anger that leads to a thirst for vengeance."

"Not emotions that I'm familiar with, Counselor."

I tried to think of my next question, knowing I was getting nowhere.

Wearing her poker face, Victoria scribbled notes on her pad.

Stirring in his chair, Solomon said, "How much more do you have, Jake? I'm not sure you're getting anywhere with this. Besides, I'm getting hungry."

-18-

Uxoricidal Rage

Steve Solomon . . .

S olomon wasn't hungry. He just wanted to end the questioning. Not that he feared Calvert would incriminate himself. That, he wished for. Rather, he felt useless. A spectator, the kid in the corner with the water bottle while Lassiter and Calvert traded punches in the boxing ring.

So far Lassiter hadn't laid a glove on the bastard. And just look at the cockiness of the guy. As if being suspected of murder juiced him. Taunting Lassiter, challenging him to come up with something—anything—to prove it.

Victoria's attitude disturbed Solomon. With clients, she always ran the show. She would never let a defendant wander off track. As usual, she had laid out the rules for Calvert before Lassiter arrived.

You don't have to prove anything, so just answer the question. Volunteer nothing. Don't try to score points and show you're smarter than Lassiter.

"But I am smarter."

"We know that," Victoria replied. "No need to prove it, Clark."

But Calvert couldn't help himself. Ignoring Victoria's instructions, baiting Lassiter, dissing Freudenstein. The "my Victoria" reference had not gone unnoticed. A totally different meaning than "my lawyer." Or how about "my lawyers"?

What am I? Chopped liver? Pickled herring? Jeez, I'm the senior partner here.

Questions dogged Solomon.

Why isn't Victoria reining Calvert in? Just what power does he hold over her? Does she still have feelings for the guy? Doesn't she see his true nature?

Criminal defense lawyers get a feel for their clients, nearly all of whom profess their innocence. A few actually are. From their first meeting with Calvert, Solomon believed the man was guilty. Victoria didn't share the feeling. For his part, Lassiter didn't have a shred of evidence, much less proof beyond a reasonable doubt.

The worst of all worlds.

"How rude of me, Stephen," Calvert said. "You're hungry. I should have offered refreshments. How about some smoked fish spread and crudités?"

Solomon shook his head. "That's okay. Don't want to spoil my appetite for a martini."

Calvert turned back to Lassiter. "Counselor, you were saying how infidelity leads to jealousy, which leads to murder. But how prevalent, really? There is so much infidelity in marriages, and so few murders."

"Occupational hazard—I see a lot them. Mostly the killers are men with seemingly massive egos, but just quivering pudding underneath. Insecurities galore, often about their masculinity."

Lassiter paused, as if waiting to see if he could get a rise out of Calvert. But the doctor just showed the same indecipherable, reptilian stare. With each passing moment, Solomon despised the guy even more.

"I would think in these days of gender equality," Calvert said, "women should be gaining in the mariticide numbers."

Using the Latin word for killing a husband, showing off. Distinctly pronouncing each syllable so it couldn't be confused with matricide. He really can't help it.

"Women usually take less drastic measures," Lassiter said. "Maybe just cut the sleeves off all their husbands' shirts."

"A Freudian might find some symbolism in that snipping." Calvert made a *click-clicking* sound with his tongue.

"A few have taken the scissors directly to their husbands' genitals. No need for symbolism there."

"Oh, how your male clients must have responded with uxoricidal rage."

Again with the five-dollar words.

"Some. That's how they became my clients."

"I imagine they saw your ads on a bus bench."

Solomon stifled a laugh. Back in the days BV, Before Victoria, he was the one with the bus bench ads, not Lassiter. The ads hadn't stirred up any business until he secured the phone number 823-3733, which translated to UBE-FREE in giant letters.

"Your clients, Mr. Lassiter," Calvert mused. "I picture a parade of grease monkeys who find their spouses in someone else's double-wide."

"What are you saying, Dr. Calvert? That you're too upper-crust to kill your wife?"

"Not precisely. Extramarital gymnastics came with the package that was Sofia. It was never a deal breaker."

"Well, aren't you the understanding one?"

"Not that I liked it. Or got off on it. I was never present. I never asked for the details. The whos and whens and wheres, I didn't want to know. If anything, we had an understanding, *sub silencio*, an unspoken agreement that she had certain freedoms, and so did I—should I choose to exercise them."

"You were unfaithful, too?"

"Such a quaint word, *unfaithful*. Religious overtones, don't you think?"

The discordant sound of a leaf blower kicked up from a neighbor's yard. Solomon looked toward Victoria. What was she thinking? What was she feeling? What was it about this supercilious prick that kept her under his spell? Why was she letting him pontificate?

Clark Calvert, oh wise philosopher. Share your wisdom.

Equal parts disgusted and fearful, Solomon would have to talk to Lassiter about it, get some advice. Before Lassiter had met Melissa, he'd had a thing for Victoria, but Solomon knew he would never act on it. Which was pretty much the definition of a friend, now that he thought about it.

"Were you tomcatting around?" Lassiter asked. "Do you like that word more?"

"Indeed, I do. It's quite vintage. Images of back alleys and stairs to third-floor walk-ups. No, Mr. Lassiter. Sofia filled all my carnal needs."

"Carnal? You play with words like a dealer shuffling cards."

"You disapprove of my vocabulary?"

"You could have said 'sensual needs.' Or 'sexual needs.' But you used the word *carnal*. You're a physician, and you drop Latin words like a butterfingered receiver with the football. My old pal Doc Charlie Riggs taught me a little of that ancient language. *Carnal* comes from the Latin word meaning 'flesh' or 'meat,' and it's related to the word *carnage*, which relates to murder and slaughter. So maybe your subconscious chose that word, and you were really saying that Sofia filled your murderous needs."

He barked a little laugh. "Bravo, Counselor! You've combined your rudimentary knowledge of Latin with your slipshod knowledge of Freud. And eureka! You've caught me. I confess. *Nolo contendere!*"

"Just so we're clear, what is it you're confessing to?"

"Not following accepted standards of behavior. Not being society's idea of a perfect husband. A capital offense, I fear." He turned toward

Victoria. "You're so fortunate you didn't marry me, Victoria. Imagine the likely consequences."

Victoria's eyes blinked, but she stayed silent.

Lassiter didn't say a word.

It was left to Solomon to say, "What consequences?"

Before Calvert could answer, Victoria said, "Steve, we're not asking the questions. Jake is."

Just great, Solomon thought. *I'm being ignored by our client and lectured by Victoria.* He looked toward Lassiter for help.

"What consequences, Doctor?" Lassiter asked, just as Solomon's eyes pleaded for him to.

"Who knows? The road not taken," Calvert said. "Opportunities left unexplored. Victoria and Clark. Who is to say what might have happened? Endless joy or endless strife. Unquestioned loyalty or embittered resentment. Possibly, eternal love." He showed that small, thin-lipped smile and looked directly at Victoria with those opaque eyes. "Or not. Who is to say which spouse cuts off the other's sleeves? Or which one pushes the other off a cliff?"

-19-

A Woman of a Million Moods

Victoria Lord . . .

Victoria sucked in a breath and didn't exhale.

What did Clark just say?

Bringing back the memory of that horrible day on the cliff near Big Sur, when he had frightened her so deeply. But what was he saying now? Admitting he killed Sofia? Or just the opposite? That he's a man who can walk that tightrope between civilized and bestial behavior. Or was this just some game, an effort to shock her? But why?

Such an odd mix of emotions just now. Sitting at a table with the man she loves and the man she first loved. She averted Clark's gaze and glanced at Steve. His big brown eyes were in puppy-dog mode. A searching, confused look.

Poor guy. Do I need to keep assuring him of my love? We're getting married! Can't he tell my devotion to him isn't threatened by my professional obligation to Clark?

In the Intracoastal, two motor yachts churned past each other, foamy wakes slapping against the seawall. The breeze was picking up, and the day, which had been sunny, then cloudy, then storming, then sunny again, threatened to change yet again. In the distance, a police siren sang against the wind.

Victoria returned her attention to Jake, who showed no signs of ending his interrogation. He had loosened his tie to half-mast, the out-of-court mode for a guy whose neck was always too big for his shirt collar. He was fifty but still a handsome man, his thick hair, once the color of sawgrass, now turning silver, the lines on his face deepening, adding character if you like that craggy look. Even the broken nose was attractive in a manly-man sort of way.

She had been worried about him. Those headaches he tried to shrug off, the experimental treatments with Dr. Melissa Gold he refused to talk about.

Typical man. Afraid of showing fear, of appearing mortal.

She was glad Melissa had come into Jake's life. A sophisticated, educated woman who cared for him. A year or so ago, Victoria had complained about Jake dating women she called "the young and the flighty." Under her prodding, Jake had agreed to stop chasing inappropriate women, though he narrowly defined the term to bail jumpers and fleeing felons.

Victoria knew that Jake was resistant to forming a deep, abiding relationship. Steve said it was because he was hung up on her, but Victoria thought it was more complex, having to do both with prior failed relationships and his uncertain medical condition.

"Let's play a game, Dr. Calvert," Jake said.

"Oh, goodie. Is money involved? Shall we wager on something?"

"Words. I'll say a name or a word, and you say the first thing that pops into your head."

"How tiresome. If you say 'cat,' and I say 'dog,' what would you make of it? Just what training did all those phys-ed courses give you for Jungian word association? Did you, in fact, learn anything at all?"

"Boxing. I learned how to throw a left-jab, right-hook combo. Wanna see?"

"Jake, please," Victoria said.

"Look, Doc. I know you gotta show you're the smartest guy on the terrazzo, but I ain't stupid."

"Ain't you now?"

Jake ground his knuckles into his forehead. Victoria didn't know if it was a meaningless gesture, like rubbing your chin, or if he was fighting off a migraine.

Jake said, "I didn't spend four years at Penn State—okay five years—to listen to your condescending bullshit."

"Fine, Counselor," Clark said. "Just get on with it before I doze off out of ennui."

"Cat."

Clark snorted and smiled. "Departed."

"Father-in-law."

"Corrupt. Wired. Always hated me."

"Dr. Calvert . . ."

"I'm sorry. You just wanted one word. Okay, what would I say about Pepe Suarez? How about 'contemptible'?"

"You thought too hard about it to come up with a single word. Let's do it your way. Don't limit yourself. Give me a phrase, a sentence, a master's thesis. Anything you want to say is fine."

"Fire away, then."

"Sofia."

"Bewitching and bewildering. Girl-woman. And very much alive."

"Your medical patients."

"Interesting specimens. Except for the boring specimens."

Jake raised an eyebrow. Victoria couldn't tell if it was intentional. Was Jake underlining the comment for her benefit? Making certain she didn't miss the point: Clark relating to human beings as things.

"Sex."

Clark laughed. "You want me to use some word associated with violence or domination, don't you, Counselor?"

"Not really. But you just did, so let's move on. State Attorney Pincher."

"Political toady."

"Detective Barrios."

"The Cuban Columbo. Without the raincoat. Or the brains."

"Steve Solomon."

"Pleasant fellow. In over his head."

Victoria winced. Why, oh why did Clark do that? And what did he mean? Over his head with the case? Or with her? She could see Steve's jaw muscles flexing. They did that when he ground his teeth.

"Victoria Lord," Jake said.

"Jake, is this necessary?" Victoria interjected.

"Let him answer, Vic," Steve said. "I'd like to hear this."

Clark cupped his chin in his hand, as if in deep thought, and said, "Unformed angel. When I met Victoria, she was so pure and angelic. So young, still a girl really. I was hoping to watch her grow into the woman she would become."

"Or were you hoping to mold her into the woman you wanted?" Jake asked. "As you later tried with Sofia."

"You're suggesting that I'm controlling—is that it?"

"I think we can all agree on 'controlling.' It's 'strangling' that's the issue."

"You don't know me, Counselor. You haven't even scratched the surface."

"Let's try. How about this one? Clark Calvert."

"Free of shackles," the doctor said.

"Shackles of marriage? Of Sofia?"

"Free of society's shackles."

"The rules don't apply to you. That it?"

"Not the stupid ones. But I wouldn't kill my wife. And I didn't."

"Forget the word associations," Jake said. "Just tell me about Sofia. In your own words."

"Whose would I use but my own?" Clark exhaled an exasperated sigh. "Lovely little thing. Well put together. Natural boobs, of course. I wouldn't let her make that mistake, though Lord knows, she wanted a couple of beach balls."

"You wouldn't let her have breast augmentation?" Jake said.

"Do you disapprove? Are you one of those men who lusts after the big melons?"

"I pretty much love all breasts. But you didn't say, 'I talked her out of it.' You said you 'wouldn't let her.'"

"In addition to your practice of amateur psychiatry, are you also a linguist, Counselor?"

"Just tell me what else I should know about Sofia."

"She loves nude sunbathing. Has a smooth tan hide and a luxurious pelt of thick, dark hair."

"Sounds like you're describing the best in show at Westminster Kennel Club."

"Indeed, she's a prize. Vivacious. Outgoing. Makes friends easily, unlike me."

"Why unlike you?"

"I'm no good at parties. Meeting people. Small talk bores me. Most people bore me."

"Did Sofia bore you?"

"Ha! You tried to trick me with the past tense. You wanted me to say, 'No, she never *bored* me.' She doesn't *bore* me, Counselor. She's alive, somewhere, and still not boring me."

"Duly noted. You found her . . . pardon me, you find her exciting?"

"A meteor streaking across the sky."

"What does that mean, exactly, Doctor?"

Clark showed a little smile. "She's hot. A firecracker. In and out of bed." He shot a look at Victoria.

What are you saying, Clark? Hoo boy, Sofia's hotter than I am?

"Beyond her looks, Sofia is a woman of a million moods. Unstable behavior that coincides with those shifting moods. A damaged self-image, which I have labored to heal. Impulsive behavior that tries the patience of anyone who cares for her. Intense episodes of anger, depression, and anxiety, and sometimes all three. Irrational fears of abandonment, feelings of emptiness that no amount of tender loving care seems to help. And a history of substance abuse and attempts at self-harm as a teenager and young adult."

"What do all those symptoms add up to, Doctor?"

"Oh, stop playing games. You know very well. Classic borderline personality disorder."

"Did you know this when the two of you met?"

"It would have been hard to miss."

"That might have scared away most men."

"Do you think I fit into that category? 'Most men.' Or would you find me more sui generis?"

"No, I don't think you're one of a kind. I've met guys like you before. Narcissists. Egomaniacs. Sociopaths."

"And did you also get a medical degree at East Bumfuck State?"

"I ask the questions, Doc. Did you marry Sofia so you could fix her?"

Clark blinked. "A surprisingly perspicacious question, Counselor. Did I underestimate you?"

"I don't know. What's *perspicacious* mean? Sweaty, like perspiration?"

He tilted his head and showed the hint of a smile. "Victoria said you were smarter than you look."

"She's told me. My brain takes it as a compliment, but my face gets pissed off."

"I suppose that subconsciously I thought I could fix Sofia. And when she comes back, I'll keep trying."

Victoria turned toward Jake. "Jake, I assume you're about finished. I think my client—"

"*Our* client," Steve interjected.

"Our client has been incredibly forthcoming. We know you have nothing. You know you have nothing. Can we just call it a day?"

"I'm almost done. Promise."

"It's okay, Victoria." Clark reached across the table and patted her hand. She flinched but didn't pull away. If it had been any other client—a man she hadn't lived with and loved and ultimately rejected—the gesture wouldn't have been so off-putting. Steve's eyes widened, watching the patty-cake.

Jake studied the three of them. Though he was expressionless, Victoria thought she saw wheels turning. Just what was he thinking? What would he do? And what would he say?

After a moment, Jake said, "Doctor, why did you kill Sofia's cat?"

-20-

The Unasked Question

Steve Solomon . . .

Lassiter's question about the cat was still pending. Steve forced himself to stay seated. He yearned to beat the crap out of the cat killer, possible wife killer, and dead-certain son of a bitch who was bird-dogging his fiancée.

"My Victoria . . ."

"Victoria and Clark. Who is to say what might have happened?"

Steve used all his self-control to keep cool and show no emotions. He surely wouldn't reveal his fondest wish: a murder conviction and a life sentence for Clark Calvert, MD.

"No segue, Mr. Lassiter?" Calvert said at last. "No song and dance? Just a rude and aggressive question?"

"The cat. Why'd you kill Escapar?" Lassiter's voice colder than it had been.

"It's hardly relevant, but if you must know, it was an accident."

"Not what Sofia told Dr. Freudenstein."

"Somewhere in Miami, there's a person walking around today whose DNA shows he's a descendant of Charlemagne."

"Not following you, Doc."

"That person's relationship to Charlemagne is closer than Sofia's relationship to the truth."

Steve looked across the table and saw Victoria smile. She probably didn't even realize she was doing it. Admiring Calvert's wit and intelligence. He imagined her saying something later.

Isn't it wonderful to have such a smart client who outfoxes Jake at every turn?

She caught his gaze and deleted the smile. *Gotcha, Vic.*

"How do you accidentally kill a cat?" Lassiter asked.

"Sofia was in one of her reclusive, can't-be-seen-in-public moods. I took Escapar to the vet for his shots. On the way home, I put his cage on the seat next to me, but I must not have latched it properly. He was strung out from the procedure, and he leapt at me, screeching. Landed on my shoulder. I swerved into the other lane, but thankfully there were no oncoming cars. I grabbed the little darling by the neck and while still driving, tried to jam him back into the cage."

"You broke his neck?"

"Apparently."

"With one of those strong hands."

"Is that a question?"

"I wonder if the same thing happened with Sofia."

"That I tried to put her in a cage?"

"Oh, we already established that. But did you accidentally kill her?"

"Jake! That's enough." Victoria scowled at Lassiter.

"No, Victoria. Let him go," Calvert said. "I'd love to hear your theory, Mr. Lassiter, if you have one."

Steve looked on, amazed. Just who was running the show, lawyer or client?

"You frequently choke Sofia during sex, isn't that right?" Lassiter asked.

"'Choke' is misleading. I never touch her windpipe. I apply pressure to her carotid artery to cut off oxygen to her brain. It enhances her orgasms. The timing is somewhat delicate. Squeeze. Release. Squeeze. Release. Knowing when to stop is essential for safety."

"Ever squeeze her neck while not having sex?"

"Why would I?"

"As a form of punishment."

"Never."

Lassiter paused, as if to decide where to go with the denial. Above the Intracoastal, seabirds chirped and swooped toward the mainland. For a moment, Steve wished he were soaring with the birds. Something gnawed at him, made him want to fly away. Then he realized what it was. The unasked question . . . and the answer he dreaded.

"Doctor, when you and Victoria Lord were involved, did you ever choke her, during sex or otherwise?"

Old-fashioned chivalry would prevent Lassiter from asking the question. He would never embarrass Victoria. But other sexual-asphyxia episodes could be used in court under pattern evidence. Lassiter knew that, of course, and could ask the question in a neutral way, omitting Victoria's name.

"What about other women, Doctor?" Lassiter asked.

You're reading my mind, old buddy.

"Other than Sofia, have you ever choked anyone or applied pressure to the carotid artery during sex or at any other time?" Lassiter continued.

A prolonged silence except for the clatter of a Boston Whaler heading out the Intracoastal. After a moment, Calvert said, "No."

Lassiter stared at him wordlessly. The trial lawyer's trick of extracting information by staying quiet. The typical witness squirms, aching to fill that quiet space with music and often makes incriminating statements. But Calvert sat there placidly, waiting.

"No?" Lassiter said. "Or, not that I can remember?"

Calvert let a small smile crease those ribbon-thin lips. "Wait! I remember now. I strangled three women during sex back in Poughkeepsie. Tossed their bodies into the Hudson."

"Clark, please." Victoria rapped her knuckles on the glass tabletop. "No joking around."

He shrugged. "Got it. No, Mr. Lassiter. No other women. And I only engaged in the oxygen-deprivation maneuver with Sofia because she asked me to. Apparently, she was well schooled in its use before we met."

"Jake," Victoria said, "we agreed to a brief interview concerning Clark and Sofia, not Clark's past. Now, you've gone far afield. Either return to the agreed-upon subject matter or we're terminating the questioning."

"Sure thing," Lassiter said.

"Counselor, I rather thought you'd want to run through the time-line of the day Sofia disappeared," Calvert said.

"If you're suggesting it, I can probably do without it."

"Don't you want to see if my story conflicts with what I told the police?"

"Aw, you're too gosh darned smart for that."

"We'd quarreled that morning. Something stupid, as quarrels usually are. Sofia wanted us to spend the next weekend on Saint Kitts with two other couples. Friends of hers, not mine. People I have nothing in common with. Without even asking me, Sofia had already told them we would go. We had a row about it."

"I got all that from the police report."

"After she stormed out of the house, cursing at me, I waited awhile, then went looking for her in all the usual places. The beaches she frequents, mostly the topless ones. Glow, the poolside bar at the Fontainebleau. She's rather fond of their cocktail called Passionate Pepper. Vodka and passion fruit spiked with jalapeño. She'd get the small pitcher for seventy dollars. Passionate Rip-Off might be a better name. The Bal Harbour Shops. Checked the fancy stores where she buys dresses she wears once, then crumples in the back of her closet."

"But you waited until the next morning to call the police."

"In the evening, I dozed off in the living room, still hoping she'd come home during the night. Maybe join me on the sofa for some makeup sex. That was our routine. When she didn't appear, I called the police first thing in the morning."

"Does that about do it, Jake?" Victoria said.

"Just a few more questions. Doctor, did you object to Sofia smoking?"

"Often, both as a physician and a husband."

"But she'd still sneak a cigarette now and then, right on this patio, wouldn't she?"

"She'd flick the butts into the water, where they'd gather against the seawall, her lipstick quite visible on the filter tips. Russian Red, the shade is called. Quite exotic."

"And what would you do, Sherlock Holmes, when you found the evidence?"

"Jake!" Victoria aimed an index finger at him. "Do I need to remind you that you're only here because Dr. Calvert graciously agreed to an interview? He didn't agree to be ridiculed."

"Sorry, Victoria. I'll save my ridicule for court."

"Victoria," Steve said, unable to keep quiet any longer, "I think we're duty bound to let Jake ask questions his way."

"*His* way is insulting and calculated to irritate and provoke. Our duty is to preserve dignity and protect our client."

"The doc's doing a pretty good job without our mucking it up. I'm just saying, let Jake be Jake. We know his bag of tricks."

Victoria's look could have left bruises, maybe even blood, Steve thought. He knew he shouldn't disagree with his cocounsel—and fiancée—in front of opposing counsel or the client, for that matter. He just couldn't help himself. He wanted Lassiter to de-nut this supercilious bastard.

"Are you two kids done?" Lassiter said. "Because now I'm getting hungry. And I'm sure you'd rather be picking out china patterns than watching this tennis match."

-21-

Let's Make a Deal

Victoria Lord . . .

Victoria cemented a smile into place. Inside she was fuming. Unable to provoke Clark, Jake was trying to sow dissension between Steve and her. And Steve had taken the bait. She vowed to keep her cool now and to set Steve straight later. Just what was wrong with him, anyway? Her long-ago relationship with Clark seemed to have more of an impact on Steve than on her.

"C'mon, Jake," Victoria said. "Just wrap it up."

"Happily. Doctor, what'd you do when you found all those cigarette butts?"

"I'd chastise Sofia. Verbally."

"She told Dr. Freudenstein you'd choke her as punishment."

"As I said, Sofia, dear heart, is capable of fabrication, especially if it garners her sympathy. That's doubtless one reason for her disappearance. Wanting people to worry about her. To fear for her. Or simply to just talk about her. As we're doing now."

"Did you similarly chastise her about her diet?"

"I asked her to cut back on sugar and carbs."

"Sofia is what, about five foot two, one hundred ten pounds?"

"One hundred seven."

"Hardly obese."

"A thin person can be quite unhealthy, Mr. Lassiter."

"Did you ever punish her for eating Ben & Jerry's?"

Clark showed a sideways smile. "Eating Ben & Jerry's what?"

"Ha!" Lassiter gave a mock laugh. "I get it. A little salacious humor. Who knew?" Jake's smile disappeared, and he pointed a finger at Clark. "Did you ever squeeze Sofia's neck to the point of unconsciousness because she ate ice cream?"

"No."

"That only occurred in bed?"

"Correct. And only once. The night I called 9-1-1."

Jake turned to Victoria. "My theory is it happened twice."

"I only care about the evidence," Victoria said, "not your theories or what you wish the evidence showed."

"But I'd love to hear it," Clark said.

"Me, too," Steve said. "You're outvoted, Victoria."

She looked at Steve in disbelief. What the hell was he doing, disagreeing with her in an adversarial setting? What a Sonny Corleone stunt!

And what does he mean 'outvoted'?

This isn't a democracy. I'm lead counsel! Steve has become a pouting whiner who needs to assert his manly authority. But I'm trapped. I can't squabble with Steve in front of our client and opposing counsel.

"Go ahead, Jake," she said. "Give it your best shot."

Jake looked straight across the table at Clark. Each man held the other's gaze. "My theory is that this was a tragic mistake. You strangled Sofia into unconsciousness during sex or while chastising her for pigging out on Chunky Monkey. This time, you squeezed too hard or too long. When you realized she was dead, you panicked."

"I never panic."

"You disposed of her body."

"Preposterous! How and where?"

"Video security shows you driving away from this house at 11:17 a.m. the day of her supposed disappearance. I presume you picked up her hundred-and-seven-pound body and put it in the trunk of your Ferrari while it was still in the garage. I don't know where you dumped it."

"Detective Barrios and his team of community-college techies combed through the car and the house and never found any evidence to support that," Clark said. "Not a hair or a fiber or a drop of my beloved's precious bodily fluids."

Clark, Clark, Clark! Why do you try so hard to be creepy?

Victoria imagined the impression he would make in court, the jurors not understanding this was merely the persona Clark presented to the world. His shtick was shocking people. It was just an act, she believed, but would a dozen strangers agree?

Jake turned to Victoria. "Involuntary manslaughter. A reckless but not intentional killing. With full confession, seven- to ten-year sentence. Actual time to be served, I don't know. We'll work out the numbers."

"In other words, Jake, you have nothing. Zilch. Zero."

She turned to her client. "Clark, if the state had anything, they wouldn't offer you a deal. But they can't even prove that Sofia is dead, much less that you killed her."

Jake stayed silent. What could he say? Victoria wagged a finger at him. "I let you do this today because we had an arrangement. If you walked out of here with nothing but lint in your pockets, you wouldn't proceed. Are you going to honor our agreement?"

"I'm not done with the interview."

"Really? Do you have more word-association games? Because I do. How about the term *prosecutorial misconduct*?"

"Motive," Jake said. "I ought to be able to inquire about motive."

"You explored infidelity, and Clark was very forthcoming. He knew all about it. He lived with it."

"I'm talking about money, not sex," Jake said.

"What money?"

"Life insurance. Three million dollars. Let's talk about that."

-22-

Three Million Buckaroos

Jake Lassiter . . .

Victoria was right. I had *nada*. There's a tired old legal expression: "If you have the facts, hammer the facts. If you have the law, hammer the law. If you have nothing, hammer the table."

Well, I didn't even have a hammer. I did have an insurance policy, however.

"The two of you had mutual insurance policies," I said. "Three million dollars."

"Do you know how much I'm worth?" Calvert said.

"From your inheritance and your own earnings and investments, we think conservatively eighteen to twenty million."

"Close enough for government work. Do you think I'd kill my wife for a lousy three million?"

"No. I already told you. I think it was an accident and then a cover-up. But maybe the best way to nail you is first-degree murder with a profit motive. Possible death penalty."

"Jesus, Jake!" Solomon's eyes went wide. "I was wrong about you. You *are* a true prosecutor. Trying to extort a plea by overcharging."

"I echo Steve's sentiments," Victoria said, ganging up on me. "This is beneath you."

"Not if we reach a fair result. As I've always said, rough justice is better than none."

Calvert regarded the three of us squabbling with a detached indifference. Then he said, "Now that I think of it, three million dollars is quite a sum of money."

Victoria's head swiveled toward him. "Clark, what are you saying?"

"To some men—most men—three million dollars is quite significant. Let's say you make sixty thousand a year. Sixty-five, tops. You lease a BMW convertible that you can't afford. You live in a crappy apartment west of the Palmetto Expressway. You're a so-called tennis pro, which is a fancy name for a guy who gives lessons to rich-bitch housewives who are so spoiled and lazy they won't bend over to pick up their own tennis balls. Now *there's* a man for whom three million buckaroos would be an answered prayer."

"You're talking about Billy Burnside at your country club," I said.

"Indeed. Billy the Kid Burnside. Master of the backhand. A suntanned Lothario of the clay courts who will soon age out of the seduction biz if multiple melanomas don't slay him first."

"What's Burnside have to do with Sofia's life insurance policy?"

Calvert reached into the briefcase at his feet and pulled out a blue-backed document, which he slid across the table to me. I looked at Victoria and then Solomon. From their expressions, they didn't know what it was. Calvert obviously liked being the quarterback and calling audibles that his teammates didn't expect. I hoped it would come back to haunt him. I let the document sit there a moment. Calvert watched me with an enigmatic smile.

"Why don't you just tell me what it is," I said. From Calvert's preamble, I figured I knew, but I'd rather study Calvert while he told me.

"Amended assignment of benefits," Calvert said. "Two months ago, roughly four weeks before Sofia disappeared, she named Billy Burnside as beneficiary of her life insurance. Cut me out completely. As you have admitted, Mr. Lassiter, three million dollars can easily be a motive for murder. Certainly, more so for Bad Boy Billy than for me, don't you think?"

"When did you learn of the change of beneficiary?"

"A couple days after she disappeared, I went through Sofia's closet, found it hidden under some lacy black panties. Little more than thongs, so they really didn't cover the document that well."

"There goes another of your theories, Jake," Victoria said.

"Not if your client is lying about when he found the document. What if he found it before Sofia disappeared? Now he's got proof of the affair that he might only have suspected. Even worse, it's proof she's in love with Billy Burnside. That's too much to take for a man of your client's towering ego. He kills Sofia, knowing the life insurance could be a motive used against Burnside."

Unruffled, Victoria smiled. "Nice attempt to recover your own fumble. But that's rank speculation without a shred of evidence."

"Gotta agree with my partner," Solomon said. "If I were you, I'd go talk to Billy Burnside and shine that flashlight of yours up his ass."

"I plan to talk to him, though probably without the proctology. I'd love to know just what Sofia told him about your client."

Even though I was talking to Solomon, I kept my eyes on Calvert. He didn't blink. He didn't flinch. He didn't smile. He didn't frown. He didn't look scared. With an air of indifference, he regarded me with those dark, bottomless eyes, as if I were no more or less interesting than the chair under my butt.

-23-

The Happiness Quotient

Victoria Lord . . .

After leaving Calvert's house, Steve and Victoria drove in silence down Pinetree Drive, hung a left on Twenty-Third Street and a right on Collins Avenue.

Finally, Victoria said, "Do you want to stop at the Raleigh for a drink?"

"Nah."

"The Delano, then? You like the starkness of the white lobby."

Steve shook his head. "Feels like a mental ward to me."

Another moment of silence, and she said, "We haven't registered yet."

"What?"

"Our wedding registry. For gifts."

"Do people still do that?"

"Of course they do."

"We already have a blender, Vic."

It could have been a joke, but Steve didn't put any humor in his voice. Victoria knew he was in one of his moods and decided to let it be.

After a moment, he said, "Let's walk on the beach and talk."

"Walk and talk. Okay, then."

Steve parked his torch-red Corvette in a garage at Seventh and Collins. They walked two blocks east toward the ocean, took off their shoes, crossed the boardwalk, and descended the stairs to the beach. They turned north when their bare feet touched moist sand at the shoreline. The wind was up, and evenly spaced whitecaps foamed on the incoming tide.

"Postmortem on the interview?" Victoria asked. "Is that what you wanted to talk about?"

"Sure. Let's start with that."

"Clark was brilliant, don't you think?"

"You say that a lot, Vic."

"Do I?"

"Last night at the Red Fish, with Jake. You said Calvert was brilliant. IQ off the charts. Speaks some zillion languages. Flies his own plane. Yada, yada, yada."

She glanced at the man she loved, but the glare of the sun, just above the horizon to the west, kept him in silhouette.

Are you jealous, Steve? Don't you know you're the only man for me, now and forever?

"Do you think I'm brilliant?" Steve asked.

She couldn't stifle a laugh.

"What was that?" His voice reflected his wounded pride.

"I'm sorry, Steve. You're very smart and very clever and a very good lawyer."

"But not brilliant."

"You got me to fall in love with you when I was engaged to someone else. That's pretty darn brilliant, isn't it?"

A pair of gray terns landed in front of them and pecked at the wet sand, hunting for treats.

"The two of you have this vibe," Steve said.

She regretted having laughed a moment earlier. Steve's usually robust ego—often too robust—had taken a battering.

"Honestly, Steve, I don't know what you mean."

"Electricity. Chemistry. I don't know, some secret language between the two of you."

"Did Jake put these thoughts in your head? Because you, of all people, know his strategy. Drive a truck between enemy platoons. He's a master at psychological warfare."

"Jake was pulling my chain last night at the Red Fish. I know that. But maybe he was onto something, without realizing it. So tell me. Do you feel a little buzz with Calvert in the room?"

"No. But knowing of my past with Clark, maybe it seems that way to you. If you didn't know he was my first guy, would you think the same thing? Or would you just think it's a good working relationship between attorney and client?"

Five hundred feet above their heads, a biplane flew along the beach, hauling a banner advertising a nightclub with cheap drinks and allegedly hip people.

"I don't know. I can only tell you what I see and how I feel."

"And I hear you. I know your concern comes from a place of love. But you must know that I have no interest in Clark Calvert and haven't since I was barely out of my teens. You, Steve Solomon, are the man for me. The only man who creates a buzz in the room." She smiled at him. "And other places."

She hoped that would settle it. They walked without speaking for several minutes, their bare feet leaving footprints in the wet sand. Ahead of them was a lifeguard stand painted a ferociously bright red and yellow. The nearly fluorescent beach shacks were the city's iconic monuments to *La Dolce Vita*. The lifeguards had gone home for the day. The sunbathers had folded their beach chairs, and except for a few joggers and seabirds, Steve and Victoria were pretty much alone.

"Last night, you said Clark called you to get your advice before he married Sofia," Steve said.

"And I told him to follow his heart."

"I asked whether you thought he was giving you a right of last refusal, marriage-wise. You evaded. You went into a story about breaking up with him all those years before, but you never answered the question, and I didn't press you."

"If you're asking again, Clark never said, 'Marry me or I'll marry her.'"

"But did you get the impression that's what he meant?"

She thought about her answer as they stopped then, in tandem, turned, and began retracing their steps southward. Some elements of their relationship were like that. Wordless agreements, a sense that each knew and shared the other's thoughts and desires. But there were times when one's thoughts seemed jarring and alien to the other.

"I had no impression other than what Clark said. I took his words at face value."

"What about subtext? That the talk of love and marriage was really about the two of you?"

"No, of course not."

She was tired of the cross-examination and hoped that would shut him up. Every couple was in sync and out of sync at times, she figured. It's the *ratio* of sameness and differences that counts, bearing in mind the importance of the issues on which they agree and disagree. She had been a pretty good math student in high school and at Princeton before turning to the less precise world of law.

As they walked in silence, she wondered if there might be a Happiness Quotient, a mathematical formula that could predict the odds of a couple's happily-ever-aftering, to borrow a phrase from *Camelot*.

She ran some rough equations through her head. Zero was a flat-line relationship, and ten a perfect score. There could also be a negative score, bottoming out at minus ten. Anything above zero was positive.

Numbers and percentages floated through her mind. Multiply the percentage of agreed-on issues times the average "importance weight" of those issues. If she and Steve agreed 70 percent of the time on issues with an average eight-out-of-ten importance weight, they scored five-point-six. Then figure they disagreed 30 percent of the time on issues with an average importance weight of four. Multiply the numbers and you get one-point-two. Subtract that number from five-point-six and you get a Happiness Quotient of four-point-four.

That's above zero, but is it high enough?

She'd have to ask her married girlfriends to run their numbers.

"Can you remember exactly what Calvert said in the call about his getting married?" Steve asked, interrupting her calculations.

"Steve, really? Is this necessary?"

"I just want to process his words myself."

She wanted to tell the truth. But she wondered, *Can Steve handle the truth?*

"He told me he loved Sofia very much, but with her history of psychological issues, he wanted to run it by me before marrying her. The conversation was almost clinical in nature, as if he were consulting his own shrink. Maybe he just had to say everything aloud to make his own decision, and I'm a pretty good listener. To answer your question, he never indicated any continuing interest in me. It was all about Sofia, nothing about me."

There is the truth, the little white lie, and the damn dirty lie, she thought. Remembering the conversation with Clark Calvert, she considered this a little white lie, an itsy-bitsy sin based on her need not to inflict pain on Steve.

"Victoria, it occurs to me that all of this is so unnecessary," Clark said after they discussed Sofia.

"How do you mean?"

"Instead of my angst over my forthcoming nuptials, we should be celebrating the two of us reconnecting."

"Clark, don't . . ."

"I've thought so much about us over these years. I have regrets. I should have given you more room to grow. You were so young. But so perfect."

"Clark, I'm not going there, and you're marrying Sofia."

"Life, my darling Victoria, is a long and winding road. Who knows when it will circle back again?"

Steve and Victoria continued along the beach, the coppery glow of the sunset washing the horizon. Victoria considered the nature of what she had told Steve.

A necessary and benevolent deception.

Sometimes, she thought, *to boost the numbers of the Happiness Quotient, it's necessary to fudge the calculations.*

-24-

The Unsworn Lie

Steve Solomon...

S teve processed the conversation as they veered across the sand to the boardwalk at Seventh Street, passing a potbellied octogenarian man sunbaked the color of cooked chestnuts. The man wore Speedos and nothing else and was waving a metal detector across the sand, hunting for lost watches and spare change.

Victoria so seldom lied; she wasn't good at it, he thought. Overall, that was a positive. But just now, it ate at him. He figured he'd been right the first time. Calvert had called Victoria, testing the water. He wanted to get back with her. She demurred, so why not just say that now?

Screw you, Clark Calvert, and your classical piano and your zillion languages and your aerobatic plane.

Victoria interrupted his thoughts. "Steve, there's something we need to talk about."

Now what? he wondered.

"Would you agree that Clark handled himself very well today?" she asked.

"Yeah, sure. He was brilliant. Genius. Best interview ever."

She ignored his sarcasm. "Well . . . he lied."

"What!"

"When Jake asked him if he ever choked any other women . . ."

"No! You?"

She exhaled a laugh. "Not me! No. Never. A young nurse he was dating in Boston after he'd left New Brunswick. They'd had an argument, and he lost it. Choked her into unconsciousness. She filed a complaint with the hospital where they both worked."

"Ho-ly shit!"

"He's very remorseful about it. Says that isn't who he is."

"Apparently it is."

"There was a hearing before the hospital board. To his credit, Clark admitted the incident. He got a warning letter placed in the file— not for the choking, but because she was on his surgical team and he shouldn't have been dating her."

"No criminal charges?"

"She never took it to the police. The hospital personnel file is confidential, and Clark says it was expunged five years later in any event."

"When did Calvert tell you about it?"

"Moments before the interview, when you were bringing Jake to the patio. He asked what he should do if Jake asked about choking other women."

"And . . . ?"

"Steve, I had so little time to process the information."

"You told him to lie?"

Her expression gave it away. "He wasn't under oath. I did nothing unethical."

"An unsworn lie is okay? That's slicing the bologna pretty thin."

"What would you have done?"

He didn't hesitate. "Same thing, but you're not me. I'm Slippery Steve. You're Miss Propriety. Or at least you were until Clark Calvert dropped into our lives."

"It was a judgment call, and I'm not sure I made the right decision. But we need to be on the same page, so there it is."

Steve stayed quiet as they climbed the stairs to the boardwalk and down the other side, heading toward the parking garage. He returned to his thoughts, picking up right where he had left off. He couldn't understand Calvert's power over Victoria. Svengali was changing her right before his eyes.

More than ever, I really hate this guy.

So how, Steve wondered, could he help Lassiter convict the son of a bitch?

-25-

The *Titanic*, Burning Coal, and Me

Jake Lassiter . . .

They were taking my blood, and I was reading about two friends who might be dying.

The *Miami Herald's* heartbreaking story reported that Nick Buoniconti, the undersize, brainy Hall of Fame linebacker, and Jim Kiick, the running back as tough as his name, were suffering from cognitive impairment. Both had symptoms of CTE, the incurable, fatal bastard of a disease caused by repeated concussions.

Buoniconti and Kiick were key players on the Miami Dolphins 1972 Super Bowl championship team. The term *perfect* was always associated with that undefeated squad. Now *CTE* and early *death* may be the watchwords. Five players had already died. Eight more appear stricken with brain damage, showing classic symptoms of dementia. With living players—including me—there can be no certain diagnosis. As Dr. Melissa Gold kept reminding me, that can only be done post-mortem in an autopsy.

I sat on the edge of an examining table in a room at the University of Miami Hospital. Melissa asked questions as a young female medical technician filled four tubes with blood from a vein in my arm. They wanted baseline readings of various substances before I started taking lithium, the neuroprotective drug being used experimentally when CTE is suspected.

"On a scale of one to ten," Melissa asked, "how would you describe the severity of your headaches?"

"On a good day, about a four. Bad day, roughly a quadrillion."

Her brow furrowed. She was wearing a white lab coat emblazoned with DR. M. GOLD in blue lettering. She held a clipboard and filled out boxes on a questionnaire filled with medical mumbo jumbo. A pair of rimless reading glasses was perched on the end of her upturned nose, giving her the look of a studious—and sexy—librarian. Her reddish-brown hair was tied back in a bun, and in the world's worst lighting—hospital fluorescent—she still looked smashing.

"Any recent episodes of confusion?" Melissa asked.

"I'm having a little trouble with names."

The medical technician removed the needle from my arm, covered the injection site with a cartoon Band-Aid—Fred Flintstone—and left the room with my vials of blood.

"You forget names or confuse them?" Melissa asked.

"Kim Jong Un and Kim Jong Il. I can't remember which is which."

She frowned, unhappy with either me or the North Koreans. "Do you find yourself growing more irritable?"

"No! Damn it!"

"It would be helpful if you took this seriously, Jake."

"Truth is, I'm feeling okay, except for the headaches and tinnitus. And maybe a general malaise I can't put my finger on."

"Try."

"It's possible I'm worried."

"About your condition?"

I nodded. "And what happens to my nephew, Kip, if I'm not around. And to you. You've raised the stakes by putting a lot of yourself into my diagnosis and treatment. Not to mention our relationship."

"*Not* to mention? Isn't that one of the things you're actually worried about?"

"I suppose so."

"Let's speak directly without euphemisms. You're worried that, if you die, it will be horribly painful for your nephew and for me."

I nodded. "I lose sleep thinking about both of you."

She took off her glasses, cocked her head, and studied me. "At least you're being real now. That's a start. What else is bothering you?"

"The case I'm investigating and supposedly prosecuting. The alleged murder of Sofia Calvert."

"It's a difficult case?"

"Impossible. There's no body. No proof the woman's even dead. I should never have agreed to prosecute."

"If there's no case, can't you just walk away?"

"I have one more interview and if nothing comes out of it, that's what I'll do. The judge says she'll let me out anytime before an indictment."

"Then you have a plan."

"Tentative plan. I'm still not sure. I'm not a quitter. Never have been."

"Is it really quitting? To drop something you don't believe in?"

"The State Attorney thinks so. He's pushing me hard to get an indictment, to hell with the evidence. So yeah, I'm stressed."

"Your work has always been stressful, and you've always handled it."

I smoothed the ridges of the Band-Aid on the inside of my elbow, Fred Flintstone looking at me with that goofy grin. "Until now I've never entertained the notion that I might be dying. Lately I've been asking, what the hell am I doing? Why am I working so hard? Why am

I taking orders from Pincher? And of course, the big one, what's it all about? Life, I mean."

Her face reflected both concern and warmth. "I'm glad you feel so comfortable with me that you can share these things."

"Yeah, well, it's something new for me. Admitting weakness."

"It's not weakness, Jake. It's simply being honest and open. Let's deal with it in small bites, starting with your legal case. It's putting a huge amount of pressure on you, and that's detrimental to your condition."

"I don't see the relationship."

A nurse poked her head inside the door, saw us, and left again. Maybe they needed the room for a paying customer, not a freeloading volunteer in an experimental study.

"You're like the *Titanic*," Melissa said.

"How?"

"The *Titanic* wasn't sunk by an iceberg."

"Sure it was."

"Not an iceberg alone. There was a smoldering fire in one of the coal bunkers below the waterline. The fire started even before the *Titanic* left Southampton."

"But the ship hit an iceberg. Everybody knows that."

"Right. By total chance, the iceberg's impact was directly on the area of the hull that had been weakened by the fire. Without that, the hull likely would have held."

"Your point being . . ."

"Reduce the number of things in your life that can add up to hurt you. Let's put out the small fires and focus on the iceberg. And maybe on the good things, too."

She watched, waiting for me to respond. "You're in my life. And that's good. Huge. Bigger than any damn iceberg." She smiled warmly. "Yesterday at South Pointe, you said your mind wandered to thoughts of me during the day. You said you cared deeply for me. I said the same about you."

"Sure. I remember."

"How deeply do you care?" she asked.

"How deep is the ocean? How high is the sky?"

"Try not to be cute, okay? Be real."

"I mean it."

"Right after you said you cared, you said, 'But . . .' And left it hanging there. Left *me* hanging there."

"But what?"

"That's what I'm asking, Jake."

"But . . ." I repeated. Women, I have long believed, remember everything you say. Perhaps they also remember everything you *almost* said.

"What gives you pause when you think about how much we care for each other?" she asked. "What's the *but* that you want to use to modify our relationship?"

I just blurted it out. "But because of my condition, I don't know if it's a good idea for our lives to become so intertwined. My future is uncertain. You've said as much. Dr. Hoch has, too. I'm betting he's been even more grim in his consultations with you."

"Wrong. You have a precursor to CTE. Neither of us can say whether that will result in the full-blown disease."

"But if it does, if the misshapen tau in my brain hardens into those fibrous tangles of sludge, I'll die. And not quietly. Or prettily. And you can't offer me any hope of treatment."

"Currently, there is none."

"And my life expectancy would be three to five years. Lousy years."

"Unless medicine makes advances."

"Like I said, Melissa, an uncertain future. It's made me get in touch with my own mortality. Meanwhile, for the past year, you and I have been getting closer. And the closer we get, the harder it will be for you if I die. And there's something else I think about late at night when you're sleeping alongside me or when I'm tossing and turning alone. The day we met, I ended up unconscious in a restaurant, and later that night, I was hooked up to monitors in an emergency room. If we'd met under ordinary circumstances—waiting for a table at Joe's, in line at the DMV, or even a blind date—would you have been attracted to me?"

"Why wouldn't I?" There was a touch of frustration in her voice. "Do you think I have feelings for you because you're ill? Because you may die? We're all going to die, Jake. And I've had lots of patients over the years, but you're the only one I've ever kissed, much less slept with. If you're thinking that I'm involved with you because of some sort of—I don't even know—medical empathy, well that's both insulting and hurtful."

Before I could say another word, she stood and left the examining room. I sat there a moment as the door slowly closed, and over the loudspeakers, a calm voice announced a Code Blue—cardiac arrest—on the third floor. It wasn't for me, of course.

Not yet. Not today. But perhaps . . . soon.

-26-

Lawyers Hungry as Locusts

The ambulance chasers were after me.

Reclining in my Barcalounger at home just after 10:00 p.m., a tumbler of Jack Daniel's in one hand, I reviewed the latest batch of unsolicited mail from "concussion lawyers," as they called themselves.

"Dear Former Player . . ."

How personal. How heartwarming.

By e-mail and snail mail, by UPS and FedEx, I was on the receiving end of epistles from these hungry-as-locusts mouthpieces.

"Register now for NFL Concussion Settlement Funds. Time is running out!"

Platoons of personal-injury lawyers would be oh-so-happy to take a bite of my apple without having to do any honest lawyering.

"Let our law firm help with doctors, testing, and paperwork."

Oh, the heavy lifting. The lawyers—or rather, their paralegals—will work themselves into a sweaty lather mailing in my paperwork, then pulling the handle on the slot machine and taking their cut when the coins jangle into the tray. Or trough, if you want to imagine the lawyers as pigs on the farm.

All of this came about because the NFL settled a class action by agreeing to pay about a billion dollars to retirees who suffered from dementia and related ailments. After denying for decades that blocking and tackling could cause traumatic brain injuries, the NFL—much like tobacco companies—finally surrendered to science. Yes, it had been wrong to rush big, tough guys like me back onto the field after sustaining concussions.

I took a long, slow pull on the Tennessee whiskey as I thought of the ramifications of all this. These lawyers were slick. They would conveniently fill in the blanks on the forms, naming themselves as my attorneys. I'd already learned from the Players' Association that some of the greedier lawyers were trying to double-dip, collecting their fees from a fund created by the NFL and then another 30 percent from their own clients. We'll see what the federal court says about that.

But do I really stand on higher moral ground?

Do I even have the right to be offended by these hounds sniffing after an easy buck? In my younger days, I used to hang out by the elevators on the fourth floor of the Justice Building. When the elevator door opened, my trained eye could separate defendants from civilians as easily as a shark could distinguish juicy groupers from poisonous rays. The ones heading for their arraignments held yellow computer printouts. Their eyes darted down the corridor. If no lawyer accompanied these lost souls, I would offer directions to the appropriate courtroom and my easily affordable services.

Credit card? Sure, I can take that.

I didn't get rich being a corridor lawyer. But that never bothered me. I never envied the heavy hitters of the profession, never lusted after their Gables Estates mansions or their trophy wives. I just wanted to do good work defending the wrongfully accused. Surprise! Turns out there were far more people rightfully accused.

I was thinking these weighty thoughts when I heard a pounding on the front door. The chimes haven't worked in years, and good friends know the door is usually unlocked. Swollen by Miami's sky-high humidity, the door will open with a sturdy shoulder or a Larry Csonka stiff arm. A cop in jackboots could do it, too.

I heard the *crunch* of the door opening.

"Jake! You here?"

It was Solomon's voice, soon followed by his corporeal presence. He hurried into my study. He wore nylon shorts, Nike running shoes, a ball cap that said "FBI," and a T-shirt emblazoned with "My Lawyer Can Kick Your Lawyer's Ass."

"What's up, Solomon?"

"I told Victoria I was going jogging."

"Well, you made it three blocks. Sometimes I wish you'd moved to Lauderdale. As long as you're here, you want a drink?"

"No time. Look, I have to tell you something, just between us."

"You're getting cold feet about the wedding. Perfectly natural. Happens all the time. You want to go to Las Vegas for the weekend?"

"Calvert lied to you yesterday."

"I knew that as soon as he said, 'Nice to meet you, Mr. Lassiter.'"

"I'm serious, Jake. He lied when he told you he'd never choked another woman."

I bounced out of the recliner so quickly, I spilled my whiskey. "Whoa, Solomon! Not another word."

"Calvert got in trouble for choking a nurse he was dating when he was on staff at a hospital in Boston."

"Shut up, damn it! I'm not listening. I was just sitting here thinking about some shysters preying on retired football players, and you come to me with the sleaziest deal I've ever heard. Just shut the hell up."

"You can find her, Jake, and you can use it."

"You can get disbarred. And for what?"

Solomon took a breath. "To get this narcissistic bastard out of my life . . . and Victoria's life."

"Calvert's no threat to you, and Victoria loves you. Why, I couldn't begin to answer. But she does. Now go home, and let's both forget you came here tonight. Okay?"

He let out a long sigh. I took it to be a yes.

"Do you want a Tennessee Mule for the road?" I asked. "I've got some ginger beer and Jack Daniel's that are dying to get together."

He shook his head. "I oughta get home."

Just before he reached the front door, I said, "How'd you find out Calvert was lying?"

"I thought we weren't gonna talk about it."

"Just this. Did he tell you personally?"

"No, he told Victoria."

"But he had to know she'd tell you."

"Sure. He knows we share everything."

I concentrated so hard I could see the pins and tumblers trying to unlock some thought in my mind.

"What is it, Jake? What are you thinking?"

"Calvert knows you don't like him."

Solomon gave me a puzzled look. "I never told him that, and I'm sure Victoria wouldn't have."

"Your body language and your facial expressions," I said. "Your words aren't the only giveaways to your attitude. Calvert's a smart guy. He knows you're threatened by him, and he knows you and I are pals."

"Not following you."

"Is it possible Calvert wanted Victoria to tell you and then have you tell me about the nurse?"

"Why would he give you a tool to convict him?"

"No idea. But he's a twisty motherfucker. And smarter than the two of us put together. You watch your ass, and I'll watch mine."

Solomon looked at me wordlessly, and his eyes got moist.

"What is it?" I said.

"Except for Victoria, you're the best friend I ever had."

"Don't hug me, Solomon. I'm not a hugger."

"I know, Jake. I know."

"And don't say—"

"I love you, pal."

"Get the hell out of here before I deck you."

-27-

Gator Shit

Sofia Calvert," I said. "You know her?"

Billy Burnside's head jerked as if I'd popped a left jab off his jaw. "Who are you?"

I introduced myself as a "specially appointed assistant state attorney," which seemed to impress him.

"Yes, sir," he said respectfully. "I know Mrs. Calvert."

Mrs. Calvert.

We talked for a few minutes, and I sized up Burnside: *Handsome. Lazy. Stupid.*

It had been a six-minute drive from my house on Poinciana in Coconut Grove to Camp Sano Country Club on Blue Road in Coral Gables. I had found Burnside in the pro shop, stringing a tennis racket. He was in his late thirties, about six-one, with the lean, muscular body of the veteran tennis player. He was right-handed, judging from his highly developed right forearm, which was significantly more muscular than his left. Streaked blond-brown surfer hair over the ears and a cinnamon suntan. From across the street, he probably still looked like king of the prom. Up close, his once-sculpted jawline had begun to sag. The pencil-line wrinkles on his sun-damaged face were a preview of the decline that was not far off. His chick-bait days were numbered.

He was one of those guys who had peaked at eighteen, when he was the number one player on his high school tennis team. College had been a disappointment. He'd been an indifferent student, and only the number four player on a midmajor program. Not nearly good enough for the tour, too short an attention span for a desk job, he'd been stringing tennis rackets for fifteen years and would do so for another twenty. He made spare cash giving club members hitting lessons and told himself he still had the goods when he banged one of their bored and ignored wives.

The pro shop was a two-room freestanding building with a window air conditioner and a few racks of tennis apparel. The stringing machine was in the adjacent room, and that's where Burnside and I talked, as the AC coughed and sputtered.

"Do you know where Sofia is?" I asked.

He shook his head, and a sprig of blond-brown hair dusted his eyes. "Like I told the detective, I haven't heard from her in almost a month. She missed a lesson with me. We were focusing on her footwork, which was really out of sync. Never called to cancel, and I haven't heard from her since."

"What did Sofia tell you about her relationship with her husband?"

"For starters, that she was afraid of him. More than once, she said to me, 'If I ever disappear, don't bother looking for me. Clark will have dumped my body in the Glades, and I'll already be gator shit.'"

He watched me a second, and when I didn't react, he added, "Can you use that in court?"

"Technically it's hearsay. There's a narrow exception in domestic abuse cases, but no telling how a judge will rule. Are you willing to testify?"

"If he killed her, you're damn right I am."

"Calvert says she's a drama queen. Did you get the impression she was exaggerating or looking for sympathy when she discussed her husband?"

"I don't like to talk smack about anyone, but Dr. Calvert? He's a scary dude. You ever shake hands with him?"

I nodded and shook my right hand, as if warding off the pain.

"Exactly," Burnside said. "I've hit about twenty million tennis balls, so my right arm is pretty developed." He flexed his fist for me, and the thick cords of his extensor muscles danced up and down his forearm. "The son of a bitch got me in a grip before I knew what he was doing, and he tried to break my knuckles."

"Was this before or after he learned you were screwing Sofia?"

He took a step back and sat down on the high stool behind the stringing machine. "Before. Look, I'm not gonna lie to you."

I stayed quiet, and like I figured, he kept talking. "I know it was stupid. Violated my own rule about not messing with members' wives. It's different if I'm doing lessons over at the Biltmore. Tourists. You see the woman two nights and never again. Doesn't matter if her husband's on the golf course or back in Cleveland. But at Campo Sano, I know better. I shouldn't shit where I eat."

"Why did Sofia think her husband might kill her?"

"Because the weekend she disappeared, she was planning to tell him the marriage was over."

That was news to me.

"She told you that?" I asked.

"She'd been saying it for weeks. Just kept putting it off because she was afraid of him. Said he was controlling and violent. Made her cut off contact with girlfriends he didn't like. Wouldn't let her take a job, even though she had a master's in social work. And he was always angry. A kettle ready to boil over, that's the way Sofia described him. Do you know about the psychiatrist's letter?"

I allowed as how I did.

134

"It really freaked me out. A doctor predicting your husband is going to kill you. How weird is that?"

"Very."

"I told her to move out when he wasn't there. Or have the cops there when she did. But she was reckless. Sometimes I thought she wanted to see how far she could push her husband. Got off on it, really."

"How did Calvert find out about the two of you?"

"Sofia thought he might have someone following her. And frankly, we weren't very careful. She'd come to my apartment, park her Mercedes out front."

"Were you her only extracurricular activity?"

"Only current one. But she led me to believe there'd been others."

From the front of the shop, a bell tinkled. Two women in their thirties in tennis togs came in and headed for a sales rack of clothing.

"Anything else you want to tell me about either one of them?" I asked.

"The doc cheats at tennis. Calls balls out where you can see the chalk dust fly where they hit the line."

He sounded offended, a tennis cheat maybe as evil as a wife killer.

"He likes to hit drop shots and little dinky-doos like Bobby Riggs," Burnside continued. "Makes you run your ass off; then when you're coming to the net, he screams 'Banzai' or some other Chinese shit . . ."

"Japanese shit."

"Whatever. Then he nails a passing shot for the point and laughs his ass off. Lousy court etiquette."

"When I asked you for anything else, I didn't mean to analyze Calvert's tennis game."

"What then? I already told the detective everything."

"The insurance policy. You didn't tell him about that."

He looked genuinely confused. "Don't know what you're talking about."

"Three million dollars. About a month before she disappeared, Sofia changed the beneficiary from her husband to you."

"No way."

"It's the truth."

"Jeez, I had no idea."

I studied him, looking for signs of deception but not finding any. Then again, I'm not a homicide detective.

"Are you surprised?" I asked.

"Totally. I mean, she never said 'I love you' or anything like that. Me, either. I never misled her. Never gave her grief about anything, and I always let her come first."

"Excellent attributes for a paramour," I said agreeably.

"I was her sport fuck. Nothing more. At least that's what I thought. Life insurance? It's pretty shocking."

"Three million dollars is a lot of money."

"No kidding. So what?"

I let his question hang there and watched thoughts cross his face like slow-moving clouds.

"You think I killed Sofia for money?"

I shrugged.

"I didn't even know about the policy."

"Calvert wants me to think you did."

"The bastard probably forged her signature to frame me."

"We'll look into that."

"And if I knew about the policy and wanted to collect, wouldn't I sure as hell leave a body somewhere? I mean, isn't it hard to collect insurance when there's no body?"

"It is, indeed, Billy Burnside. It takes years. And off the record, I don't think you're a lady-killer, at least not in the meaning that involves a corpse."

He let out a long breath I didn't know he'd been holding.

"Do you think the doc killed her?" Burnside asked.

136

"I'm not even convinced she's dead."

He scratched his chin with the knuckles of his right hand and said gravely, "I am, Mr. Lassiter."

"Go on."

"She used to call me almost every day. Just for a few minutes. Usually while she was driving somewhere. To pass the time, I guess, because the conversations weren't meaningful. Just chitchat, the way women do. She's been missing, what, almost a month now? If she were alive, she'd call me. I know she would. I keep thinking back to what she said, and if I were you, I'd be looking in the Everglades for some fat and happy gator."

-28-

The Timeline

Detective George Barrios asked me to meet him for lunch at Versailles, the classic Cuban restaurant on Calle Ocho. Barrios had a fondness for *rabo encendido*, the oxtail stew. He also enjoyed eavesdropping on tourists from Kansas trying to speak Spanish to the servers.

Sure enough, at the next table, a portly Anglo man was staring into his Frommer's guide and telling the waiter, *"Tendré el sándwich Cubano con mayonesa."*

The waiter winced at the mention of mayonnaise, said his *"Gracias,"* and headed toward the kitchen.

"There might be a break in the investigation," Barrios said.

That jump-started my pulse like a double shot of Cuban coffee. "Tell me, George."

"The timeline of the day Sofia disappeared has always been incomplete, and once Calvert hired David and Maddie, he's been uncooperative."

"Moonlighting. Nice reference. You oughta be on *Jeopardy!*, George."

"What Calvert did tell us was this. They argued after breakfast, and she stormed out of the house, leaving by the front door at roughly nine thirty a.m."

"But the security camera at the front door wasn't working, so there's nothing to corroborate that story," I said, remembering the missing-persons report.

"Right. She had a ten a.m. Pilates class, and he thought that's where she was going. He figured she'd cool down after the workout."

"Did she usually walk to Pilates?"

"Class was on Arthur Godfrey Road. Maybe a ten-minute stroll from their house on North Bay Road. About ten twenty a.m., Calvert says a friend of Sofia's calls the house. Tells him that Sofia isn't at the class. The two women were supposed to go shopping afterward, and Sofia isn't answering the cell. He tells the woman they'd quarreled, and he suspects she's walking it off, getting it out of her system. Or maybe she took an Uber to Haulover Beach, where she liked to hang out topless. Or maybe she went shopping alone."

"Does the call check out?"

"Sofia's girlfriend confirms it to the letter."

"Did she notice anything unusual about Calvert on the phone?"

"Good question, Counselor. You should have been a cop." He paused a moment as a server delivered our meals: oxtail beef simmering in a broth of wine and tomato sauce for Barrios, plantain pie with *picadillo*—ground beef with raisins—for me, with a guava milkshake to wash it down. "She said he was the same old Clark, distant, aloof, detached."

"So what's the break in the investigation?"

"Slow down, Jake. When you make a stew, you have to stir the broth." With that, he plucked a piece of oxtail beef from the stew and plopped it into his mouth, making a purring sound of contentment. "Calvert says he left the house in his Ferrari between eleven and eleven thirty, and in fact, the security video outside of the garage, which was working, shows him pulling out at eleven seventeen a.m. He says he came back home around nine o'clock that night, and the camera records the Ferrari pulling in at nine-oh-seven p.m."

"He went looking for her. You've already told me this."

"Patience, counselor. Patience. Can I have a bite of your *picadillo*?"

He didn't wait for an answer. Just stuck his fork into the middle of my bowl, where a mound of sweet ground beef simmered on top of a pile of mashed plantains.

"Before he lawyered up and clammed up, Calvert told me his movements that day. Claimed he drove to Haulover Beach, then to Bal Harbour Shops, back down to the Fontainebleau, and checked out all their bars and restaurants."

"Told me the same thing. Basically, he stayed on the beach."

"By the way, if you were looking for your missing wife, wouldn't you be calling her on your cell while you drove around town?"

"Yeah. I'd call her and her friends."

"Zero calls on his cell phone once he left his house. Why do you suppose?"

"He knows cops could later pinpoint his location from the towers picking up his calls."

"Leading you to believe?"

"He lied. He didn't stay on Miami Beach all day."

"I'm recommending you to the cop academy." Barrios took a second bite of my lunch and continued, "I asked him for permission to remove the SunPass transmitter from his Ferrari, and lo and behold, he tells me it's missing. Probably stolen when he left the car unlocked on Alton outside Epicure market. Or so he said."

"You subpoena the DOT?"

"Of course. Took them a while. But yesterday I got the printout. The last time Calvert's SunPass rang any bells was that very morning at eleven fifty-four a.m. when he entered the turnpike at Golden Glades."

I pictured his route, thirty-seven minutes from his house to the turnpike entrance. "He went across one of the causeways, north on I-95, and then onto the turnpike. No Haulover Beach. No Bal Harbour. No looking for Sofia."

"I figure he didn't have to look for her if he'd put her dead body in the trunk before he left the house."

"That'd be a better theory if his trunk hadn't been clean of fibers and blood."

"He's a neat doc, not a messy one. Oh, I also figure he killed her the night before."

"What's the evidence of that?"

He pointed to his head with an empty fork. "Experience. Very few men kill their wives at nine in the morning."

I filed that information away. "You're keeping me in suspense. Where'd Calvert exit the turnpike?"

"It's not readily apparent."

That puzzled me. "The SunPass pings when you exit. It would be in the DOT database."

"You weren't listening. I said the last time the SunPass was used, Calvert was getting on the turnpike."

It took me a second. "Oh, shit. I see what happened."

At the next table, Tourist Guy was waving to the server with his empty glass of iced tea, saying, *"Té helado, por favor."* Pronouncing it "fave-er."

"Go ahead, Counselor. What's your theory?"

"Calvert enters the turnpike, hears the beep, and realizes his SunPass just recorded his location. For a smart guy, he did a dumb thing. Probably cursed himself out. But if he'd killed his wife and her body's in the trunk, he's a little flustered. Realizing what he's done, he rips the transmitter off his windshield and tosses it out the window. Or stows it in a trash can at the Fort Pierce rest stop. Either way, it's gone by the time he pulls off an exit."

"Which is where, Counselor?"

"How would I know? He's got enough time to drive up to Pahokee, bury the body in a levee on Lake Okeechobee, and get home by nine at night."

"You thinking Calvert buried her in broad daylight?" Barrios said. "That's your theory?"

"I don't know, George. There are some pretty remote places up there."

"I don't think Calvert went that far north." He gave me a little cop grin. "You want some dessert?"

"*Tres leches* cake. What's another thousand calories?"

"Double-egg-yolk flan for me," Barrios said.

I signaled for our server and gave the order.

"Okay, George. You've had your fun. Do you know where Calvert got off the turnpike?"

"Every exit has a camera that takes photos of license plates. Files are uploaded to the cloud, kept for ninety days, then deleted. If you know the license plate you're looking for . . ."

"It would take a lot of manpower to check photos at all the exits for a couple hundred miles."

"Manpower, Jake? You're living in the past. You plug in the license plate number and hit the 'Search' button. Maybe two minutes of work for each exit."

"Tell me, damn it, before these clogged arteries kill me."

"How you feeling, by the way?"

"Fine, George! What exit?"

"Number sixty-seven. Pompano Beach. At twelve fifty-one p.m."

"Which way did he turn? East or west?"

He shrugged. "Camera doesn't show that."

"Where the hell did he go? What was he doing for the next eight hours before he got home?"

"How's your geography? What's around there?"

I thought about it just as my *tres leches* arrived. A heavy sponge cake made with condensed milk, evaporated milk, and heavy cream, topped by whipped cream in the event you needed more saturated fat.

142

I speared some whipped cream, then dug my fork into the soggy cake underneath.

"The landmass there is just a thin corridor between bodies of water," I said. "The ocean is maybe five miles to the east, the Everglades less than ten miles to the west. Plus, hundreds of lakes and canals in between." Reality was setting in, and it was depressing. "We'll never find her body, George. We'll never have a case."

-29-

The Titty Trap

Detective Barrios had changed his mind. I wouldn't make a good cop, after all. At least not a good homicide detective.

"Don't say, 'We'll never have a case.' It takes patience, Jake. This isn't an hour TV show where a clue falls into your lap after the third commercial."

He gave me a lecture about the power of pounding the pavement, even in these days when computers and cell towers and security cameras keep track of what we eat and drink, where we travel and sleep, who we screw, when we leave the house, and down what forbidden road Google has taken us.

Ask not for whom the hard drive tolls; it tolls for thee.

Maybe it was the sugar from the Cuban desserts, but Barrios became animated. He had a plan, which was more than I had. We would drive separately north on the turnpike to Exit 67. I would head east toward the ocean, and he would head west toward the Everglades.

"What the hell are we looking for?" I asked.

"If I knew that, we'd both go together right to the spot. Just drive and keep your eyes open. We're retracing Calvert's steps. You never know what you might find."

Barrios was right . . . the second time. I'd make a lousy cop.

I fired up my ancient Cadillac, turned the AC on high, and drove north on I-95, snarled in endless traffic. It took thirty-five minutes to get out of the city and through the Golden Glades interchange, where I picked up the turnpike, just as Calvert had done the day Sofia disappeared.

This was useless.

A waste of time and gasoline.

My lower back was seizing up as I passed Hard Rock Stadium, where the Dolphins play, or pretend to. That's where I plied my trade, though not very well, and it's where I got my brain dinged. Funny, I look back on those days with wistfulness and joy and few regrets. I still call it Joe Robbie Stadium, because that was the original name, and Robbie was the guy who brought the team into existence back in the days of the American Football League. After Robbie died, the new owner sold naming rights to Pro Player, basically an underwear company that had the good sense to go bankrupt. Then the name reverted to Dolphins Stadium, and a year later, the *s* was dropped, so it became Dolphin Stadium. I don't know why. Maybe a shorter name saved money on the electricity bill. Then came Land Shark Stadium, named after the beer supposedly made by Jimmy Buffett, but in reality, just another Anheuser-Busch watery brew that's sold at the concerts of our Florida troubadour. One year later, say hello to Sun Life Stadium, named after an insurance company. And now, with more money changing hands, it's Hard Rock Stadium.

The stadium's shifting identity perfectly mirrors South Florida, home to shallow traditions and feigned loyalties, fast-buck artists and fly-by-night businesses. This alleged tropical paradise is built on the shifting sands of impermanence and the frail coastline of rising tides.

I passed Calder Race Course, where I've lost money betting favorites and long shots alike. Traffic moved smoother here, lots of motorists taking the exits for 595, heading east into Fort Lauderdale. I lost sight of Barrios in his city-owned Chrysler. He was cruising at about eighty-five, immune from the tickets of state troopers.

I started paying attention to the billboards just to take my mind off the plug-ugly nature of flat, soggy Florida, as seen from the turnpike. Billboards for churches with antiabortion messages, billboards for lawyers who will make millions for you if you're crushed by a cement truck, billboards for payday lenders, eager to hand you cash.

And billboards for strip clubs.

As I neared Pompano Beach, the strip-club signs leered at me.

CHEETAH.

4PLAY.

DIAMOND DOLLS.

THE TITTY TRAP.

Northern Broward County was crawling with lap-dance joints. I hadn't been in one in ages. Back in my playing days, I may have been a benchwarmer on Sundays, but the rest of the week, I starred on the All-Pro, All-Party team, leading the league in broken curfews. After practice at the training camp in Davie in the southern part of the county, a few of us would head north for an evening meal, a few brews, and, of course, naked ladies.

Okay, I was young and stupid with an extra dose of testosterone, so shoot me.

As I neared Pompano Beach, I remembered something Dr. Freudenstein had said to me: *"Calvert also has a penchant for getting lap dances at strip clubs. Sofia complained about it, and he admitted it."*

I slowed and took Exit 67, which looped south for a few hundred yards. At the traffic light, I looked to the west. Coconut Creek Parkway. Barrios would be headed that way, so I would go in the other direction. I looked to the east and immediately saw the two-story sign.

THE TITTY TRAP

Right there. Dan Marino could fire a pass from where my car sat growling and knock out a window on the strip club.

It can't be this easy, I told myself. But maybe it is. Then I wondered how much cash I was carrying, and what they were charging for lap dances these days.

-30-

Amber, Autumn, Venus, and Delilah

I ordered an eight-dollar beer, a local hoppy brew, and chatted up the bartender, a woman in her forties in a blue chambray halter top and cutoffs, a straw hat, and cowboy boots. Her false eyelashes were long enough to sweep the bar of peanut shells. She could have been the MILF featured player in a cattle-ranch porn video. I figured her as a former stripper whose knees were shot and whose tips diminished along with the tautness of her thighs.

She drew the beer from a tap. "Haven't seen you in here before, pardner."

I loosened my tie and draped my suit coat over the railing, as if I might stay a spell. "Friend recommended the place. A doctor."

She gave me a gap-toothed smile. "We get a lot of doctors. Couple plastic surgeons give discounts to the girls."

"And make house calls."

"More like VIP room calls." She motioned toward the back, where a beaded curtain provided privacy for lap dances. "You hungry? We got a lunch special."

"Lemme guess. Strip steak?"

"You *have* been here before."

"Nah, my pal told me. Maybe you know him. Clark Calvert, doctor down in Miami."

Her eyes hardened. "I'm not good with names."

She moved down the bar, as if to serve two guys in ball caps and T-shirts. But they didn't need anything. They were tossing two-dollar bills to a stripper who cat-crawled along the bar, wiggling her butt, alternately purring and snarling, naked except for her shiny red platform heels. She picked up two of the bills, stood, and somehow managed to balance the greenbacks on the tips of her nipples while swaying to the music.

I tried to get the bartender's attention, but she ignored me. I'd screwed up.

I'd moved too fast and asked the wrong person. She was a lifer in places like this and could smell bullshit before it hit the ground.

Barrios wouldn't have made that mistake. But then, Barrios owned the street, and I was just a tourist. What had he advised me?

Patience.

Four elevated stages were scattered around the big room. I swung around on my bar stool and checked them out. Three stages were empty and dark. One was occupied by a nude stripper on a pole. She was a pale young woman with a blonde-and-pink mullet hairdo. Her legs were encircled by red-and-green tattoos from her ankles to her nether regions. As the sound system blasted Journey's "Lovin', Touchin', Squeezin'," she swung upside down, one ankle high over her head wrapped around the pole, her other leg parallel to the floor. Four men were scattered around the stage, pressed close to the rail, studying her as if they were gymnastics judges at the Olympics.

I sipped my brew, and a young brunette in a red thong and matching push-up bra slid onto the adjacent bar stool as gracefully as a cowboy hopping onto a saddle. She had a coppery complexion, thanks to a couple layers of makeup that might have been applied with a spatula, like icing on a cake. I was willing to bet her name was Amber, Autumn, Venus, or Delilah.

"Hi," she said. "I'm Trouble."

"Small *t* or capital *T*?"

"Both."

"Ha, good one." I smiled broadly and idiotically, as if I were the friendliest, dumbest traveling salesman ever to take a detour off the turnpike.

The music stopped long enough for a gravelly-voiced DJ, hidden behind darkened glass, to inform us that Amber—I knew there had to be one!—had one more pole dance and that Summer was on deck. Standing off to the side, Summer took a bow. She had blonde pigtails and wore a short plaid skirt, white blouse, and black patent-leather shoes. Tortoiseshell eyeglasses completed the parochial-schoolgirl look.

The DJ went quiet, and Def Leppard's "Pour Some Sugar on Me" pulsed out of the speakers.

"How 'bout a lap dance?" Trouble asked. "Full friction."

"Tell me more, capital *T* for *Trouble*."

"Only twenty bucks. Early-bird special."

"Sweet deal."

"But that's only one dance. We call it the stimulation. We recommend three dances for completion. Only fifty bucks."

"Volume discount." I nodded appreciatively, a man who knows a bargain. I handed her a fifty. She shot a glance at the cowgirl bartender, slipped off the bar stool, and took my hand, leading me behind the beaded curtains, where the speakers roared even louder.

I eased onto a red vinyl bench, and Trouble swayed to the music, her long dark hair brushing her shoulders. She was thin and slim-hipped with outsize breasts as round as volleyballs, courtesy of those discount plastic surgeons, I figured. She whirled around and waved her skinny butt in my face, giving me a view of several tattoos on her back: a butterfly, a hawk, and several snakes. A real animal lover.

Just before she lowered her butt into my lap, I grabbed her elbow.

"Hey, no touching!" she said, spinning away.

"Sorry, I didn't mean anything. I just—"

"Didn't you see the sign? No touching, spanking, groping, or grabbing."

"I don't want a lap dance. Just sit down and talk to me."

"Oh, one of those. Sure."

"I'm looking for a friend of mine. His name is Clark Calvert, but I don't know if he goes by that name in here, or by any name, for that matter."

"Doesn't ring a bell." Sitting alongside me, she still moved to the music.

"He's a doctor in Miami." I reached into my suit pocket and pulled out a three-by-five head shot Barrios had given me. I showed it to Trouble and immediately saw her eyes widen just a bit.

"Maybe I know him," she said.

"Maybe I have another Ulysses S. Grant in my pocket."

"A pair of them will do."

I handed over the money, and she said, "Sawbones. That's what he likes to be called."

"Is he a regular?"

Before she could answer, the beaded curtain flew open, and an elephant barged into the VIP room. Okay, not an elephant. A man in black jeans and a gray pin-striped vest with no shirt underneath. He had massive sloping shoulders covered with curly black hair. His arms were slabs of beef. Not much definition, but if he could throw a punch, it would land like a sledgehammer. Sticking out of the front pocket of his vest were four plastic-wrapped Slim Jims.

"It's okay, Corky," Trouble said.

Corky? I'd been thinking something along the line of Bruiser.

"He's not touching me or nothing," she said.

The cowgirl bartender was standing off to the side, nearly obscured by one of Corky's hairy shoulders.

"Beat it, T," Corky said.

Trouble slithered off the sofa and ducked past him and through the beaded curtain. The bartender followed.

"You're asking a lot of questions," Corky said, once we were alone.

I spotted a camera mounted on the wall near the ceiling. There'd be a microphone somewhere, too, everything wired into the manager's office. I took Corky to be the manager-bouncer-guy-who-unloads-beer-kegs-two-at-a-time.

"Just tracking down a guy," I said.

"You a cop?"

"Close. Assistant State Attorney."

"We cooperate with the law. We pay our taxes, run a clean place. No drugs, no prostitution. No underage girls or patrons."

"I appreciate that."

"You got ID?"

I reached inside my suit pocket and pulled out a genuine imitation leather billfold and handed it over. Inside was a similarly genuine imitation gold star with the seal of Miami-Dade County. The seal portrays a Spanish sailing ship approaching the sun-drenched virginal shore of Florida but omits any imagery of the sailors bringing syphilis to the natives.

Corky took a moment examining the slip of flimsy paper with my name and title handwritten in ink. "This is dated last week."

"I was just appointed. I'm special, that is, specially appointed for one case."

"So you're a temp?"

"I didn't think of it that way, but sure. A part-timer. A freelancer. A temp."

"Like some of my girls who go to community college during the week and can only work weekend shifts here."

"Same principle."

On the speakers, the DJ was advising patrons to get change at the bar. Two-dollar bills for their tips. Or as he put it, "Ten Tom Jeffersons in return for a twenty."

"Sometimes cops come in here," Corky said, "and we give them free lap dances. Maybe someday they can do us a favor. But you're down in Miami and just a temp, so . . ."

"I can't ever do you a favor."

"So why should I help you?"

"Maybe 'cause you're a concerned citizen." I handed him the head shot and waited.

"Sawbones," Corky said. "I doubt he's a criminal."

"I just need to know if he was in here on Saturday, June 3."

"That's almost a month ago. No one's gonna remember."

On the speakers, R. Kelly was wailing "Feelin' on Yo Booty."

"You have a video security system, right?"

"Everywhere but the restrooms, and if you got a subpoena in your other pocket, we're in business."

"I can get one and have you served tomorrow, or you can just take a few minutes and go through the hard drive now."

"Cloud. It's in the cloud."

"Isn't everything? It won't take long, and I'll be out of here."

He shifted his weight from one foot to the other, and the building didn't collapse. "Your ID says Jacob Lassiter."

"Guilty as charged."

"There was a Jake Lassiter who played for the Dolphins when I was a kid."

"You must have been a hell of a fan. I never started a game unless two guys were hurt. Usually I sat so far down the bench, my ass was in Kissimmee."

"But you were a holy terror on the suicide squads. Made your share of tackles."

"Only way I could stay on the roster was to sacrifice my body."

"My old man couldn't afford tickets, but we watched every Dolphins game on TV. He was a bettor, but not a very good one. Would bet the rent money, the food money, money he borrowed, money he swiped from the collection plate at church. When I was about twelve, he says to me, 'Corky, I'm gonna buy you a pair of Air Jordans with the money I win today.' He'd scraped together five or six hundred bucks, a fortune for him, and he had this feeling about the Dolphins game on the road against the Jets."

Oh, shit. I know where this is going.

"December game at the Meadowlands?" I said. "Frozen turf. Swirling snow. Misty fog."

"Yeah, that's the one. Crazy day. Like the game was being played on the moon."

Why, God? Why does the past cling to me like mud on rusty cleats?

"Jets led by six late in the game," Corky said, "and the Dolphins scored to take a one-point lead. On the kickoff, you made a helmet-to-helmet tackle we could hear on the TV. Like a tank hitting a brick wall."

So that's what a concussion sounds like from the outside. From inside, it's strangely silent.

Corky said, "The Jets' returner fumbles. The ball spins on the ground like a top. You're staggering around, but somehow you pick up the ball. Remember what happens next?"

In truth, I don't remember the play, or anything else that happened that day, but I've seen the video a hundred times. My mind will probably replay it on my deathbed.

"Vaguely," I said.

"You get turned around and run to the wrong end zone, where about six Jets pile on top of you. Two points! Safety. Jets win by one."

"I'm sorry, Corky," I said. "Sorry your dad lost all that money."

"Lost? He took the Jets straight up. And I got my Air Jordans."

Corky laughed so hard the wall behind him shook. "C'mon back to my office, and we'll look for the video."

He led me out of the VIP room and into a dark corridor that led to a small office in the back of the building.

"You say June 3 was a Saturday?" he asked.

"It was. Does that make any difference?"

"Not with the recording system, but that's the day he usually brought her along."

"Who?"

"His wife. On Saturdays, Sawbones usually brought his wife along."

-31-

Blowing Smoke

One day after Corky gave me the proof that Calvert had lied about his whereabouts the day Sofia disappeared, I walked into an office where three men were sucking on Cuban cigars. The big, fat, expensive Cohiba.

I just hoped no one would start waxing ecstatic about the Cohiba's pungent coffee flavor or its earthy spices. I don't know which group is more insufferable, wine snobs or cigar aficionados.

Leaning back in his black leather chair, his shiny black wingtips perched on his desk, Ray Pincher, the duly elected state attorney of Miami-Dade County, waved his cigar in my direction and said, "Jake, this is Pedro Suarez."

"Call me Pepe." Suarez sat in one of the deeply upholstered client chairs, his shrewd eyes studying me. "Thank you for everything you're doing on behalf of my daughter."

"Pleased to meet you, Pepe," I said. "Sorry it has to be under these circumstances."

His hair was combed straight back and was the same color as the cigar smoke. His suit was a shimmering blue, probably light wool, and custom tailored to disguise his blocky build. Handsome man, early fifties, plain gold wedding band and a diamond pinky ring. A jagged scar ran from the corner of his right eye toward his ear, and then back again, stopping an inch from his mouth. It occurred to me that a plastic surgeon could repair the scar, but Suarez must have chosen not to do it. Maybe it was a negotiating tactic. Let the bankers or competing sugar barons or EPA investigators know they were dealing with a tough *hombre*.

Suarez gestured toward the large, bearded man sitting next to him. "This is JT."

I said, "Howdy," maybe because the man wore scuffed cowboy boots. Big guy in his late forties, blue jeans and a khaki shirt with epaulets and military pockets. If he stood up, he would probably be around six-four, and I guessed 250 pounds. I pegged him as head of security for Suarez Farms. "Nice to meet you, JT."

The big man grunted a "Hullo" back at me.

Examining the glowing tip of his cigar, Pincher said, "Jake has some good news for you, Pepe."

"Potentially good news," I corrected him. Like all politicians, Pincher puts topspin on his first serve. I didn't want him making promises I couldn't keep. "A couple days ago, frankly, we had nothing but suspicion. Now we have something."

"Let's hear it." Suarez was not a man given to long preambles.

"Calvert lied to the police about his whereabouts on the day Sofia went missing. He didn't spend the day looking for her, didn't even stay on Miami Beach. We can prove that."

"That son of a bitch. That's huge."

"It can be, but we need to know why he lied. Sometimes there are innocent reasons."

"Jesus, Jake!" Pincher thundered. "Stop talking like a defense lawyer. Forget the nuance."

"You're right, Ray. Old habit. What I should be saying is generally one lie leads to another and another, and at the end of that trail is the truth. We're following that trail."

"Just tell me what you've got," Suarez said.

I told him about the good detective work of George Barrios in establishing when Calvert left the house, when he got on the turnpike, and where he got off. I told him about my lucky guesswork at where he went—at least his first stop—in Pompano Beach. I filled him in on Corky's story. Calvert was a regular at the Titty Trap. On weekends, Sofia would often come along. She'd join him in the so-called VIP lounge, where he'd buy lap dances. Mostly she'd watch. Sometimes she'd kiss and fondle him while the stripper was grinding his lap.

"That damn weirdo perverted her," Suarez said.

"Security video shows Calvert pulling into the parking lot at twelve fifty-three p.m. on June 3 and leaving just thirty-one minutes later. He was alone. He had one nonalcoholic drink at the bar, exchanged pleasantries with the barmaid, and paid for a single three-song lap dance with a stripper who calls herself Trouble. Tipped her fifty dollars. He didn't seem nervous or agitated. There was nothing unusual about the visit, except he stayed a shorter time than usual. Detective Barrios theorizes the reason he left so soon . . ."

"He had Sofia in the trunk," Suarez said grimly. "The dirtbag was disposing of her body and stopped to get jerked off. Jesus!"

"That's the theory," I said.

"Sick bastard. Where'd he go from the strip club?"

"That's the next stop on the trail, but we're not there yet. We only know that at nine-oh-seven p.m., seven hours and forty-three minutes later, the Ferrari pulls back into his garage on North Bay Road."

Suarez spit out a fleck of tobacco. "Bastard could have gone hundreds of miles."

"Or just a few," Pincher said. "You've got the ocean, what, twenty minutes away?"

"Less," I said. "Barrios is checking boat rentals for that day up and down the coast. He's had a couple cases over the years where husbands drop their wives' bodies in the Gulf Stream."

Pincher's cigar had flamed out. He struck a wooden match with the tip of his thumbnail and relighted. "Jake, tell Pepe what else you've got."

"Did you know that Sofia was involved with the tennis pro at their country club?"

Suarez shrugged. "Who the hell could blame her? And now you got a motive to play with. Jealous husband takes revenge."

"Like a lot of evidence, it cuts both ways. Sofia recently made the tennis pro the beneficiary of her life insurance policy. If you ask me, the guy's not a killer. But that won't keep the defense from pounding the table and claiming Burnside is a suspect we overlooked."

"Is that it?" Suarez asked. "That's all that's new?"

"The nurse," Pincher said. "Jake, tell Pepe about the nurse."

Damn. I had told Pincher in confidence, leaving out that the tip came from Solomon.

"Just a rumor," I said. "There's a nurse, someone involved with Calvert before he married Sofia. Back when he was on staff at a hospital in Boston. She filed a complaint that he choked her into unconsciousness."

"You have a name?" Suarez asked.

"Not yet. It could be a blind alley. But it could also mean there are other women out there. Look at the Bill Cosby case. First one, then a torrent. Same with Harvey Weinstein and all those other guys."

Suarez was quiet a moment. Then he pointed his cigar at me, as if dotting an *i.*

"I gotta be honest with you, Lassiter. I was skeptical when Ray told me he was appointing you."

"Yeah?"

"Now I'm sure I was right and Ray was wrong. You're all wishy-washy. Following a trail. Evidence cutting both ways. Stuck in blind alleys, taking your sweet time, and meanwhile Calvert is flying to Vietnam . . . When, Ray?"

Pincher exhaled a puff of smoke. "Two days."

"He's coming back," I said. "He's not setting up a practice in Ho Chi Minh City."

"Just answer this," Suarez ordered. "Can you indict by tomorrow?"

"No," I said, just as Pincher said, "Yes."

"Ray, you guys gotta get your shit together."

Before Pincher could dig a deeper hole for me, I said, "We need time."

"Time is what you don't have. Ray told me you can indict now."

"Getting the grand jury to indict is easy," I said. "The problem's securing a conviction. If we charge without sufficient evidence, the defense will demand a speedy trial and beat the tar out of us."

"Indict his ass and worry about that later."

"Not the way the process works," I said.

"'Process'? I don't give a shit about process. I care about results." Suarez nailed me with a withering look, then swiveled his head toward Pincher. "Ray, I warned you. This guy's a burnout, a punch-drunk, de-nutted wuss of an ex-jock."

Wow. I've been insulted multiple times over multiple decades but seldom so many times in one sentence.

Pincher held up one hand, like a crossing guard in front of a school. "Now, Pepe."

"Don't 'Now, Pepe' me! This is who you give me to go after my daughter's killer."

"Lassiter has his own way of doing things, but once we get into court, I swear, he's the man we want. He's dynamite on his feet, and jurors love him."

"Bullshit! This stiff is painting by the numbers when I need a Picasso." Suarez turned to the large man who had been silent since grunting hello. "I'm getting JT involved."

160

"Pepe, that could come back to bite us in the ass."

"You telling me what I can and can't do, Ray? Do you want to be governor, or dogcatcher of Calhoun County?"

Pincher stayed silent, the Cohiba drooping from the corner of his mouth, the phallic symbol gone limp.

"I take that as acquiescence," Suarez said. "JT, you're gonna handle the street operation and report only to me. First item of business. You make sure Calvert doesn't get on a plane to Vietnam or anywhere else."

"Whoa," I said. "Who the hell is this guy?"

The big man stirred in his chair, uncrossing his legs and leaning forward. He smiled for the first time, his teeth gapped as gravestones and jagged, as if he'd been gnawing on bones to suck out the marrow. "We've met before, Lassiter. Don't you remember?"

-32-

Of Spitting and Pissing

Pincher tapped ashes from his Cohiba into his black onyx ashtray. Suarez craned his neck upward, exhaling a blue-gray smoke ring. JT sat there with his jagged-tooth, shit-eating grin, waiting for me to try to remember who the hell he was.

I studied his face, came up empty, shook my head. "My memory's not what it used to be."

The man said, "I didn't have the beard then. J. T. Wetherall. Ring a bell?"

A distant chime, but I still couldn't place him. Normal aging, maybe. Sometimes I forget the names of ex-teammates and former lady friends. Then again, maybe misshapen brain protein was clogging my memory banks.

"Sorry, JT, you seem familiar, but . . ."

"No worries, Lassiter. Long time ago. Criminal case in Orange County. Started as a business dispute between two brothers who owned a citrus grove. Then one of them got busted with a stash of cocaine in his pickup. You defended him."

"Ah, there it is. *Deputy* Wetherall."

"Sheriff's department. That was me."

It came back then. Wetherall on the witness stand, smirking at me, daring me to call him a liar. "You planted evidence, Wetherall. You were a dirty cop."

"So you claimed. Jury disagreed."

"Another failing of the so-called justice system. Or maybe I wasn't good enough to show them the darkness sitting right in front of them. You lied so easily, so naturally, that it was a wonder to—"

"Jeez, Jake," Pincher stopped me. "We're all on the same side here."

"Right, Ray. I remember. 'The sunny side of justice.' That's what you called this office when you drafted me."

Wetherall puffed on his own cigar and blew smoke in my direction. I felt a headache brewing, pressure building behind my eyes like steam in a boiler.

"When you cross-examined me," Wetherall said, "you got real close to the witness stand. The judge warned you a couple times to step back, but you kept inching up, raising your voice. You were waving my personnel file at me. Had a couple demerits in there for excessive force. You taunted me. Shouted at me. Your spittle hit me in the face."

They ought to teach it in law school. If you want the spit to fly, drink two glasses of water, use a lot of *s* words, and get close to your target.

"I wanted you to lose it, Wetherall, to come off the witness stand and take a swing at me."

"If I'd done it, you would have regretted that decision, friend."

"I was in dire need of a mistrial, so yeah, I would have given you a free one."

"See what I told you, Pepe?" Pincher said. "Lassiter will take a punch for a client."

Poor Ray sounded desperate to please his major donor and major-domo. I felt sorry for Pincher, so I didn't point out that the people of Florida were my clients, not filthy-rich Pepe Suarez.

"The judge called Lassiter up to the bench," Wetherall continued, enjoying the limelight. "Chewed his ass out. You remember, Counselor?"

"Nope."

That was a lie. I've flirted with contempt and danced with disbarment so many times I've forgotten most of them, but the judge's angry whispers that day came back to me.

"Mr. Lassiter, I don't know how they practice law down in Sin City, but in Orange County, lawyers don't spit on witnesses."

"Respectfully, Your Honor, if I could, I'd piss on this guy just to extinguish the steaming turds coming out of his mouth."

"Five hundred bucks for your vulgarity, Mr. Lassiter. You can pay the court clerk at the recess. No credit cards."

"Wetherall, correct me if I'm wrong," I said. "Didn't you get booted off the force?"

"That's enough, you two," Suarez said. "Lassiter, JT's my chief of security now. When my son-of-a-bitch son-in-law called to say Sofia was missing, JT set up surveillance teams and other stuff you don't need to know about."

"Wiretapping," I guessed. "Ray must have told you he didn't have probable cause to get a warrant, so you had Claude do it the old-fashioned way."

"Claude?" Suarez said. "You mean JT."

"Sorry, I was thinking of Claude Mulvihill in *Chinatown*. Noah Cross's big, stupid hired goon. Only difference I see, Claude wore cheap suits and smoked cheap stogies."

"Screw you, Lassiter," Wetherall said.

"But you didn't turn up anything, did you, Claude? If you had, your boss would have told Ray, who would have told me, and we'd be off to the races. You risked blowing the entire case with illegal wiretaps and got nothing out of it." I turned to Suarez. "Now you want this slug to run a 'street operation'? What the hell does that mean?"

Pincher got up from his desk and walked past a wall festooned with plaques and photos attesting to his civic greatness. "I'm gonna take a piss. Why don't the three of you hash this out?"

Oh, thanks a lot, Ray. Keeping your dainty hands clean as the shit piles up in the barnyard.

Suarez watched smoke swirl to the ceiling and waited for the door to close behind Pincher. "Lassiter, I didn't always own fifty thousand acres of sugarcane. Didn't always wear Italian suits. See this?" He pointed to the scar on his face. "Got this back in high school. Know how?"

"You got fresh with your prom date, and she let you have it with her fingernails."

His eyes hardened. "Haitian kid, migrant worker. I was chopping alongside him in the cane field. He was quicker with a machete than I was. At first, that is . . ."

He let it hang there, waiting for me to ask what happened next. Screw him.

"Are you following me, Lassiter?"

"Before you get carried away with this working-class-hero crap," I said, "wasn't this your old man's sugar plantation?"

"So what? Can you figure out what I did to the Haitian kid?"

I didn't like Suarez's tone. I didn't like his attitude. In fact, there was nothing I liked about him.

"I'm a pretty smart guy, Pepe," I said. "I passed the bar exam on my fourth try. If a team gains three yards on first and ten, I know it's now second and seven. So, yeah, I think I know what you did to the Haitian kid. But I figure it took you and three or four of your father's hired hands."

"Fertilizer, Lassiter. I helped the Haitian kid reach his highest and best use. Fertilizing the sugarcane."

"Is that supposed to make me think you're a tough guy?"

"I don't give a shit what you think. If you don't indict the bastard by tomorrow, JT is taking over."

"Great. I can't wait to hear his opening statement."

"He's gonna roust Calvert by any means necessary." Suarez turned toward Wetherall. "JT, I don't care if you use a cattle prod to his scrotum or a baseball bat to his knees. But you get him to talk."

"Why the fancy choreography?" I asked. "You obviously told Pincher this before he excused himself to go to the ladies' room. Why am I even here?"

"To let you know what you're dealing with, Lassiter. My level of commitment."

"This isn't gonna end well. Not well at all."

"I'm not a thug, Lassiter. I'm a businessman and a father. I don't want any innocent people getting hurt."

"What innocent people?"

"I know you're friends with the lawyers representing Calvert. They've been spending a lot of time with him, day and night. Especially the woman lawyer."

I pointed an index finger at him. "Are you threatening them? Because if Claude here pulls any shit, I'll kick his worthless ass and then come straight for you."

"Calm down. Just tell your friends it might be smart not to hang around Calvert so much."

"How the hell am I gonna do that without telling them what I know?"

"You said you're a smart guy. Figure it out."

·33·

The Essence of Partnership and Love

Victoria Lord . . .

Victoria had just hung up the phone and was staring out the window at the bay and Key Biscayne in the distance. A dozen sailboats were puffing along on the downwind leg of a race, their multicolored spinnakers ballooning in the steady easterly breeze.

The fledgling law firm of Solomon & Lord had recently rented a small but luxurious office on the eighteenth floor of a Brickell Avenue high-rise. The view was spectacular, the rent crushing. It had been Steve's idea, of course.

"Gotta spend dough to make dough, Vic."

Victoria didn't think their clients cared about the provenance of the glass sculptures in the waiting room or the Brazilian teak on the walls. As the only one of the partners who could balance a checkbook, she was burdened with juggling accounts and paying bills. Making the monthly nut was her worry, not Steve's.

The six-figure retainer from Clark Calvert had put them in the black for this month and possibly the entire summer, but when you're humping a major homicide case, you're not out hustling for others. No time for lawyer lunches with colleagues who are likely to refer clients. That's why *winning* the Calvert case was so important. Beating the state in murder trials, that's how you build reputations.

For the good of Solomon & Lord, it was necessary that Clark be charged. This caused Victoria cognitive dissonance. She wanted Clark to be a free man, but she also wanted her little law firm to be a success, and the two goals were not entirely consistent . . . unless Clark was charged and acquitted in a highly publicized trial.

While she was mulling these conflicting thoughts and watching the sailboats carve their way across the turquoise water, her partner and fiancé barreled into her office.

No knock-knock.

No "Am I interrupting you?"

Just Full-Speed Steve, a thousand-horsepower boat swamping the sailing craft in his wake.

"Hey, Vic, your door's closed," he said.

"*Was* closed."

"Were you on the phone?"

His way of asking, "Who were you talking to?"

"Yes, I was," she said. "It's a highly useful instrument of communication."

Make him squirm; force him to be direct.

"With Calvert?" he asked.

"Sit down. We need to talk."

Steve plopped down into a client chair, a modern Ligne Roset imported from France. The chair had a heavy-duty lumbar support and a heavier-duty price tag. Steve's idea, of course.

"Shit, who'd he kill now?" he asked.

She considered how to disclose what she knew. Clark's case had altered the way they communicated. Their discussions—both personal and professional—had always been free and open. She had held nothing back and believed the same of Steve.

But now . . .

Steve had been acting so squirrelly. Jealous of a man who was no threat to him, causing her to parcel out information, to withhold or delay until she figured how to package the news. This was no way to defend a case . . . or nourish a relationship.

Now she just blurted it out. "Clark lied to the police about his whereabouts on the day Sofia went missing."

"What!"

"He didn't drive up and down Collins Avenue checking her favorite places all day."

"Where was he, digging a grave in the Everglades?"

She ignored the crack. "A strip club in Pompano Beach. Getting a lap dance, to be more specific."

She expected another cheap shot, but instead Steve silently stood and walked to the window. He faced the racing sailboats in the bay, but his gaze seemed to reach to the distant horizon. "When did he tell you this?"

She could lie and say just now. But one would lead to another, and somewhere along the trail of interlocking fabrications, the chain would break. "The day of Jake's interview."

He turned from the window to face her. "Afterward?"

She shook her head. "Before. When you walked to the front of the house to bring Jake to the patio."

"The same time he told you about his choking the nurse. Unbelievable!"

"I'm sorry, Steve."

He sat on the edge of her desk, his face halfway between shock and anger. "Let me guess. He asked you whether to repeat the lie to Jake. And instead of huddling with me to reach a joint decision—a partnership decision—you told him to lie. Again!"

"I told him to keep his story consistent with what he told the police."

"And you kept me in the dark. About this and the nurse."

"I made a mistake. Two mistakes."

"This is so unlike you, Vic. Calvert's messed with your head."

"That was him on the phone just now. Jake found the strip club. Knows when Clark got there and when he left. Knows who he talked to and who gave him a lap dance."

Steve processed the information. He was good at this, she knew, staying calm under pressure. When he spoke, there was wonder in his voice. "Of all the strip joints in all the world, Jake finds the stripper who was twerking on our client the day his wife disappeared."

"He'll run with it," Victoria said. "I don't know where it will take him, but he'll make his point in a dramatic way."

"Dog with a bone. How'd Calvert find out Jake knows?"

"The stripper called him. Apparently, he's a regular and a big tipper."

"Why'd he lie to the cops in the first place?"

"He was embarrassed. His wife goes missing, and instead of looking for her, he's getting a lap dance."

"It could have been explained. She'd only been gone a few hours. No reason to believe she'd been snatched or was in any danger. But once he lied to the cops . . ."

"He was stuck with the story."

This is more like it, she thought. *Finishing each other's sentences, humming along in sync. Relationships are hard and need constant work, but they're not impossible.*

"Let's put ourselves in Jake's shoes," Steve said. "If he knows Calvert was at the strip club, what's his next question?"

"Where'd you go from there, Doctor? Where were you until you got home that night?"

"Exactly. What's the answer?"

"Clark won't tell me."

"What! Tell him he has to tell us or we can't defend him properly."

"I've told him, Steve. He simply refuses to tell me where he went."

"You know what that means? He's guilty."

"Not necessarily."

"How do you figure?"

She looked into the eyes of the man she loved. He was clueless. Maybe that made her love him even more. "Clark knows you hate him."

"I don't—"

She held up a hand to shush him. "He doesn't trust you to keep his confidence. I told him that you would never betray him, but he claims to have a sixth sense about these things."

Steve kept quiet, and she continued, "If Jake could prove where he went and what he did, Clark says he'd be convicted, even though he's innocent."

"With all due respect to our saintly client, that sounds like a crock of shit."

"Either way, it's the crock we're stuck with."

Looking troubled, Steve said, "I have a confession, Vic."

"Yeah?"

"I do hate Calvert."

"I know."

"But I'd never betray him."

She studied his eyes, which blinked twice. Meaning what? *Nothing*, she thought. And hoped.

"I know that, Steve. The man I love could never do such a thing."

-34-

Ethics 101

Jake Lassiter . . .

I was supposed to be in my astronaut's bed, inhaling 100 percent pure oxygen and curing my traumatic brain disease, if any there be. Oh, it's not really an astronaut's bed. It just looks like one of those glass-topped, torpedo-shaped compartments in sci-fi films, the ones where astronauts travel for eighty years and wake up feeling spry and not even needing mouthwash. It's a pressurized hyperbaric oxygen chamber where I inhale pure oxy for two hours three times a week. It cuts into a guy's schedule.

Today I was missing my appointment because of a pressing personal matter: I wouldn't participate in thuggery or the flat-out perversion of the judicial process. When I left Pincher's lair, feeling as if I needed a shower to wash off the scum, I called Judge Melvia Duckworth's chambers. Her Honor had left for the day. She had an 8:00 a.m. motion calendar tomorrow and a specially set hearing at ten. She could squeeze me in at eleven thirty. I would be there to turn in my sword, which is to say, tender my resignation and get her official blessing for my return to civilian life.

Next, as my old Caddy crossed the 12th Avenue bridge over the Miami River, I dialed Pincher's cell. As the phone rang, I caught sight of Marlins Park, where it sits like a tombstone on the site of the late and lamented Orange Bowl.

"I assume you've finished powdering your nose, Ray," I said when he answered.

"Jesus, Jake, you make my job a helluva lot harder than it should be."

"Always about you, isn't it? How can we get Sugar Ray to the governor's mansion without passing 'Go,' or rather, without landing in jail?"

"I thought you'd be more of a team player."

"And I thought you'd recused yourself! Why are you butting in?"

"Because you're puttering around, and an important citizen's daughter is dead."

"Appointing me was a charade to give you political cover. I'm quitting. Consider this my courtesy of giving you a heads-up. Get some other sucker to stand by and watch Pepe Suarez and his thug run the show."

"C'mon, Jake. I've got a better idea."

"Better than Suarez's thug kidnapping and torturing Clark Calvert?"

"That would be a mistake, I grant you. But there's a way to head it off. A preemptive legal strike to head off an illegal one."

Waiting for Pincher's brilliant idea, I passed Calle Ocho, only three blocks from Azucar, the Cuban ice-cream shop. I usually stop for a double scoop of *El Mani Loco*, crazy peanut, and *Platano Maduro*, sweet plantain, but right now, I was more in a Tennessee-whiskey mood.

"Grand jury convenes in the morning," Pincher said. "They're investigating elder abuse at nursing homes, but they'd be happy to shift gears to a juicy homicide. Bring in Dr. Freudenstein. He'll come without a subpoena. Hell, he'll camp out tonight for the chance to talk. With no one to cross-examine him, and with what you already have—Calvert's lie, his wife's fear of him—you can get an indictment. If Calvert's in the can, Pepe will step back."

"You're thinking tactically, Ray. I'm thinking strategically. How do you suggest I get Freudenstein's testimony into evidence at trial?"

"Jeez, show some cojones. Where's the old Jake? What did you used to say? 'Buckle your chin strap. Law is a contact sport.'"

"A sport with rules, Ray. I can't be a party to Suarez's thuggery, to illegal wiretaps, and to forced confessions. I can't use inadmissible evidence in front of the grand jury and just hope for the best at trial."

"Don't lecture me on ethics, Jake. You're the guy who considers the canons mere suggestions."

"I may violate a rule now and then, but only little ones."

"Yeah, yeah, I know. You don't mind getting your hands dirty as long as the stains come out. But you know what? You don't get to pick which rules you consider worthy of your fealty. The stains don't come out. You *are* dirty. You're just too damn sanctimonious to admit it."

The phone line clicked, and he was gone. That left me heading toward Coconut Grove without ice cream or whiskey or salvation. I considered the tongue-lashing I had just taken. Had I been fooling myself? Is there a bright, clearly defined ethical line separating black from white? Was it foolish of me to stake my claim in the gray?

Just what role did my medical condition play in all this? These days, I sensed my own mortality in a way that would have seemed foreign a short time ago. Subconsciously, did I want to make amends for the crap I'd done in my past?

I had no idea. But I was certain of one thing: I couldn't let my friends be hurt through my actions or inactions. I had been driving home, but now I hung a left on US 1 and looped back toward Brickell Avenue. I needed to talk to Solomon and Lord, and what I had to tell them couldn't be said on the phone.

·35·

Best Friends Forever . . . or for a While

Helluva view, Victoria." I watched a freighter docking at the Port of Miami across the inlet. "How much you paying a square foot?"

"Too much," she said.

"Not that much," Solomon said.

Some things don't change.

"Not like you to drop in without calling," Victoria said.

"I didn't want to use the phone," I said.

They gave me their puzzled looks.

"You both should have your office and home swept for bugs and your cars checked for any GPS tracking devices," I said. "Tell your client to do the same. Plus, he ought to get out of his house and check into a hotel until he goes on that trip to Vietnam."

"Holy . . ." Solomon said.

"Moly . . ." Victoria said. "You want to tell us what's happening and who's doing it?"

"It's not official, by which I mean, it's not Pincher or Barrios or any state agents. All extrajudicial, all illegal. I have to leave it at that."

"Pepe Suarez," Victoria said.

PAUL LEVINE

"Said all I'm going to about that. Tomorrow morning, I'm resigning my commission and going back home to the farm."

"Honoring the commitment you made to us," Victoria said.

"Does this mean you believe Calvert is innocent?" Solomon asked.

"Insufficient evidence doesn't equal innocence. But I'm not bailing because of our agreement."

"So why, then?" Solomon asked.

"Because—"

"Because you're swimming in the ocean," Victoria interrupted, "and you see a massive oil spill headed your way. An endless sea of muck and slime that will pull you under."

"Overly dramatic, but not far off," I said.

Everyone was quiet for a moment. Outside the high-rise windows, a passenger jet from MIA crossed the bay and gained altitude, heading toward the ocean.

"Okay, we respect your decision," Victoria said.

I gave them a small smile. "I guess you guys were right all along."

"How's that?" Solomon asked.

"You told me it wasn't in my nature to be a prosecutor. You said prosecutors had no empathy."

Victoria's brow furrowed. "Steve said that. I think you could have been a prosecutor with a heart, but they wouldn't let you."

"Either way, I'm out. And I just want you two to be safe." I stood, preparing to go.

Victoria gave me a warm look. "We love you, too, Jake."

Solomon clopped me on the shoulder. "Best friends forever, Jake. Or until somebody better comes along. C'mon, pal. I'll walk you to the elevator."

When we were in the corridor, Solomon lowered his voice to a whisper. "Stuff's been happening with Calvert."

I didn't respond.

"I've tried to keep my personal feelings out of it, Jake. My love for Vic, I mean, and Calvert's past with her. But from the very beginning, I've sensed there was something off with that guy."

"Solomon, you oughta stop now."

"You're getting out of the case. What difference does it make?"

"It just doesn't seem right."

"You're my best friend. I need to talk to you."

"I'm not your therapist."

"Hear me out. I'm not saying I have evidence Calvert killed his wife. He certainly hasn't confessed. But deep inside, I know it. I feel it. The son of a bitch is a murderer."

"Barrios said the same thing from day one. But I'm out, Solomon."

"I sort of wish you'd stay in."

"Why?"

"Victoria still has feelings for Calvert. Same deal. I just know it deep inside. And without you, who the hell is gonna help me with that?"

-36-

Mindfulness for Dummies

Melissa Gold *ooohed* and *aaahed* and purred like a cat. We were on the sofa in my living room, her shapely legs propped in my lap, and I was giving her a foot massage, which she might say is the second-best thing I do.

"Aaah," she cooed. "I could get used to this."

"That's my game plan, Doctor."

"Oooh, right there. *Flexor digitorum longus.*"

"What's with the Gregorian chant?"

"The muscle you're digging into on the bottom of my foot. Heaven. What did I do to deserve this?"

"You didn't yell at me when I told you I missed my astronaut-under-glass appointment."

"Hyperbaric oxygen? That's okay. Dr. Hoch doubts it has any effect on the tau proteins that cause CTE."

"But you prescribed it."

"It's what you would call a Hail Mary."

"I didn't know we were down to the last few seconds of the game."

"End of the first half is all, Jake. I should watch my football analogies."

I ran my right thumb along a tendon that stretched from Melissa's heel all the way to her arch. The thumb has been broken three times, the last when I smacked a tight end on his helmet, both to get his attention and to keep him from running a slant over the middle. It hurt now, but the pleasurable purr in Melissa's throat diminished the pain.

"I saw Joe Namath at an Old Timers' dinner," I said. "He had a hundred twenty sessions of pure oxygen and thought it helped him think clearer."

"But Nick Buoniconti tried it at UM Hospital with no positive results." She shifted her position and flexed her foot, exposing more of the tendons and muscles. "Have you increased the CBD?"

"Smoking more weed, absolutely."

She made a *tut-tut* sound. "How many times do I have to tell you? Stick to the prescription. You only need the CBD, not the psychoactive THC."

"That's like thinking about sex without actually doing it. Which is pretty much what's going on at this very moment."

"Keep rubbing, buster. Your time will come. You can warm up the Sade channel on Pandora anytime now, smooth operator."

I loved that switcheroo, from an esteemed neuropathologist to a sexy bedmate in a Miami minute. That prompted me to move from deep tissue to a lighter, more sensual touch, letting my fingers glide up her calf. She pursed her lips and made a soft *mmm*-ing sound.

"Have you been trying to stay in the moment and not worry about the future?" she asked.

"Mostly I've been living in the past."

"Seriously, Jake, have you gotten into mindfulness and meditation, as I suggested?" she asked.

"I bought the book *Mindfulness for Dummies*."

"Bought it? Did you read it?"

"Tried, but I found myself skipping chapters to see what comes next."

179

I laughed at my little joke, but she didn't.

Melissa said, "Oh, how those college cheerleaders must have found you so charming and witty."

My hand was caressing the soft flesh behind her knee. I heard another coo, another *mmm*, and I let my fingers dance a little higher.

"Have you had any luck in reducing stress?" she asked.

"Just the opposite. But tomorrow I'm turning everything around."

I summarized the case for her. The puzzling Dr. Calvert, the devious Ray Pincher, the smarmy Pepe Suarez, and the thuggish J. T. Wetherall. Told her that I'd be getting out of the case and resuming a normal life, or a reasonable facsimile thereof.

"I'm sorry it didn't work out, Jake. I had thought that switching sides might be good for you. A new challenge that could get your mind off all the medical uncertainties."

"I remember. You said change can be very therapeutic."

She reached down and clamped my hand, which was halfway up her thigh. "Are you blaming me? Holding me responsible for your decision?"

"No, not at all. I've known Ray Pincher for a long time. I should have seen this coming. He's a man of secret agendas. Always has been."

"Okay, then." She released my hand. I withdrew it from under her summery dress, and she swung her legs to the floor and scooted closer to me on the sofa. It seemed like an excellent time to move from touching to kissing, accompanied by Sade's "No Ordinary Love."

"Has Mr. Pincher agreed to your withdrawing from the case?" she asked.

"He doesn't want me to, but it's not up to him. Judge Duckworth has final say, and she told me I could bail anytime before an indictment was returned."

"But from what you say about Mr. Pincher and his agendas, might he not have something up his sleeve?"

Her question made me think of a saloon in one of those old Western movies. There's a poker game with whiskey bottles on the table and cowboys all around. Plus one professional gambler, a villainous mustachioed guy in a black hat. Sure enough, when he deals from the bottom of the deck and is threatened, he's got something up his sleeve. A single-shot derringer.

"I hadn't thought of that," I admitted. "But you're right. Pincher never lets go of what he wants. And if there are two paths toward reaching his goal, he always takes the winding road."

Melissa frowned, and little lines furrowed in her forehead. "Sorry I brought that up. I'm sure everything will be okay tomorrow, just the way you've planned it."

We kissed, and Sade claimed she gave her man "all the love I got." I closed my eyes, trying to stay in the moment, but damn it, I kept seeing the barrel of a derringer pointed straight at me.

·37·

The Fall Guy

Bruno paced around the judge's chambers, panting and slobbering. He was Judge Melvia Duckworth's beloved English bulldog.

The judge sat at her gleaming mahogany desk, looking into a handheld mirror, patting her graying Afro. I sat in a leather armchair, squirming, wanting to get this over with. If the judge didn't hurry up, I might join Bruno in pacing and panting, if not slobbering.

"How do I look, Jake?" Judge Duckworth asked.

"Like a million bucks, Your Honor."

"In trial, you're a helluva lot better liar than that feeble effort. I've got bags under my eyes and old-lady wrinkles that have their own baby wrinkles."

"I swear, Judge. You look like a college coed."

"Ha! You know Jackson Pettibone, runs the probation office?"

"Good man. Always gives my clients the benefit of the doubt."

"He lost his wife two years ago, about eighteen months after cancer took my Henry. Anyway, Jackson invited me to lunch." She lowered the mirror and looked at me. "Truluck's on Brickell."

I made an appreciative sound, approving of Jackson Pettibone's good taste. "Try the seafood primavera. Shrimp, crab, and calamari over linguine."

"Might be too messy for a first date."

"Your Honor, the reason I'm here—"

"Maybe just a broiled salmon fillet. Keep it simple, eh?"

"Sure. Sounds good. The reason I'm—"

"Why so antsy, Jake?"

Bruno took that moment to expel a deadly bulldog fart and then continued slobbering.

"Maybe you can walk Bruno when I go to lunch," the judge said.

"Happy to, Your Honor."

"Now, what were you saying?"

"To put it in military terms," I said to the judge, appealing to her background as an army JAG officer, "I want to be mustered out. Resign my commission."

She eyed me with concern. "Your brain on the fritz, Jake? Delusions, dementia, and whatnot?"

"It's not that, Your Honor. I'm just not cut out to be a prosecutor. At least not on this case. Not with—"

"Ray Pincher looking over your shoulder."

"More like breathing down my neck."

"What happened to the Chinese wall with Pincher on the outside?"

"It turned into the Maginot Line."

"I told you Pincher was a slippery one, but you knew that, Jake." She sighed and looked at me with even more concern. "Okay, let me get Cynthia in here with the paperwork so I can go to lunch with the handsome Mr. Pettibone."

The judge's phone buzzed, and she picked it up. "Okay, put him on." She gave me a look and raised her eyebrows. "Hello, Raymond. Yes, always good to speak with you, but I haven't seen you in church in ages. Uh-huh. Uh-huh. I see."

She hung up and looked at me, regret saddening her eyes. "My dear Jake. As you might have gleaned, that was the State Attorney. I'm afraid you're a dollar short and twenty minutes late. The grand jury just indicted Dr. Clark Calvert for the murder of his wife."

"That's not possible, Your Honor. I haven't even said hello to the jurors. Haven't set a foot in their room."

"Then this takes runaway grand juries to a new level."

"Makes no sense, Judge."

"I'm sorry, Jake, but as I told you in the beginning, I can't muster you out post-indictment. And I'd caution you against going AWOL."

"I don't get it. How'd they render an indictment? Who presented the evidence?"

"Raymond didn't say. He knew you were in here, by the way."

Pepe Suarez and J. T. Wetherall. Following me as if I were the enemy. And maybe I am.

"I can't win this trial. No one can, and Pincher knows it."

"Then why's he doing this?"

"He needs someone to blame. I'm his fall guy."

IN THE CIRCUIT COURT OF THE ELEVENTH JUDICIAL CIRCUIT IN AND FOR MIAMI-DADE COUNTY, FLORIDA—SUMMER TERM 2017

INDICTMENT
MURDER SECOND DEGREE Fla. Stat 782.04 (2)
STATE OF FLORIDA
vs.
CLARK GORDON CALVERT

IN THE NAME AND BY THE AUTHORITY OF THE STATE OF FLORIDA:

The Grand Jurors of the State of Florida, duly called, impaneled and sworn to inquire and true presentment make in and for the County of Miami-Dade, upon their oaths, present that on or about the third day of June 2017, within the County of Miami-Dade, State of Florida, CLARK G. CALVERT evincing a depraved mind, did unlawfully and feloniously, by an act imminently dangerous, kill a human being, to wit: SOFIA SUAREZ-CALVERT, by strangulation of said SOFIA SUAREZ-CALVERT, in violation of Fla. Stat. 782.04(2), to the evil example of all others in like cases, offending and against the peace and dignity of the State of Florida.

Laura M. Dunlap
Foreperson of the Grand Jury

·38·

The Lion in Winter

I cleared the metal detectors and the armed guards using my ID card as a specially appointed prosecutor, a "temp," as Corky called me. I burst into Ray Pincher's office and unloaded. "What the hell were you doing in the grand jury? You're supposed to be out of the case."

He didn't even look up. He was sitting at his desk, signing a stack of direct Informations, the charging documents in cases that don't go to the grand jury. The stack was a foot high.

"I haven't left my office all morning." Pincher kept on signing.

"But I was there," a voice said.

In one of the client chairs, Phil Flury turned around to face me. I hadn't seen the little weasel. "With Calvert planning to leave the country, it seemed prudent to push the matter." He stood and handed me a document, making a show of blowing on it. "The foreperson's signature is still wet."

I took a quick look. "Strangulation? Tell me, Flury. Was Sofia's hyoid bone fractured?"

"Who knows? We don't have a body."

"And therefore, no bruises on the neck. No fingerprints or fingernail marks you can tie to Calvert."

"No."

"Or Calvert's DNA under Sofia's fingernails."

"Obviously not."

"What sucker's gonna prosecute this smelly fart of a case?" I said, still thinking of Bruno the bulldog.

"I've got faith in you, Jake." Pincher finally looked up from his busywork. "Phil tells me that Dr. Freudenstein held the grand jurors spellbound. The old shrink performed brilliantly."

"A trained seal can perform brilliantly when it's not being attacked by a shark," I said.

"Ah, you mean cross-examination," Flury said.

"Solomon and Lord will eat Freudenstein alive if the judge admits his testimony, which is a long shot in itself."

"Give the judge some of that Lassiter mumbo jumbo." Flury was smirking, enjoying my predicament.

"Ray, Freudenstein can't withstand cross. It'll be a bloodbath."

"I wouldn't be too sure," Flury said, even though I wasn't talking to him. "You should have seen the grand jurors' faces, especially the women, when Freudenstein read his *Tarasoff* letter: 'Mrs. Calvert, it is my considered medical opinion that you are in danger of great bodily harm or death if you continue to reside with your husband.'"

"Yeah, I've read it."

"Make sure you pack the jury with women, Lassiter."

"Really, Flu Bug, I hadn't thought of that. When you do some more heavy thinking, tell me how to get that damn letter into evidence."

"It's not just the letter. Freudenstein was quite persuasive with the house, tree, person test."

"That's crap! Calvert was playing him. And Freudenstein didn't even keep copies of the drawings."

"He can recite them from memory."

"Flury, you're an idiot. That'd be like a cop saying he confiscated heroin from the defendant but lost it on the way to the police station."

"Calm down, Jake," Pincher said. "Someday you'll thank Phil for teeing the ball up for you."

"Someday, I'll kick his ass from here to Sopchoppy! And as for you, Ray . . ."

I couldn't form the words. The room swayed like a dinghy in a squall. I reached out and steadied myself by leaning on a credenza, my hand knocking over a framed photo of Pincher with some politicos at a black-tie gala.

"Jake, you okay?" Pincher's voice echoed in the distance. *"Oka-a-a-a-ay."*

I felt my knees buckle. Pincher bounded out of his high-backed chair. The little ex-boxer still had a lot of quick, and he grabbed my shoulder before I toppled forward.

"What is it, Jake? You want an ambulance?"

I regained my footing by holding on to him.

How humiliating.

Rescued by my tormentor.

"I'm fine, Ray. Fine."

"You sure, pal? You want some water? Bourbon? Anything?"

"I don't know, Ray. I feel like I just stepped into a gator hole, and I don't know if I'm gonna lose a foot or an entire leg."

Pincher turned to Flury and barked, "Phil, get outta here. Go push some papers."

"Yes, sir," Flury said.

When the weasel was gone, Pincher directed me into a client chair and sat on the corner of his desk, studying me with a look of concern that seemed genuine. "We go back a long way, Jake, and I always liked and respected you."

I kept quiet, declining to return the compliment.

"I know you're having a hard time right now with the illness and all, and I'm feeling some regret."

"For what, Ray? Inviting me to your party as your personal piñata?"

He sighed and stared at his wall of fame, the photos and plaques attesting to his civic-mindedness and, shall we say, self-importance. "Pepe Suarez put me under tremendous pressure, Jake. If he withholds support for my gubernatorial run, I'm dead in the water. If I run for reelection as state attorney and he backs someone else, same deal."

"You're supposed to do your job, Ray, and not sell your office to the highest bidder."

"Didn't know you were such an idealist. Look, this is all about time and distance."

"No idea what you're talking about, Ray."

"The time until the next election and the distance between me and the losing prosecution."

"Go on."

"I think Calvert killed his wife, but I admit the proof is weak. We're never gonna find her body, never gonna have any forensics. Ever since Sofia disappeared, my choice has been whether to piss off Suarez every day for the next year while the investigation goes nowhere, or to get it over with."

"Lose quick or lose slow," I said.

"Exactly, Jake. If we lose quick, I'll have eighteen months to mend fences before the election. That's the 'time' I'm talking about. It's why I pushed so hard for the indictment now. And I appointed you to have some distance between the case and me, should everything go south."

"You feel better telling me this, Ray? Ease some of the guilt?"

"Some. But I've been thinking. You've got the tennis pro who'll testify Sofia was terrified of her husband. You caught Calvert in a lie. The bastard's getting a lap dance the day his wife disappears. Maybe you'll find that other woman he choked into unconsciousness. And if you get Dr. Freudenstein's testimony in, you've got a fighting chance, if he can hold his own on cross."

Suddenly I felt exhausted, my energy drained. If Pincher wanted to argue, he would have to do it with himself. What had happened to my vigor, my stamina? Where was my fighting spirit to go along with that fighting chance Pincher was trying to sell me?

"I don't know, Ray. I feel old. The lion in winter. Too slow to catch the wildebeest, too weak to chew through bone."

"Wrong! You may be the lion in winter. But, Jake, my friend, you are still the lion."

Stephen Solomon

and

Victoria Lord

request the honour of your presence at their
marriage

on Saturday, the twenty-first day of October

Two Thousand and Seventeen

at six o'clock in the evening

Vizcaya Gardens

3251 South Miami Avenue

Miami, Florida 33129

Black-Tie Dinner to Follow

-39-

The Rabbi, the Minister, and the Disbarred Judge

Victoria Lord . . .

Y ou want your father to preside at our wedding?" Victoria asked. "Are you serious?"

"I think he's a good compromise," Steve said.

What a clever and sneaky negotiator, she thought, feeling a mini-squabble coming on. They were jogging south on Le Jeune Road, nearing the circle where Sunset Drive meets Old Cutler Road and the entrance to Cocoplum. It was late afternoon, and a storm had threatened, but it had been a false promise. Although sheet lightning flashed in the distance, the sky only dripped and drooled, an old man spitting out his soup.

"How is your father a compromise?" she asked. "I'd like a minister. You'd like a rabbi."

"A *reformed* rabbi. So reformed he's practically Episcopalian."

"And we compromise on a disbarred judge? Is he even qualified to officiate?"

"Dad still has his notary license, so sure. It would mean the world to the old guy. Who knows how long he has left?"

"Doesn't your dad still catch spiny lobsters with a bag and tickle stick in fifteen feet of water?"

"Sure. He's been a snorkeler and a bug hunter his whole life."

"And doesn't he still haul in a couple dozen over the legal limit?"

"What's your point, Vic?"

"Your dad is going to outlive all of us!"

"Okay, okay. It was just a thought. Meanwhile, Jake's mad about the wedding date."

"Why?"

"It's the night of the Penn State–Michigan game."

"Oh, tell him to grow up."

Victoria's cell rang. She slipped it out of shorts, saw Clark Calvert was calling, and slid the 'Answer' button.

"Victoria," he said, his voice tight, "there are three police cars in my driveway."

-40-

How Many Women?

Steve Solomon . . .

T here are rats in here!" Calvert's voice was ragged with fear. For a moment, Steve thought he meant snitches. Informers.

They were in a ground-floor lawyer's room—actually a barred cell—at the Miami-Dade County jail. The place smelled of disinfectant and oily lubricants, body odor and urine. Solomon had long believed that if you brought every twelve-year-old boy in the county here for one day, the crime rate would drop precipitously in the coming years.

"Rats as big as cats," Calvert continued. "Jesus. The conditions are inhumane."

"Steve is working on bail." Victoria paused, waiting for her partner to speak up, but he was lost in thought.

Steve was fighting a war within himself. He wanted to win the trial because, well, he was a competitor who always wanted to win. But he despised their client, and deep in his heart, he would love to see Calvert go to prison. Talk about cognitive dissonance! How would it play out when given a chance to win—or lose—the case? He didn't know.

He asked himself: *What would Jake do?* The big guy was his role model, not that Solomon would ever admit it. He remembered their conversation outside Calvert's house. He'd admitted that Calvert had unnerved him, had made him feel threatened about his relationship with Victoria. Jake gave him no sympathy.

"Solomon, you gotta toughen up. Victoria loves you. God knows why, but she does."

It was solid advice. Man up! Women despise weakness. And just what was he afraid of? The wedding invitations had been sent out, the cake with bride and groom and a scales of justice had been ordered. The Solomon-Lord life plan was set in motion, and their weasel client couldn't do anything about it.

In the same situation, Jake would take charge. Show strength. Betray no fear. Hell, he'd break down doors to win the case, even if he despised his client. *Because that's what lawyers do. We're soldiers of the Constitution,* Solomon thought. *Not to get all misty about it, but we're the infantry, defending the individual against the heavy artillery of the state.* Solomon felt like snapping off a salute, but instead got down to business.

"I've got a bail hearing scheduled for the morning," he told Calvert. "For now, just chill."

"Please. Please get me out of here." Calvert's voice, usually so cocky, had become a whimper.

So much for all that intellectual bravado. Cutter of bones. Pilot of planes. Pianist, linguist, and all-around Big Fucking Deal!

Processing at the jail had taken hours. It was nearly 10:00 p.m. Steve imagined what Calvert was feeling. How the sounds, the smells, the garish lighting, the barking guards, the prisoners' stares made him feel. Terrified, for one thing.

Piss your pants for all I care. I'll show you, Calvert. I'll show Victoria, show Jake, show the whole damn world who's in control.

"I got Jake to agree to a million dollars cash bail." A note of pride in Steve's voice. "The judge will go along."

"Steve hopped right on it," Victoria said, giving him the credit he deserved.

"Thank you. Both of you." Calvert's eyes darted to the corner of the cell, as if expecting to see a rat the size of Pepé Le Pew. "A million dollars. I can do that."

He was wearing an orange jumpsuit that was a couple of sizes too large and flip-flops that squeaked on the concrete floor. His hands were cuffed in front of his chest. He looked small, pale, afraid.

"This so dehumanizing," Calvert said. "They try to make you feel like a criminal so that you will believe you are, or at the very least, so that everyone else will think you are."

"Get through tonight," Victoria said, "and tomorrow you'll be home. Then we'll start preparing in earnest."

"You'll surrender your passport," Solomon said, "and wear an ankle bracelet and monitor."

Calvert nodded. Solomon knew their client would agree to anything rather than stay in this palace of horrors. He had a pretty damn good idea what Calvert was thinking: *You want my left arm, take it at the elbow. Just get me out of here!*

"The case has become very real," Steve said, "and we have to move quickly."

"Tomorrow," Victoria said. "Let's let Clark get some sleep."

"When a doctor is charged with killing his wife, it makes news," he persisted. "Sam Sheppard in Ohio. Carl Coppolino in Florida. Robert Bierenbaum in New York. Jeffrey MacDonald, the Green Beret surgeon, in North Carolina. These days, with the Internet and social media and all those true-crime shows, this is going to hit everywhere, fast and hard."

"And your point is?" Calvert asked.

"You told Victoria about a nurse in Boston who accused you of choking her into unconsciousness during sex. Are there any others?

What are their names? Where are they located? If they hear about the case, are they likely to contact the prosecution?"

Firing off the questions, *rat-a-tat-tat*, a commander of troops.

Calvert didn't immediately answer. His shoulders hunched, and he seemed to withdraw even farther into himself. Outside the cell, a buzzer blared, a discordant sound, and a steel door clanged shut.

"Ste-phen," Victoria said, dragging out his name, "perhaps we should have discussed this before you bring it up on what is perhaps the worst day in Clark's life."

"Sorry. But I thought the day Sofia disappeared would have been the worst day."

"You know very well what I mean."

"Actually, I don't. With any other client, you put the case first. Feeling down because you were arrested today? Get over it! The lawyer's job isn't to pamper the client but to protect him—from the state and from himself." He turned toward Calvert. "So I'm sorry if you've had a shitty day. I want . . . we want to keep you from having forty shitty years. Okay?"

Calvert raised both cuffed hands in what looked like a gesture of surrender. "Okay. Please. Victoria. Steve. We're all on the same team."

My team, Steve thought. *Victoria has been acting as if this is her case alone. Did she forget we're partners in life and law? And my name is first on the letterhead.*

Still hunched over, looking at the cuffed hands in his lap, Calvert spoke in a whisper. "There might be more than one woman out there."

"Let's start with the nurse in Boston," Steve said matter-of-factly, wondering just how many names there would be. He shot a glance at Victoria to see if she registered shock or surprise, disappointment or disgust. No, she maintained her poker face. A professional, adhering to the first rule of lawyering: don't act judgmental toward your client.

Calvert said, "Her name is Lisa Hardt. A nurse at Mass General. That's where I went after University Hospital in New Jersey. We dated.

We were intimate. She greatly enjoyed the enhanced orgasms induced by cutting off the oxygen supply. She pretty much demanded that I do it."

"Quite a coincidence," Steve said. "You told us the choking was also Sofia's idea."

"Her idea. My idea. Does it matter if the high jinks were consensual?"

"Maybe, if the high jinks led to death."

"With Lisa, there was only one incident when she lost consciousness. After we broke up, she complained about it to the hospital board. Claimed she didn't consent to either the sex or the airflow restrictions. The board correctly determined that she was a woman scorned who was seeking her revenge."

Another moment of quiet, except for a man's screams from somewhere on the first floor. *"Lemmeeeee out! Lemmeeeee out!"*

Another buzzer, another steel door slamming, and a voice on an intercom, the sound scratchy and indecipherable.

"Do you need to know anything else about her? And there might be two others."

"We'll get to the others. Do you know where Lisa Hardt is today?"

"Oh, sorry. I nearly forgot. You're worried she might call Mr. Lassiter and offer to testify."

"Exactly."

"No chance of that. Lisa, poor dear, drowned."

"Oh, God. That's terrible," Victoria said.

Steve just waited, didn't ask the obvious question. He'd learned interview techniques from Lassiter, who'd long preached that silence is sometimes the best question.

A few seconds later, just as he had hoped, Calvert continued speaking. "About three months after we broke up, she went swimming off Cape Cod. Late at night. Alone. There was a riptide."

"What did the autopsy show?" Steve asked.

"There wasn't one," Calvert answered. "They never found her body."

-41-

The Curvy Ethical Road

Three months later
Jake Lassiter . . .

Summer turned to well, endless summer. September used to be the soggiest month. The buggiest month. The crappiest month. Now the rain and heat last deep into October. For some reason, the downpour usually catches me in my car, the staccato drumbeats against the canvas top so loud I can barely hear Johnny Cash ruing the day he shot a man in Reno just to watch him die. Me? In October, I get the Miami Blues.

The rain does not relieve the heat, which rises in steamy waves from the pavement. Bugs abound. Mosquitoes breed in every puddle, threatening Zika virus. No-see-um gnats buzz your ears and nose. Cockroaches we euphemistically call palmetto bugs, but these guys are as big as roller skates.

One bright note. When the sea levels rise enough, we can return South Florida to the gators and the birds, the bugs and the rodents.

If the days are broiling, the nights are simply dank and sweaty, with barely a breath of moving air. One consolation: in my Coconut Grove neighborhood, the scent of jasmine is so lush and sweet it will make you woozy. Not that I needed the jasmine. I'd been vertiginous, off and on, for the past few weeks. Usually, it would come at night, my mind clouding, a rug slipping out from under my feet.

I never fell. Never lost consciousness. Just a bit of dizziness. My headaches had increased in number and worsened in degree. Oh, one more irksome matter. A couple of times in the past few weeks, I had trouble forming words. My brain knew what I wanted to say, but my mouth couldn't spit it out.

"How are you feeling?" Melissa Gold asked me every day.

"Tip-top," I usually replied. Unless I said, "Never better." Occasionally, just to break the monotony, I'd say, "Peachy."

So, yeah, basically I lied.

At Melissa's urging, I continued to undergo tests. A new MRI seemed to rule out atrophy in my frontal lobes, a cause for some celebration. A different result would have indicated full-blown CTE or Alzheimer's. Choose your poison.

Melissa and her colleague Dr. Hoch kept poking me with needles and pestering me with questions. Based on their conversations with me and each other, I learned that, should I honestly disclose all my symptoms, they would send me to the hospital for a spinal tap. They'd insert a needle into the spinal canal to steal some fluid and test it for abnormalities.

I didn't want to do it. Not that I'm not afraid of needles. Back in the day, I had more painkiller injections than I can remember. I've had large-gauge needles jolt both knees with cortisone. I've had needles punched into my pelvis to withdraw bone marrow that was later injected into both my shoulders in futile attempts to fix my rotator cuffs. But just now, with the Calvert trial looming, I decided to call a halt to all the doctor visits other than house calls—and booty calls—after-hours by the lovely Melissa Gold.

As for the Calvert case, Solomon and Lord had moved for a speedy trial, as I had expected. That's what the defense does when it's confident the state doesn't have the evidence. Get the case under way before a body pops up from the bottom of the bay.

Judge Erwin Gridley had scheduled the trial for next week. I'd been working with Detective Barrios, getting my witnesses prepared, but we were in no better shape than the day the indictment was returned.

Tonight Melissa had stopped by, bringing takeout from Havana Harry's. Fried yucca with mojo sauce, tostones laced with pork and onions, topped by queso fresco, and chicken *vaca frita* that we shared. I provided the tequila. The good stuff, Don Julio 1942. It's pricey, but life is too short for liquor that singes the throat.

Melissa had an early meeting at the hospital tomorrow, so she didn't sleep over. I dozed off in my recliner around 11:00 p.m. and was awakened by a piercing headache a few hours later. I staggered into the kitchen and grabbed a bottle of some exotic pain reliever Melissa had prescribed. I washed down three pills with the last few drops of Don Julio from the tall triangular bottle.

That's when I heard the noise.

From the porch at the rear of the house.

A scraping sound, as if someone had bumped into a chair in the dark. Or maybe it was just the neighborhood possum rooting around, looking for leftover potato chips and beef jerky. I hadn't turned on the lights, so whoever was out there—man or possum—couldn't see me in the darkened kitchen.

I stayed still and quiet. There was no sound other than the buzz of nighttime insects. Then a faraway barking dog.

Then footsteps. An unmistakable sound on the wooden floorboards of the porch. The AC kicked on then and drowned out the sounds.

I padded barefoot to the foyer closet, pulled out my black-barreled baseball bat made of hard maple. The Barry Bonds model. Hey, if it was good enough to hit seventy-three home runs in a year, it ought to be able to crack the skull of a trespasser, burglar, or whatever night-crawling lowlife was on my property.

I slipped out a side door that was shielded from the porch by a row of purple bougainvillea. Holding the bat in my right hand, I brushed back the thorny vines with my left hand as I made my way around the corner of the house.

I saw a figure silhouetted by the mercury vapor lamp that sits on the property line. The figure was on my back porch, leaning over. I couldn't make out whether it was a man or woman, large or small. Just then my right foot caught on the garden hose, and I tumbled facedown into the dirt. My bat went flying, and I let out a *whoomph* as I landed.

Footsteps again, the figure dashing off the porch and across the yard. When I looked up, it was gone.

A moment later, I found something.

An eight-by-eleven manila envelope on the porch, propped up against the door to the kitchen. My visitor wasn't a burglar. He or she was making a delivery, but of what?

I carried the envelope back into the house and turned on the kitchen lights. The envelope was blank. I opened the clasp and looked inside. A single sheet of white paper. A name was typed on the page.

Ann Cavendish.

And a phone number with a 404 area code, which I knew to be Atlanta. And one typewritten sentence.

She would love to talk to you about Clark Calvert.

I looked into the darkness toward the rear of my lot, where the figure had disappeared. Keep going two blocks and you'd practically be in Solomon and Lord's front yard.

Steve Solomon.

You crazy bastard! Risking your license! And tempting me into the valley of the shadow of disbarment.

I figured that Ann Cavendish of Atlanta was the nurse Solomon already told me about, a woman Calvert choked into unconsciousness back in Boston. Or if not her, another woman with a similar tale. It made sense. Sofia would not have been the first. A man doesn't wait till his forties to start getting kinky.

Calvert likely had been getting his jollies in that dangerous game for a long time. And sure, I'd love to have a couple of other witnesses. I'd love to establish the choking as "pattern evidence." If he did such a thing in the past, chances are he did it now as well. That's the theory that allows into evidence what lawyers call "prior bad acts."

But as much as I'd like to find Ann Cavendish of Atlanta, I couldn't do it.

I'll steer clear of that ethical minefield. Won't I?

I thought about it some more.

Was there a way I could take advantage of the information without violating my oath? Okay, let's be honest. I couldn't, though I might find a way I could rationalize. Might as well be frank about it. Knowledge of self is acquired through a shattered mirror, certain features obscured. A searing thought, then. Was Pincher right?

"You are dirty. You're just too damn sanctimonious to admit it."

Aw, to hell with it, Ray.

I would create a buffer between Ann Cavendish and me. Put one curve in the road between Solomon's grievously unethical act and my mildly shady one.

I wouldn't call Ann Cavendish. Detective Barrios would do it for me.

-42-

Tar and Feathers

heard a woman's scream.

Only it wasn't a woman. It was a peacock that must have weighed fifty pounds. A male. It flapped its wings and half jumped, half flew from my backyard to the lowest edge of my roof, where it spread its tail and shook its six-foot-long iridescent feathers.

It screamed again, and I saw two female peacocks in the yard below. *Aha. Mating season.* In my youth, I, too, was guilty of show-off behavior to garner female attention. Lacking iridescent feathers, I once leapt from a fifth-floor hotel balcony into a swimming pool, missing the concrete deck by perhaps six inches.

I didn't have to look up at the male peacock. I was above him, tiptoeing up the hitch of the roof, trying not to break the barrel tiles under my size-thirteen-and-a-half, triple-E feet. Trying also not to slip down the steep slope, crash through the chinaberry bush, and break my neck.

My recent dizzy spells made roof work an iffy proposition, especially with the tiles still wet from a morning storm, as I worked my way across the ridge toward the chimney. Yeah, my old coral-rock bungalow has a fireplace, which is as useful hereabouts as a snowplow.

My roof's been leaking after heavy rains. From experience, I know it's the metal flashing around the base of the chimney, which is why I was tiptoeing across the roof tiles, carrying a bucket of hot tar and a small mop. The physical labor also took my mind away from the Calvert case. Melissa had prescribed an honest day's work as therapy, though she meant sweeping the driveway and porch, not dancing across the roof.

My cell phone rang. I wouldn't have answered, but with the trial looming, you just never know when you'll get an important call.

"Mr. Lassiter, this is Samuel Merrick Buchanan," said the caller in a booming voice.

"I didn't sleep with your client's wife," I replied.

"Ha! Good one. But not the first time I've heard it."

Sam Buchanan was Miami's leading divorce lawyer. When representing the husband, he was legendary for smearing the wife's name. When representing the wife, he usually found hidden piles of the husband's money.

"What can I do for you, Mr. Buchanan?"

"You're prosecuting the case against Dr. Clark Calvert."

I sat down on the ridge at the highest point of the roof, keeping the can of tar steady with one hand. "I'm gonna take a wild guess here. Did Sofia Calvert retain you for a divorce before she disappeared?"

"I've been struggling with what I can ethically tell you. As you know, the attorney-client privilege survives death."

"It's been a long time since I barely passed the bar exam, but the fact that Sofia Calvert retained you is not privileged, while what she said to you is. You could testify that you are a divorce lawyer and she hired you. The jury could reach its own conclusions."

He exhaled a sigh and said, "Do you believe my testimony, circumscribed as it may be, will be useful to the prosecution?"

Sweat was coursing down my face, down my back, down my arms, down my legs. Between the heat of the Miami sun and the steaming bucket of tar, it was quite possible I would just melt into a puddle of liquid protoplasm.

"We'd need to prove Calvert knew she hired you," I said. "If he did, it's evidence of motive. If he didn't know, it's just prejudicial testimony without probative value."

"Put me on your witness list. I'll do the best I can."

"Thanks for making the call."

"I feel terrible about that poor woman. Maybe if I'd pushed her to file and move out, this never would have happened."

"Not your fault, Mr. Buchanan."

"I'll help the prosecution as much as I can, but it's a sticky situation."

Like hot tar on a Miami roof, I thought.

He lowered his voice as if someone might be listening. "Between us, Mr. Lassiter, Sofia was terrified of her husband. I doubt you can get this into evidence, but as she walked out my office door, she said, 'Sam, if I ever go missing, don't even bother looking for me. I'll be dead and buried, and Clark will have made certain no one will ever find me.'"

It didn't surprise me but still landed with a wallop. Sofia was a woman living in fear. I had empathy for her and needed the jurors to feel the same way. Unfortunately, the Rules of Evidence—from doctor-patient privilege to attorney-client privilege to hearsay rules—conspired to keep the jury in the dark.

"She told her tennis pro virtually the same thing," I said.

He wished me luck. I thanked him again, then made my way gingerly to the corner of the roof where the chimney sat astride the ridge. I couldn't tell exactly where the flashing was leaking, so I decided to do a big, sloppy job that would be certain to cover the spot and likely a good number of tiles, too. I dipped the fiberglass mop into the hot tar and lathered it on.

My cell rang again. Leaning on the mop, I checked the display. Detective George Barrios.

"I found Ann Cavendish," he said when I answered.

"Yeah?"

"She was stunned when I asked about Calvert. She said, and I quote, 'I don't want to talk about that man. I don't want to see that man. And please don't call me again.' Then she hung up and wouldn't answer when I redialed."

"And what did you gather from that?"

"She's scared witless. Of Calvert, not me."

"You have her address?"

"Suburb of Atlanta."

"You're gonna have to knock on her door, George."

"No kidding. You oughta be a cop. Where do you think I am right now?"

As if on cue, I heard the voice on the loudspeaker. The Delta flight to Atlanta was ready for boarding.

-43-

Dirty Money

The first goal in trying any case—civil or criminal—is not to make an ass of yourself. The second is to win. The goals are related, of course. It's difficult, though not impossible, to win even if you knock over the courtroom spittoon. That's what happened to the legendary Texas mouthpiece Racehorse Haynes in his very first trial as a greenhorn lawyer. He nervously got to his feet and knocked over the spittoon where lawyers spat out their chewing tobacco. And, yes, he won, maybe having gained sympathy from the jury for his klutziness.

We don't chew or spit in court anymore, though we surely blow smoke, so I would have to come up with another way to warm jurors' hearts.

It was early evening, and I was in my temporary office—courtesy of the state of Florida—the Calvert file fanned out in front of me on the war-room table. Detective Barrios had not called me back, and I fought the urge to pester him. If he had anything positive, he would call.

The after-hours receptionist at the front desk buzzed me. She sat behind bulletproof glass because not all visitors to the State Attorney's office were saints and heavenly angels.

"Señor Pepe Suarez to see you," the receptionist said in heavily accented English.

A moment later, Suarez threw open the door to the conference room, not bothering to thank the security guard who had escorted him in. He slammed the door and tossed a document on the table.

"Your friends served me with this shit," he said, meaning Solomon and Lord.

I examined the document. A subpoena duces tecum requiring Suarez to appear at trial and bring documents related to a trust he had formed for Sofia.

"I assume you didn't know this was coming, Lassiter." He made it sound like an allegation.

"What's this about a trust?"

"A father creates a trust for his daughter. What business is that of the lawyers defending the man who killed the poor girl?"

Translation. Suarez doesn't want to talk about the trust.

I asked him to sit down and offered coffee, which he declined. Suarez plopped into a chair and put his cordovan loafers on my conference table. He wore no socks and bird's-egg-blue slacks. He patted his sport coat just above his heart and didn't find what he was looking for, which I assumed was a cigar.

"Tell me about the trust," I said.

It took about ten minutes of bobbing and weaving, but I got the story out of him. He had created a spendthrift trust for Sofia when she was still a teenager. At twenty-one, she got a small portion, another at twenty-five. At thirty, she would get everything. And her thirtieth birthday, it turns out, was this month.

"How much money is in the trust?" I asked.

"That's where it gets muddy."

I was intrigued by *muddy*. Like plumbers, lawyers make our living wading hip-deep in other people's filthy water.

"The trust documents allow me to put money in and withdraw it at my discretion, as long as I have Sofia's written consent," he said. "In reality, while some of the money is Sofia's, or will be when she turns thirty, a majority is mine. That's not what's shown on the books, of course."

"What kind of a trust is that?"

"Cayman Islands. That's where the assets are held. Cayman laws apply."

"How much are we talking about?"

"Sofia's portion is worth roughly six million. But on the books, the Cayman bank would show assets of roughly forty million. The difference is my money."

It took me only a second to figure out the scam. "Thirty-four million bucks you've hidden from the IRS. Dirty money that you launder through the trust. Now you want to quietly get it out before it goes through Sofia's estate and the tax man wants most of it."

"What's that got to do with Calvert's trial? Why should I have to show the trust documents in open court?"

Through the sealed windows, I could hear a police siren. We were, after all, a stone's throw from the jail and some dicey neighborhoods.

"What happens if Sofia dies before her thirtieth birthday?" I asked.

"The trust assets would go to her children, if she had any . . ."

"Which she doesn't."

"In that case, everything reverts to me."

"That's what I thought. Did you ask Sofia's permission to remove your money from the trust before her birthday?"

He didn't answer, which was answer enough. He'd asked; she'd said no.

Finally, he said, "She wouldn't talk to me about it, so I had Wetherall lean on her. That was a mistake. Scared her. Clarified things for her, she said. That's the word she used the last time we spoke. Wetherall came on too strong. Told her if she showed up at that bank in the Caymans, she'd better look both ways down the street because he'd be there. Sofia

213

accused me of threatening her life, said I'd stop at nothing to get the money back. But that's not true, Lassiter! Jesus, she's my daughter. But do you see the dilemma? She's ripping me off."

"When did your relationship with your daughter go south?" I asked.

"When do you think? When she married that bastard! All of a sudden, I was a polluter. A robber baron. An abuser of migrant workers. Jesus, Lassiter. We'd been close, and he turned her against me."

"If we looked at Sofia's phone records, how many times would we find she called you in the last few years?"

"Practically none."

"How many holidays have you shared?"

"Same answer."

"Making it easy to prove the two of you are estranged."

"What's all that have to do with the trial?"

I knew the answer would outrage him. Sometimes, the trick to keep people from yelling is to speak softly yourself.

"You're a straw man," I whispered.

"Meaning what?"

"Something I taught Solomon and Lord. When you're defending a homicide case, look for a straw man. Someone else with a motive to kill the victim."

"What! Kill my daughter? Are you insane?"

"Here's what they can prove. You cheat on your taxes. You have no relationship with your daughter, and she refused to give you the money you skimmed from your business. If she's dead, you get all that money and hers, too. The defense will contend that you have a motive to kill your estranged daughter, and that raises a reasonable doubt that Calvert killed her."

"Bastards! Sons of bitches! Motherfuckers! You can't let them do that to me."

"Actually, Mr. Suarez, I can't stop them."

-44-

The Third Plane

After Suarez stormed out of the conference room promising to call Ray Pincher at home and nail my hide to the barn door, I got back to work. I shuffled my witness files, trying to arrange my order of proof. Detective Barrios would be an early witness, perhaps right after the paramedics who responded to the 9-1-1 call the first time Calvert choked Sofia into unconsciousness.

Barrios would relate Calvert's story of how he spent the day on Miami Beach, looking for Sofia. Then, boom, Corky from the Titty Trap and his video recordings would prove Calvert was a liar. Liar does not necessarily equal murderer, but it's the first building block on the path toward conviction.

I needed to plant in the jurors' minds the idea that Calvert was getting a lap dance while his wife's limbs were going into rigor mortis in the trunk of the Ferrari. But Sofia's body would only be there if he was going to dispose of it somewhere.

Where? Where did Calvert go after spending thirty-one minutes at the strip club?

That's what the jurors would want to know. And that's what I didn't have.

In the old days, I would have spread a road map of South Florida across the table. Now I brought Google Maps onto the computer monitor. I zoomed in to Pompano Beach so that the Florida Turnpike was on the western border of my screen and I-95 on the east. It's a distance of only about two miles. The Titty Trap was near the western boundary, just off the turnpike exchange. What was near there? A mobile home park, a truck stop, a bunch of fast-food restaurants on Hammondville Road. Nothing promising. I zoomed in closer to check out the north-south thoroughfares, Powerline Road and Andrews Avenue. Still, nothing of interest.

I widened the view on my screen. East of I-95, I spotted a gray space with no apparent buildings and three intersecting streets. *No, wait. Those aren't streets. Runways.*

Pompano Beach Airpark.

I Googled the place. A tiny, nondescript general aviation airport. Three runways, all under five thousand feet in length. An aircraft control tower operated under contract with the FAA. Meaning there would be records of takeoffs and landings. If Calvert had stuffed the dead body of his petite wife into the luggage, he could easily have dumped her in the ocean.

Okay, it was just a hunch, but I've made my living on hunches. I grabbed my cell phone and dialed a number.

"Jake, I was just gonna call you," Detective Barrios said, answering the phone.

"I have some potentially good news, George."

"Me, too. But you first."

"There are two acrobatic planes registered in Calvert's name, right?"

"Aerobatic planes, to use the correct term. A Marchetti SF.260 trainer and a cute little biplane, an Eagle Talon 1. Both at Tamiami Airport. And neither flown the last six months."

"Solomon told me Calvert flies almost every weekend."

"Not those planes he doesn't."

"Right. But what else do we know he does on weekends?"

"Visits the Titty Trap."

"Exactly. And guess what? There's a general aviation airport five miles away. Pompano Beach Airpark."

"Like I said, Jake, his two planes are down south at Tamiami Airport."

"Yeah, the ones he owns. If he's leasing a plane, would your records search have turned it up?"

"Long-term lease, yes. He doesn't have one."

"Maybe he rents each time he flies out of Pompano. Or borrows a friend's plane. There's gotta be a third plane, George, and it's at Pompano Beach Airpark. When can you go up there and flash your badge around?"

"Tomorrow. I'm at Hartsfield right now, buying a second ticket to Miami."

"Why? Did you put on weight?"

"You can thank me later, smart-ass."

I waited a moment, then heard a woman's voice. "Hello, Mr. Lassiter. This is Ann Cavendish. I'm going to help you put that maniac Clark Calvert behind bars."

-45-

The Sword of Justice

With the trial looming, it was all coming together. That happens sometimes. Other times you ride into battle on a spavined steed, waving a rusty sword. That's what I'd expected in the case against Clark Calvert. But the sword in my scabbard seemed to have magically turned into King Arthur's Excalibur. Powerful and magical, call it the Sword of Justice, if you don't mind a little hyperbole.

The morning after returning from Atlanta, Detective Barrios headed to Pompano Beach Airpark. By 11:00 a.m. he'd called with the news I'd been hoping for. Clark Calvert was well known to the guys in the hangars, the maintenance shops, and the tower. He frequently flew a Bellanca Citabria, a little single-engine, two-seat aircraft. The plane was owned by a friend, a Boston physician with a winter home in Palm Beach. The friend allowed Calvert to take out the plane as often as he pleased, and, yes, the guys frequently saw him on weekends, sometimes with his wife, sometimes alone. When they were together, the Calverts flew to Bimini or Nassau for weekends or day trips. Other times, Calvert would just go out for a few hours by himself.

"On June 3," Barrios said, "at two sixteen p.m., fifty-two minutes after he left the Titty Trap, Calvert took off for points unknown. He didn't file a flight plan."

"I don't suppose there's video of him getting into the cockpit, carrying an oversize duffel," I said.

"Ha. You don't ask for much. No security cameras where the Citabria was parked. He touched down again at Pompano at five forty-seven p.m."

"Three and a half hours. Divide it in two for the outbound and the return. He could have covered a lot of ground, or water, before dumping the body."

"I figure he chose the Gulf Stream," Barrios said. "If the cargo didn't sink, the bones might wash up on a beach in Greenland."

"You peek into the cockpit?"

"Nothing in plain view to report. Would love to have the techs up here tomorrow with their tweezers and flashlights and luminol."

"The search-warrant application will be awaiting your signature when you get your butt back here."

"Ann Cavendish there?"

"I told her to get some sun at the hotel pool and a good lunch, courtesy of the state of Florida, and I'd see her this afternoon with you."

"You're making me feel indispensable, Lassiter."

"It's you and me, buddy. We took this stinking pile of roadkill and turned it into a murder case. No body. No forensics. Squeaky-clean defendant with no priors. Shaky motive. Purely circumstantial case with lousy circumstances. And look where we are."

"Yeah?"

"If Ann Cavendish pans out, we're gonna win, George!"

-46-

Dream Witness

Ann Cavendish strolled into my office after lunch, along with Detective Barrios. While I asked questions, he would evaluate her answers and compare them to what she'd told him the day before. It's useful to tag-team witnesses.

She was a striking thirty-six-year-old with a torrent of dark hair falling over her shoulders in waves. I had thought she was the nurse from Mass General, the woman who complained to the hospital that Calvert had choked her into unconsciousness during otherwise consensual sex. But that was someone else, meaning there was yet another woman out there. At least one, possibly more—an enticing fact.

Before I could focus on that, I needed to turn my attention, full bore, to Ann Cavendish, who had been a surgical-instrument sales rep in Boston when Calvert practiced medicine there a dozen years ago.

As I listened to her heartfelt tale, well told, I began to think I had the dream witness.

"I'm a midwestern girl," she began. "Iowa."

She told me she'd been a local beauty queen runner-up and quickly realized that would get her nowhere. She had a two-year degree from a community college but couldn't get a decent-paying job. Moved to

Chicago and did some catalog modeling, then latched on to a position as a sales-rep trainee for a manufacturer of surgical instruments. Those companies liked hot young women, going back to the days when the vast majority of surgeons were men. She'd graduated to full-fledged sales rep in the company's Boston headquarters just before she met Calvert.

She called on him at his medical office, pitching hip-replacement gear. He asked her out. First date, no problem. He was a gentleman. Charming, erudite, thoughtful. Interested in her. Lots of questions about her background. Second date, no problems, either. Dinner, a long walk, and a pleasant demur to his suggestion she come up to his penthouse condo and enjoy the view. She had figured the view he meant was his bedroom ceiling, and she still had some of her midwestern innocence.

Third date, she agreed to go to his place for a drink. Nothing more. Okay, some kiss-kiss, but no bang-bang. She remembered being on the sofa as they kissed, fully clothed. He clasped a strong hand around her neck. It barely hurt. She didn't choke. She wasn't gasping for breath. He must have been applying pressure to her carotid artery, she later figured. She awoke in his bed. He was atop her and inside her. She tried pushing him off, but he continued thrusting until he ejaculated.

Furious and humiliated, she gathered her clothing, dressed, and fled. He called her several times, but she refused to answer. She would spot his car outside her apartment, a chilling sight. She had no close friends in Boston. No support group. She didn't report Calvert to the police. Didn't tell anyone. Alone and afraid and ashamed, her life crumbled. She would burst into tears during a sales call. Within weeks, she was fired.

She fell into a deep depression but never sought therapy. She decided to start over, prompting the move to Atlanta. First thing she did was change her name. The lawful way, with a petition to the local court. She knew it sounded a bit paranoid, but she was afraid of Calvert locating her. She rebuilt her life, and currently worked as a freelance sales rep, handling surgical instruments.

"I admire your courage," I told her.

"It's not easy. I never wanted to hear Clark Calvert's name again. But the way I was raised, we help our neighbors. If Calvert goes free, he'll just prey on another woman, and another one after that. I couldn't live with myself if I didn't step up."

I called a taxi for Ann and sent her back to the hotel with instructions to charge a mammoth steak-and-martini dinner to my temporary employer. Then I did my postmortem with Detective Barrios.

"She's credible, Jake," the homicide detective said. "Told the same story to me yesterday, but not word for word. No sign of rehearsal or coaching."

"I wish she'd reported the rape to the police. Or to a friend or a therapist. Anyone."

"You play the cards you're dealt, partner."

"How much of her story could you confirm?"

"The name change, for starters. I've copied the courthouse file. In Boston, she was Jane Smith. Really. She said that Ann Cavendish sounded more exotic, and her name was always so plain. Her apartment is filled with those charts you see in doctors' offices. Spinal column, that sort of thing. Plus, several briefcases that look like your trial bags, but inside are surgical tools. Forceps, retractors, drill bits, bone clamps, knee and hip joints."

Something was bothering me, but what?

Barrios was an intuitive detective, as the best ones are. He studied me a moment. "What's eating you, Jake?"

"She changed her name so Calvert couldn't find her."

"Yeah?"

"If Calvert came clean with Solomon and Lord, he would have said, 'There's a woman out there somewhere who might say nasty things about me. Her name's Jane Smith. But the note Solomon left outside my house said, 'Ann Cavendish.'"

"What do you figure, Jake?"

"Only two possibilities. Either Calvert tracked her down under her new name, which is pretty creepy. Or it wasn't Solomon who gave me the name."

-47-

Pedantic Semantics

I filed my "Amended Witness List," adding Ann Cavendish, and had a messenger hand-deliver a copy to Solomon and Lord at their home at precisely 7:00 p.m.

I waited for the inevitable call.

Which came at 7:06 p.m.

I was sitting on my back porch in a weathered Adirondack chair, listening to the peacocks screech and the crickets chirp and the Metrorail train toot its horn. Did I mention that I was sipping Jack Daniel's?

"What's this bullshit, Jake?" Solomon yelled into the phone.

"To what particular bullshit do you refer?" I inquired politely.

"Too late to add a witness, buddy."

Are you putting on an act, buddy?

That's what I couldn't figure out. If Solomon was the one who gave me Ann Cavendish's name, then he couldn't be surprised that I added her to the witness list. He would expect her to testify, would want her to testify, would want Calvert to be convicted. At the same time, he had to put up a front for Victoria, had to profess shock at this turn of developments.

"Steve, old chum, are you perchance talking about Ann Cavendish of Atlanta, Georgia? The Peachtree State."

"Who is she, Jake?" Victoria's voice. They were on a speaker.

"I expect you'll learn when you take her depo. But in the spirit of collegiality, let's just say she's another woman whose neck found itself in your client's unyielding grip. In fact, he raped her."

"Bull feathers! It never happened."

"Did you just say 'bull feathers'?"

"Besides, it's too late to add a witness. I'll move to strike her from your list."

In the background, I heard Solomon say, "*We'll* move to strike her."

"Consider this newly discovered evidence," I said, "permitting her addition to the cast of the show. I'll produce her for depo tomorrow if you'd like. There's no prejudice to the defense."

I heard whispering at the other end of the line. Then Victoria's voice. "We just spoke to our client. He's never heard of Ann Cavendish."

Now it was my turn to whisper. To myself.

Yet another ethical dilemma. If Calvert is telling Solomon and Lord the truth, it's because he only knew the woman as Jane Smith of Boston. I could tell my friends this, but frankly, I'm under no legal obligation to spill my guts. At the same time, how could Solomon be the source if Calvert didn't know the woman as Ann Cavendish?

"Then Calvert has nothing to worry about," I said. "Where do you want to depose her, your place or mine?"

"That won't be necessary, Jake," Victoria said.

Hmm. Not like her. Ms. Preparation. She never liked to wing it in court.

"Victoria, you're puzzling me."

"Good."

"Either you're supremely confident—"

"Aren't you the one who taught me never to show fear to the opposition?"

"Hey, Vic! That was me!" Solomon protesting in his whiny voice.

"Or you have something up your sleeve," I continued.

"We'll file a motion to strike your new witness. Both on grounds of timeliness and admissibility. Even if true, she's talking about an unrelated event that's not relevant to whether Clark killed Sofia."

"Prior bad acts. Pattern evidence. Such a murky area of the law, don't you think?"

"Not in this case."

"The court has wide discretion," I said. "In Bill Cosby's first trial in Pennsylvania, the judge only allowed one of the other alleged victims to testify. I thought that was a little stingy, don't you?"

"You won't even get one."

I cleared my throat and spoke in stentorian tones. "Florida Statute Section ninety-point-four-zero-four, subsection two. Other crimes, wrongs, and acts."

"Since when do you read the law books?" Solomon challenged me.

"Today, five o'clock."

"I know the statute by heart," Victoria said.

"Of course you do, dear."

"Don't call my fiancée 'dear,'" Solomon ordered.

"You're right, pal. I apologize. That was a semisexist statement, only spoken under the influence of my second whiskey. Or perhaps my third."

"You've been drinking too much, Jake."

"Bull feathers! I'm as healthy as the next guy, as long as the next guy is sitting on a bar stool."

Victoria said, "The statute is clear. The state can't introduce evidence of other wrongful acts to demonstrate bad character or a propensity to commit a similar act."

"Oh, fussy, fussy, fussy, Victoria."

"What!"

"Your semantics are so pedantic."

PAUL LEVINE

"I'm simply telling you the clear meaning of the statute."

"You've just gone from Miss Congeniality to Miss Technicality."

Solomon said, "He's just pulling your chain, Vic."

"I know that, but, Jake, must you be so insufferable?"

"It's called lawyering, sweet cheeks."

"What!" Solomon exploded. "What did you just call my fiancée?"

"You've gone too far, Jake," Victoria said. "Really. Shame on you."

What had I done? The words just came out. No premeditation. No control. Melissa had told me that loss of inhibition was a symptom of traumatic brain injury.

"I'm sorry, Victoria," I said. "Blame my frontal lobes. Or maybe the NFL for not outlawing spearing until my playing days were done. To tell you the truth, I haven't been myself lately."

"That concerns me, Jake."

"Me, too," Solomon chimed in.

"No sympathy, please. That would just make it worse. But honestly, it's all pretty confusing. I just don't know what's happening to me."

-48-

Natural-Born Persecutor

I awoke with a headache that might be called a migraine, unless there's another name for the feeling of two steak knives jammed into your temples. I couldn't eat my breakfast of bacon, scrambled eggs, and toast because chewing exacerbated the pain. Melissa, who had spent the night, played helpful nurse and made a smoothie of fresh papaya, mango, strawberries, and yogurt. I had breakfast through a straw.

Melissa also gave me an unmarked bottle of pills. "Only take these in dire circumstances," she whispered, as if the DEA might be listening.

I massaged my forehead with my knuckles. "These days, all my circumstances are pretty damn dire."

"Really, Jake, the pills are the last resort. Only take them if you'd rather jump off a bridge than take another breath. And only one a day. Don't double up, no matter how bad the pain. Let me know at once if you have side effects."

"Such as?"

"The pills will lower your blood pressure. Some people become dizzy and faint. So never drive after taking the medication. And don't go to court. You could end up speaking gibberish."

"Who will notice the difference?" I asked.

"I don't want you held in contempt when you tell a judge he has a face like an orangutan's anus."

"Got a couple like that. But contempt doesn't scare me. A lawyer who's afraid of jail is like a surgeon who's afraid of blood."

"Just promise to be careful."

"Okay. What the hell are these pills, anyway?"

"I'm not at liberty to say. They're not approved, but they've been found to be effective for migraines and might have some ability to halt the advance of tau proteins."

Oh, brother. Another experiment with yours truly, the big, fat guinea pig.

I opened the bottle of unmarked pills, tapped one into the palm of my hand.

"Wait," she said. "I want to take your blood pressure for a baseline today."

"I know what it was around midnight. A zillion over a quintillion. These pills aren't going to interfere with . . . you know . . . are they?"

"I wouldn't worry about blood going that direction," she advised with a smile.

As she took my blood pressure, I examined the pill. It was about three times as large as an aspirin. No markings. I'm not sure what I was looking for. A skull and crossbones, maybe. I washed it down with the remains of the smoothie.

Sure enough, within twenty minutes, my headache had subsided from mortal stab wounds to a dull ache that could have been caused by a football helmet one size too small.

Melissa left for the hospital, and I aimed the old Caddy toward the Justice Building complex and my temporary digs in the State Attorney's office. I arrived in the war room at 8:30 a.m. In twenty-four hours, we would pick a jury. The *State vs. Calvert* file was spread out on the scarred and sweat-stained conference table. The only sound was an old-fashioned coffee percolator that was pure Maxwell House.

Detective George Barrios entered, carrying a cup of a Starbucks Frappuccino with whipped cream on top. For a guy approaching retirement, he was way more au courant than I was.

"Crime scene techs turned up zilch inside the cockpit and the storage space," Barrios said.

"Not surprising," I said. "If Calvert had strangled Sofia and smushed her body into some extrasize duffel, there likely wouldn't be any blood or bodily fluids. Just like at the house."

"Hair, Jake. Sofia frequently flew with him in the Citabria. I would have expected a couple strands of her hair plus prints. No latents in the cockpit, not even Calvert's. The storage-space carpeting was freshly vacuumed and practically antiseptic. Not a grain of sand, a leaf, a blade of grass. No scuff marks from luggage on the bulkhead. Showroom new."

"Can you get a tech to testify that the scene looks tampered with?"

He took a sip of his frothy drink. "Sure, I can. Then the defense moves to strike because it's total speculation."

"But the jury will have heard it. All I care about."

Barrios laughed. "You got the hang of this side of the courtroom real quick."

"Maybe I'm a natural-born per-se-cutor."

"You feeling okay, Jake?"

"Tip-top. Why you asking?"

"'Cause you're swaying a little bit."

"What?" I honestly didn't know.

"Not a lot. Sort of like Stevie Wonder singing 'Signed, Sealed, Delivered.'"

Somehow I made it through the day and worked through most of the night with last-minute preparation. You're never fully prepared for trial. There is always one more thing that can be done. Trial dates arrive with amazing speed. One moment you're buried in files, gathering evidence, and you think you can never be ready, and the next moment, it's showtime.

-49-

A Trout in the Tub

G ood morning, ladies and gentlemen. My name is Jake Lassiter. I'm a specially appointed assistant state attorney."

Making myself sound very special, indeed.

"As such, I represent the people of the great state of Florida, more particularly the people of Miami-Dade County. Your friends, your neighbors, even yourselves."

Judge Erwin Gridley whistled. Really. He put his lips together and blew. Pretty darn close to the sound of an official's whistle in a football game. Which made sense, because Judge Gridley was a part-time college football referee. He was in his early sixties, with wispy white hair on a mostly bald head. Looking sternly at me, he formed the letter *T* with both hands. *Time-out.* Meaning get your ass up here for a sidebar.

I nodded to the prospective panel and sidestepped to the end of the bench away from the jury box. Steve Solomon and Victoria Lord slipped away from the defense table to join me.

Judge Gridley stared at me over the top of his rimless trifocals. He never wore the glasses when officiating games, which might explain how he once called encroachment on the Florida State mascot, which happens to be a horse.

"It isn't often I flag a lawyer when he introduces himself to the jury in voir dire." Judge Gridley gave me an admonishing look. "But, Jake, did I just hear you say you represented the jurors?"

"I believe I may have inadvertently implied that in some fashion," I semi-admitted.

"What in the name of Amos Alonzo Stagg are you doing?"

"No idea, Your Honor. I've never been on this side of the courtroom. I guess I misspoke."

"Illegal procedure, Jake. Now settle down."

It's true I was a little nervous. Jumpy. If you watch football players on the sideline just before kickoff, you'll see them hopping up and down in place. That's not part of the pregame warm-ups. They've already stretched and jogged and run mythical plays. Now their adrenaline is flowing, and they're blowing off steam like a kettle on the stove. I always needed that first physical contact on the kickoff to settle my nerves. Same thing in the courtroom, except I couldn't hit juror number one with a forearm smash to the Adam's apple.

"Thank you, Your Honor," I said, as if he'd just complimented my trial skills or the cut of my off-the-rack suit. Courtroom protocol. A judge could call you an illiterate chimpanzee with bad breath, and you bow slightly and say, "Thank You, Your Honor."

"Word downtown is you got your brain rattled one too many times," the judge whispered.

"Baseless rumors, Your Honor."

Judge Gridley turned to Solomon and Lord. "You two got anything to add?"

Both shook their heads and said, in unison, "No, Your Honor."

"Fine. Git on back to your tables, and let's pick us a jury."

Some lawyers think you win or lose cases in jury selection. I'm not sure I agree, but voir dire is surely crucial. To convict Clark Calvert, I needed jurors who didn't expect perfection in the state's case.

"Do you understand that a real murder trial isn't like a TV show?" I asked the panel, which murmured its acquiescence.

"Real cases don't always have fingerprints and DNA. Real cases usually don't have eyewitnesses or a confession. Not every murder trial has a body. Do you understand it's still possible to convict a defendant under all those circumstances?"

I got a few nods of the head and a few blank stares.

"Have you all heard the term *circumstantial evidence?*"

Everybody had. I knew better than to ask if the jurors could define the term. They couldn't. So I gave my own example.

"Suppose Mary walks into the bathroom and finds a trout swimming in the bathtub. Does she have a circumstantial case that her husband, Joe, put it there?"

The jurors all shook their heads no.

"That's right. It's a very weak case, at best. But what if I told you that Mary and Joe live out in the country, thirty miles from the nearest neighbor? They have no children. No houseguests. No visitors for months. Joe's an avid fisherman who just this morning said he'd love fresh fish for dinner. A stream loaded with trout flows through their property. When Mary comes home, she sees Joe's waders on the front porch, still wet. And there in the bathtub is that live trout. Now does Mary have a solid case that Joe went fishing and caught that fish?"

A bunch of smiles and nods.

"I agree. Mary has every right to yell, 'Darn it, Joe! You promised to fix the garage door today, not go fishing.'"

More smiles and a few knowing laughs. Yes, they understood the concept of a strong circumstantial case.

I kept at it for a while, winnowing out people I figured wouldn't be open to the state's case. In other words, people I would have wanted if I were defending the case. After about ninety minutes, I thanked all the potential jurors for doing their patriotic duty by driving to the civic center through rush-hour traffic, making them sound as heroic as Navy SEALs attacking Osama bin Laden's compound.

When I was finished, Victoria Lord stood and introduced herself. After a few preliminaries, she said, "There's a problem with circumstantial cases. Add one more fact, one more circumstance, and the case collapses like a house of cards."

Where was she going with this? A slight smile at the corners of her mouth told me I wouldn't like the destination.

"Suppose Mr. Lassiter left out this fact. Joe's best friend lives on the other side of the trout stream. That day, Joe put on his waders, forded the stream, and visited his neighbor, who gave him a fresh trout from his catch. Joe splashes back home, puts the trout in the bathtub, and fixes the garage door. Mary's circumstantial case that Joe went fishing is as leaky as a trout net."

Touché.

Victoria glanced at me, her eyes twinkling with self-satisfied delight. Next to her, Calvert peeled his thin lips back to reveal his mortician's smile.

I gave Victoria an appreciative nod. *Nice work.* I admire sculptors who carve statues from chunks of stone, composers who translate the music in their heads to notes on the page, and lawyers who can turn tin into gold.

At the defense table, Solomon stared at me with a look I couldn't decipher. Maybe it was, *"Do something!"* But that would mean he really wanted to tank the case, wanted Calvert to be convicted. And now I wasn't sure about that. Was he really the one who'd given me Ann Cavendish's name? But if he didn't, who did?

Solomon's facial expression could just as easily have meant, *"How about that, Jake?"* Meaning his fiancée was a step quicker and would dance circles around me in the courtroom.

As things now stood, I couldn't disagree.

-50-
Ready, Willing, and Able

At eight the next morning, Victoria Lord stunned me with a trick play. The three of us—Solomon, Lord, and little old me—were huddled in Judge Gridley's chambers, sipping coffee from paper cups and taking care of housekeeping before opening statements. The chambers were a minimuseum to Gridley's alma mater, the University of Florida. The carpet was orange and blue. A plaque on the wall was testament to the fact that Erwin Gridley was a "Bull Gator Emeritus." On his desk was a stuffed alligator head, mouth open, jagged teeth exposed, like a ravenous lawyer.

"The defense has filed three motions in limine," Judge Gridley said. "First one seeks to preclude Dr. Harold Freudenstein from testifying to certain matters on grounds of doctor-patient privilege."

"We withdraw that motion, Your Honor," Victoria said.

I nearly spilled my coffee.

"Really?" The judge peered at Victoria above the eyeglasses perched on his nose, his bushy eyebrows curling upward. "Next is the defense motion to limit inquiries from a Mr. William Burnside as to hearsay statements made by the alleged victim concerning her fear of the defendant."

"Withdrawn," Victoria said. "Let Mr. Burnside have his say."

I took a gulp of my coffee rather than spill it on the snarling alligator woven into the carpeting. It was my fourth cup since five o'clock, when I'd awoken from a restless sleep. A headache startled me awake, and I took one of those no-name experimental pills. The pain subsided, but I was left feeling groggy and slow, as if walking through a vat of pudding.

Now I was trying to assess Victoria's strategy and getting nowhere. The look on her face was inscrutable. I glanced at Solomon, who hadn't spoken a word. He was taking notes, or maybe completing a crossword puzzle.

"Very well, Ms. Lord," Judge Gridley said. "I was rather looking forward to Mr. Lassiter's argument that the statements are admissible under the hearsay exception in spousal-abuse cases. Just wondering if a homicide case fits that category."

"If murder isn't abuse, I don't know what is," I said.

"We'll save that for another day. Ms. Lord, you've also moved to bar the testimony of a Ms. Ann Cavendish. Mr. Lassiter, do you intend to elicit testimony from this witness as to an unrelated assault by the defendant?"

"I do, Your Honor. A prior bad act is admissible under an exception to—"

"Slippery slope, Jake. Slipperier than Lambeau Field in January."

"We withdraw that motion, also," Victoria said. "Let Mr. Lassiter take his best shot with all the witnesses he can muster."

"Okeydokey." The judge took off his eyeglasses and chewed on the stem. "Ms. Lord, I'm not sure what razzle-dazzle you have cooked up. The fumblerooski or maybe a double reverse with a dipsy-doodle. But it seems like you're giving old Jake the ball at your own ten-yard line."

"We have an excellent goal-line defense, Your Honor," Victoria said.

While I tried to decipher that, the judge addressed both of us. "Seems to me you folks get along so well I don't have to remind you of the rules once we get into the courtroom. But they're simple enough. No arguing my calls. No hitting after the whistle. And no playing to the crowd, by which I mean the jury. Play hard but play clean. So, if the pregame rituals are over, shall we trot onto the field and kick off?"

"State's ready, Your Honor." That's what I said, but was it the truth? Just what was up Victoria's sleeve? The dreaded derringer?

"Defense is ready, willing, and able," Victoria said. "Locked and loaded, ready to rock and roll." She shot me a look along with a fetching smile. Those were my words, my usual patter at the start of a trial. I'd forgotten to use the line, so Victoria unabashedly stole it.

Take that, Jake, she seemed to be saying. Leaving me wondering if I'd ever be ready, willing, and able again.

-51-

Salacious Evil

Nearly sixty years ago, Fidel Castro gave a speech at the United Nations that lasted four hours and twenty-nine minutes. Just imagine the fun of listening to the United States being bashed for 269 minutes for its imperialism, colonialism, and general rude manners. It was awful then and would be unthinkable now.

People nowadays have attention spans the approximate length of a tweet. Knowing this, I have tailored my opening statements and closing arguments accordingly.

Start fast. Score points. Sit down.

The boring, outdated gasbag style would be to take your sweet time warming up, then start with the disclaimer, "Now, what I'm about to say is not evidence . . ."

Though true, why say it? Might as well begin, "What I'm about to say is not important. You may begin your snooze now."

I want the jurors to think every word I say is a thunderbolt from Zeus himself.

Some lawyers resort to this oldie but not goodie: "The opening statement is like the table of contents of a book . . ."

Books are boring! Put on a show, not a book report.

Then, there's that old saw, repeated each time you refer to a witness's expected testimony: "The evidence will show that . . ."

Oh, spare me your technicalities.

I stood, bowed slightly to Judge Gridley, more to stretch my lower back than to show respect, then positioned myself at an angle to the jury box that blocked the defense table from view. If Solomon and Lord wanted to see, let them scoot to the corner rail of the gallery where the television camera whirred away, interfering with their hearing.

At my request, the court clerk had placed a thirty-by-forty-inch head shot of Sofia at one end of the jury box and one of Calvert at the other. I had chosen a color photograph of Sofia in a bright-turquoise peasant blouse. Her smile was so wide, her eyes so bright, she might have been laughing. The overall impression: a pretty young woman full of life. I had found a dour black-and-white shot of Calvert on the Internet. He'd been speaking at some sawbones convention. The lighting made his complexion gray. His impenetrable eyes were even darker than in person. He looked as if he needed a shave, and his mouth was the narrow slash of a switchblade. The overall impression: the funeral director will see you now.

I waggled my neck, always tight in a dress shirt and tie. I didn't say thank you. I didn't say good morning. I believe in getting right to the point and doing it in plain, straightforward language, preferably with one- and two-syllable words.

"This is a simple case," I began. "The husband killed the wife's cat, and then he killed her."

I let that sink in a moment. "On June 3, 2017, in their home on Miami Beach, Clark Gordon Calvert strangled his wife, Sofia. He placed her dead body in the trunk of his Ferrari and drove to a strip club in Pompano Beach. He paid for and received one lap dance, and after ejaculating into his pants, returned to his car and drove four miles to a small airport. He placed Sofia's body in the cockpit of a single-engine aircraft and took off for parts unknown . . . but not mission unknown.

He dumped her lifeless body, most likely in an oversize duffel, somewhere in the Atlantic Ocean. He then returned to the airport and drove home to Miami Beach. The next day, with the body disposed of, Clark Gordon Calvert called the police to report his wife missing."

I pivoted at an angle to the jury box, opening the view to the defense table. As I expected and hoped for, neither Solomon nor Lord was sitting there. They had taken up positions where they could watch me. Calvert was alone, again just as I wanted.

"That is the defendant, Clark Gordon Calvert." I pointed an index finger at him, as if it were a rapier.

Clark Gordon Calvert.

Conveying the image of other three-named fellows. John Wilkes Booth. Lee Harvey Oswald. James Earl Ray. John Wayne Gacy.

"The man you see sitting there is a murderer."

I paused and took measure of the jurors. No one had fallen asleep. Every juror was staring at Calvert. Three seemed to be glaring at him. Calvert kept his chin up and looked at them head-on with his own dark-eyed gaze. I hoped the jurors found his demeanor as chilling as I did.

"Let me tell you about the Calverts' marriage," I continued. "A marriage between a controlling man with a violent temper and an insecure, emotionally unstable woman. A dysfunctional, toxic mix. And let me be clear about something. Sofia Calvert was no saint. But she did not deserve to die a horrible death at the hands of her husband."

I paused and shifted my weight. I had been standing motionless, sturdy as a slab of granite. Some lawyers like to prance back and forth in front of the jury box. It forces the jurors to become spectators at a tennis tournament. I hold their attention with my voice, a throaty baritone, and my size, roughly that of the pillars of the courthouse.

The jurors were waiting now.

Just what did he mean, the victim is no saint?

I would keep them in suspense and hold their attention while they waited for an answer.

"The fatal flaw of this marriage—and I do mean fatal—was the defendant's overwhelming need to control his wife in every aspect of her life. Who could be her friends, what she could eat, whether she could take a job, and what would be expected of her in bed."

Yep, they were still listening.

"The defendant disapproved of Sofia's friends and family, so she stopped seeing them. He forbade her from having ice cream, and when she disobeyed him, he choked her into twilight unconsciousness. He refused to allow her to get a job outside the home. And during sex, he insisted on choking off the carotid artery in her neck on the pretense that she desired it, when in fact, it was for his own sadistic pleasure."

I would come back to the phrase *sadistic pleasure* again in closing arguments. The words echoed with salacious evil.

Now, what had I overlooked?

"Oh, there's one more thing Clark Gordon Calvert sought to control. What pet could Sofia have? To be clear, he didn't prevent her from acquiring a pet. He killed the one she had! Strangled her beloved cat, Escapar."

Several jurors appeared stricken, including one whose Prius had a PETA sticker on the bumper. Yeah, before voir dire, I had Barrios assign a rookie cop to surveil the juror parking lot.

I was suddenly aware that I had lost my place. Working without notes, I couldn't remember where I had planned to go next. Seconds passed. I knew my order of proof. The first 9-1-1 call would kick off the testimony. So that's where I would go now.

"You will hear two 9-1-1 calls made by the defendant. The first came in March, not quite three months before Sofia disappeared. You will hear from paramedics called to the house after the defendant choked Sofia into unconsciousness. He squeezed her neck so severely that the blood stopped flowing to her brain, and she stopped breathing.

She could have died on that occasion. You might ask yourselves: Was that a dress rehearsal?"

"Objection!" Victoria vaulted out of her chair. "Mr. Lassiter is commenting on the evidence."

"Sustained. The state is reminded that this is opening statement. Run the ball up the middle. No double reverses, no hook and ladders."

"Thank you, Your Honor," I said, nodding politely.

"Now, I've been using the term *choked* a little loosely," I said to the jurors. "You'll hear testimony from a physician that what the defendant used was a 'vascular hold,' a grip to cut off the flow of blood from arteries to the brain. Police departments used to do this to restrain unruly suspects . . . until the suspects started dying."

Again, I lost my train of thought. For more than twenty years, I'd done opening statements without a legal pad or notes of any kind. Closing arguments, too. I wanted the jurors to think I believed what I was saying, not just reading from a script. But now I needed cue cards. Where was I?

I looked around the courtroom, as if seeking guidance. I was aware of the clock mounted on the wall above the door at the rear of the gallery. The clock face was fuzzy, the second hand moving way too slowly, as if plowing its way through a snowbank. I blinked once, twice, three times. And the clock came into focus. Conscious thought returned. I took a breath, exhaled, recovered some semblance of a train of thought, and got back to business.

"Despite the troubles, Sofia Calvert did not give up on the marriage. She went to a noted and experienced psychiatrist, Dr. Harold Freudenstein, who formerly was on the staff at Mount Sinai."

Before he was shitcanned and now practices out of a chickee hut while stoned out of his gourd.

"Dr. Freudenstein analyzed both husband and wife."

"Talked a couple of hours" is probably more accurate than "analyzed," but a lawyer shades the truth the way an eclipse shades the sun.

"The doctor concluded that Sofia suffered from borderline personality disorder and lived in constant fear of abandonment. The defendant is both a narcissist and a psycho-sociopath who feels unbound by the laws of society and had a propensity for violence. So those were the diagnoses. Then the doctor made a startling prognosis."

They waited, and I milked the moment. But the moment stretched on. I had lost my way yet again.

What the hell is going on?

One explanation: I wasn't prepared to discuss Dr. Freudenstein. I never would have mentioned him in opening if Victoria hadn't surprisingly waived her objections to his testimony. Oldest rule in the book: never promise what you can't deliver. Another explanation: my brain was not operating on all cylinders.

"Mr. Lassiter," Judge Gridley said, "would you kindly continue?"

"Of course, Your Honor."

But my mind was as blank as a slate-gray sky.

"Mr. Lassiter, I believe you were about to tell the jury the psychiatrist's prognosis," the judge prodded me. "'Startling prognosis,' you mentioned."

"Yes, of course, Your Honor."

I had notes back at the prosecution table, but fumbling through them would make me look ill prepared, a bumbler. Just what the hell was I going to do?

-52-

Two Prophecies Fulfilled

After thirty excruciating seconds that seemed like hours, I had no choice but to walk back to the prosecution table. I did so purposefully, as if I'd always intended to pick up a file. I felt a presence beside me and turned. Victoria Lord leaned close to me.

"Are you all right, Jake?" she whispered.

"What are you doing? Sit down."

"You just seem confused."

"Trial tactic."

"Do you want a recess?"

"Stop hovering!"

She placed a hand on my arm, and I swung around to meet her gaze. "Please take care of yourself, Jake. It's just another case."

"Is it? For you, I mean."

With that, Victoria's jaw went slack. She returned to the defense table, where Solomon sat, looking as confused as I felt.

What just happened? Was Victoria messing with me? No, her eyes showed real concern. And why did I say that to her? I don't feel in full control.

"Mr. Lassiter," the judge said, "are you ready to continue?"

I scanned my table. On top of a stack of documents was Dr. Freudenstein's letter. *Ah, that will do.*

"You bet, Your Honor," I said.

I picked up the letter and turned back to the jury. In a tone that conveyed both solemnity and sadness, I said, "Dr. Freudenstein's prognosis was chilling. He concluded that Clark Gordon Calvert was likely to kill Sofia. Kill her!"

The jurors were back in the game. Wide-eyed, waiting for more. And I seemed to have a grip on myself, for the moment at least.

"The doctor did not just say this idly. He signed his name to it! Yes, he put his reputation on the line, perhaps all of psychiatry on the line. You will see the entire letter when he testifies, but for now, I'll give you a preview." I read aloud.

"Mrs. Calvert, it is my considered medical opinion that you are in danger of great bodily harm or death if you continue to reside with your husband. I urge you to immediately separate and refrain from all personal contact.

"Dr. Calvert, it is my further medical opinion that you constitute a clear and present danger to your wife's safety and indeed her life."

I watched the jurors exchange *Holy shit* glances. If Freudenstein didn't come off like some hippie-pothead-guru on the stand, maybe this strategy would work.

"So very sad to say, the learned Dr. Freudenstein was correct. His prognosis was prophetic."

I let the jurors feel their own sadness a moment, then continued, "Let me take you now to the first week of June of this year. Much was happening in the Calvert household. Tired of her husband's controlling nature and abusive conduct, Sofia had decided to leave him. She told this to a man named Billy Burnside, one of the state's witnesses. Billy was Sofia's tennis instructor, but he was more, too. He was her friend, her confidante, and, yes, as someone who would listen and let her be herself, Billy became her lover."

None of the jurors scowled or appeared ready to mark Sofia with a giant red *A*. I had prepared them by saying she was no saint, but now who could blame her for seeking solace outside the marital bed?

I glanced toward the bench. Judge Gridley appeared to be listening. Usually he reads the sports section of the *Miami Herald* during the parts of trial where his constant attention isn't a necessity.

"Sofia told Billy a few days before she disappeared that she would tell her husband that weekend the marriage was over. She had already consulted with a divorce lawyer. Now Billy urged her to leave, not to remain in harm's way. But tragically she stayed, and we now know what happened."

At least that's my theory. We don't really "know" anything.

A couple of jurors shook their heads sadly, and I decided to play up the moment. "Mr. Burnside will testify to something else Sofia told him, and it's a crucial piece of evidence."

At the word *crucial*, three jurors straightened in their seats. I had them. I could feel it. If I were a preacher asking for millions to build a cathedral, they'd be reaching for their checkbooks.

"Sofia said, 'Billy, if I ever disappear, don't bother looking for me. Clark will have dumped my body in the Glades, and I'll already be gator shit.' Unfortunately, Sofia did not follow Billy's advice or her psychiatrist's advice. Like so many abused women, she stayed in that lion's den a day too long. She told her husband she was leaving him. And how did he react, this controlling man with a narcissistic personality, this man with an inflated sense of his own importance, this man with a habit of choking his wife into unconsciousness?"

The jurors waited. Some seemed to be holding their breaths.

"He killed her!"

At least two jurors gasped. I don't like to repeat myself, but sometimes it's useful to underline the high points.

"What, then, have we heard?" I asked the jurors. "A noted psychiatrist predicted the defendant would harm his wife, perhaps kill her. And she predicted that if he did so, her body would never be found.

245

And now, ladies and gentlemen, just look where we are. Two prophecies fulfilled."

I paused again. When you're drinking fine liquor, you don't guzzle it. When you make a point in opening or closing, give the jury a few seconds to digest it.

"As I told you in voir dire, this is a circumstantial case. Now let me tell you, before Ms. Lord and Mr. Solomon do, what we don't have. We don't have a body or body parts. We don't have blood or fingerprints. We don't have bloody clothes or a murder weapon or an autopsy. But we don't need any of those things. We need only to prove that Sofia is dead, and she is dead because the defendant killed her. And that is precisely what we will prove. That Sofia told her husband she was leaving him, that he decided to wipe her off the face of the earth, and that he did so. We shall prove the charge beyond and to the exclusion of every reasonable doubt."

I sneaked a peek into the gallery. At least a dozen journalists. Newspapers, television, Internet outlets. Pepe Suarez and his thug, J. T. Wetherall, sat in the front row, grim looks on their faces. For the first time, I noticed Ray Pincher standing just inside the door to the courtroom, arms folded across his chest. He smiled at me.

Yeah, Ray. Just like you told me, this old lion still has his teeth.

"What should you be looking for in this case?" I asked the jury. "One thing is to examine the credibility of the defendant. If a man's wife disappears, shouldn't he be truthful when he speaks to the police? Surely an innocent man would want his wife to be found, while a guilty man would not."

"Objection!" Solomon popped out of his chair. "Mr. Lassiter is arguing the case."

"Sustained," Judge Gridley said. "Save it for closing, Mr. Lassiter."

I turned back to the panel. "Remember when I told you a few minutes ago what the defendant did the day his wife disappeared?" I was pretty sure they remembered, but I would remind them. "He went to a strip club sixty miles from his house. Bought himself a lap dance, with his wife's corpse in the trunk of his car. Who does that? A socio-psycho-path, as described by Dr. Freudenstein. The defendant stayed at the strip club thirty-one minutes, then drove to the airport. But that's not what he told the police. He lied about his whereabouts. He claimed to have stayed on Miami Beach all day, looking for Sofia in her favorite places. Stores, the beach, restaurants. One lie after another. All meant to cover his true whereabouts and his actions, the disposing of his wife's body."

Out of the corner of my eye, I saw Solomon leaning forward, so I switched gears before he could lob another objection, like a hand grenade, into my foxhole. I told the jury they would hear from an expert witness, a pilot, hired by the state for an experiment. He had filled a large duffel bag with 110 pounds of sand and placed it on the passenger seat on a Bellanca Citabria, the same model plane used by Calvert. He took off from Pompano Beach Airpark, flew northeast over the Atlantic, and with the plane on autopilot, successfully tossed the bag into the Gulf Stream. I told the jury they would see a video of this demonstration, and in my heart, I knew they would think of Sofia sleeping with the fishes when they saw it.

I wandered back to the prosecution table and saw a yellow Post-it with one word scribbled on it: *Cavendish*. Jeez, I'd forgotten. So now I told the jurors they would hear from a woman named Ann Cavendish who would describe how the defendant also rendered her unconscious several years earlier in an incident that could only be called date rape. That caused two jurors—both middle-aged women—to exchange glances. I think they were ready to hang Calvert, perhaps even before I was finished. Time to round up the horses, head back to the barn, and call it a day.

"Ladies and gentlemen, I won't directly speak to you again until all the evidence is in. After each side has argued its case, Judge Gridley will instruct you on the law, and you will retire to the jury room. I have no doubt at that time that you will conclude that Clark Gordon Calvert is responsible for Sofia's death by an act of murder in the second degree."

-53-

Last Rodeo

When I sat down, Victoria Lord surprised me yet again. "The defense reserves opening for the beginning of its case," she told Judge Gridley.

It's not unheard of, but I never do it when I'm on that side of the courtroom. After the state talks trash about my client, I spring to my feet and counterpunch. I don't want the jury to go days—or weeks—without hearing my theory of the case.

Just what are you up to, Victoria? What's the student's secret strategy for defeating her teacher?

I wasn't expecting any twisty tactics. For the defense, this was a traditional reasonable-doubt case. With the state lacking a body, forensics, and clear motive, there could hardly be a better strategy. Cross-examine the state's witnesses, poke holes in their stories, expose gaps in the evidence. Then fire up the smudge pots and create a smoke screen. Pepe Suarez and Billy Burnside had financial motives to want Sofia dead, enough to create flickers of doubt. No need for fancy footwork.

Judge Gridley called for the lunch recess, and I headed for the lawyers' lounge. No time during trial for the drive to Brickell or South Beach or even downtown for margaritas and grilled snapper. Detective

Barrios was waiting for me with two grease-stained paper sacks. Cheeseburgers and fries.

We found a quiet corner table and set upon the food like ravenous wolves. "All the witnesses subpoenaed?" I asked between bites.

"Third time you asked. Answer's still yes."

"Everyone knows what day and time to show up?"

"Affirmative."

"You tell Billy Burnside not to wear tennis shorts?"

"Jeez, Jake, you think I'm a rookie?"

"Sorry. I know. I know. Not your first rodeo."

Barrios took a long pull on an iced coffee. "But probably my last."

"Huh?"

"Gonna put in my papers. Take the pension and go fishing in the Keys until I'm dead or they run out of snapper."

"Aw, you been saying that for years."

"I've lost a step, Jake. And it's not as much fun as it used to be. Too much staring into computer screens instead of pounding the pavement."

I finished off my burger and wiped the grease off my lips with a paper napkin. "We're gonna be a poorer society without you. All I can say."

"Thank you, Jake. Now what else can I help you with?"

"How's Ann Cavendish holding up?"

"Fine. Last I saw her, she was drinking piña coladas at the hotel pool."

"You ran through the questions again?"

"She's fine, Jake. Trust me."

"Billy Burnside. Did he confirm for tomorrow morning?"

"Aw, shit, see what I'm saying. Forgot to tell you. He's been served, so I'm not gonna worry about him showing up, but he didn't return my call. Two calls, really."

"Damn! Send a uniform over to the pro shop at the club—make sure he's not getting cold feet."

"My guy's on the way. No worries, Jake."

But a trial is nothing but worries. A murder trial has a thousand moving parts. Any one of them breaks, the whole damn thing can fall apart. There was a time when I could keep most everything in my head. Dates, times, witness stories, the thrust and parry of tactics, an entire closing argument.

Like Barrios, I might have lost a step getting to first base. I just prayed I didn't fall flat on my face rounding the bases.

-54-

Infusion Confusion

After court, I headed straight to the hospital, where a physician who looked too young to shave jabbed me with a needle connected to an infusion bag of fluid, which began its *drip-drip-drip* into a vein.

"What's in the bag?" I asked.

"A new cocktail," the young doctor said.

"Yeah?"

"Lithium and a secret sauce of protein antibodies."

"Why the secret?"

"Infusion X-7 is experimental. Not quite approved."

"Then what's new? I've been taking lithium and protein antibodies."

"Maybe I should answer in terms you can understand."

Doogie Howser, MD, gave me such a condescending look I was tempted to pull out the needle and take an experimental, not-quite-approved swing at him. "Okay, try me, Doc."

"This is a different recipe. More gin, less vermouth."

"Pretty good, Doogie. Thanks. I take back all the shitty thoughts I had about you."

***

That night at home, I listened to Tom Russell singing the red-dirt, Tex-Mex classic "Tonight We Ride" as my headache returned with the ferocity of stampeding stallions. The song tells the tale of US General John Pershing's horseback soldiers chasing Pancho Villa over the border into Mexico. If the troops caught the *bandido*, they promised to skin him alive and make chaps out of his hide. I developed my respect for the justice system from such keen observations of law and order in the West.

I took one of the new pills Melissa had given me, and the pain subsided. An hour later, she came by and asked how it had gone at the hospital.

"Some junior high school kid injected me with a bag of martinis," I said.

"Infusion X-7. We're very hopeful about it."

I'd heard that before, many times, but I kept my mouth shut. Melissa was doing the best she could. All the doctors were trying.

"Do you still have some marijuana around?" she asked.

"Do I? Are the Kardashians annoying? I've got sativa, indica, hybrids, buds, oils, honey. Care to join me?"

She skipped the usual lecture about not needing psychoactive THC. Instead, she said, "Let's smoke some Mendocino Thunderhump, have sex, watch SportsCenter, and go to sleep."

"Are you real or did I invent you?" I asked.

-55-

A Tale of Two Calls

At 9:05 a.m. the next day, still buzzing with weed but thankfully no headache, I presented my first witness, Gladys Estefan, a communications officer from the Miami Beach Police Department. She played two tapes for the jury. First was Calvert's 9-1-1 call on March 7, roughly three months before Sofia disappeared.

"My wife's unconscious! Low pulse, abnormally slow respiration. I'm performing CPR, but I need paramedics with oxygen!"

"You've taken hundreds of 9-1-1 calls?" I asked the witness.

"Thousands," she said.

"Did Dr. Calvert sound truly alarmed?"

An objectionable question on multiple grounds, but Solomon and Lord remained silent. Why wouldn't they? Calvert's voice was pinched, the pitch high, the words firing quickly, and his breaths audible. He sounded like a man scared to death.

"Yes, his voice was consistent with that of many calls from people with stricken family members."

We played the 9-1-1 call from June 4, the day after Sofia disappeared.

"This is Dr. Clark Calvert. My wife. Her name is Sofia. She left yesterday morning. From my house. Our house. And I'm not sure . . . uh . . . she hasn't called me."

His voice halting. Seeming distracted somehow. No sense of urgency.

"Officer Estefan, does that sound like a man who's alarmed that his wife has disappeared?"

"Objection!" Victoria bounced to her feet quickly for someone in heels. "Leading, calls for speculation, improper foundation, and ridiculously self-serving."

"Sustained," Judge Gridley said. "Move along, Mr. Lassiter."

I didn't care. I'd already gotten what I wanted, my question emphasizing what the jurors already heard. The first call, Calvert was afraid Sofia was dying. The second time, he already knew she was dead. At least, that's the impression I wanted to convey.

Next came the paramedics who showed up at the Calvert home in response to the first call. By the time they arrived, Sofia had regained consciousness but was groggy. They administered oxygen and stayed an hour until they were certain she didn't need hospitalization. Calvert freely admitted he had rendered Sofia unconscious with a vascular hold, compressing the carotid artery.

"'Consensual sexual asphyxia,' he called it," one paramedic testified. "I've seen autoerotic-asphyxia deaths, so I warned him to refrain from the practice."

"And the defendant's response?" I asked.

"He said, 'I have a medical degree from Harvard and multiple fellowships. You have what, a first-aid course from a community college and you work out of a firehouse?' He was rather arrogant."

"That's sounds like an understatement."

"Mis-ter Lassiter!" Judge Gridley said in his scolding voice. "You know better than to comment on the testimony. Next time you do it, I'm calling unsportsmanlike conduct and fifteen yards."

Meaning contempt and a $1,500 fine.

"Understood, Your Honor," I said humbly, and returned my attention to the witness. "What else did the defendant say?"

"Dr. Calvert seemed to blame his wife for passing out."

"How so?"

"He said his practice is to stop applying pressure to the neck as soon as Ms. Calvert achieves orgasm. But that night, she was too slow and therefore he kept squeezing. His exact words were, 'Sofia was late to the party.'"

Not wishing to write a check to the clerk of the court, I restrained myself from saying, "What a sensitive fellow."

"Did Mrs. Calvert say anything while you were in their home?" I asked.

"Objection, hearsay!" Victoria got the words out even before she stood up.

"Spousal-abuse exception," I fired back.

Judge Gridley removed his spectacles, breathed on the lenses, wiped them on his robe, and put them back on. "Overruled. The March incident fits into spousal-abuse territory. The witness may answer."

"At first, Mrs. Calvert wasn't really able to talk. Then, quite hoarsely, she thanked us."

"Anything else?"

"She exchanged words with her husband."

"Go on."

"Dr. Calvert told us he only performed the vascular hold at his wife's request. He said, 'She's a sexual masochist.' And Mrs. Calvert, quite hoarsely, said, 'Fuck you, Clark. You're a sexual sadist.'"

I shot a glance toward the defense table. Solomon and Lord wore their poker faces, just as I'd taught them. *If a witness stabs you in the eye, don't even blink. Never let the jury see your pain.*

Next to them, Calvert wasn't as stoic. His features had hardened into an unpleasant look. Cold and mean. I hoped the jurors were watching. Turning to my pals, I said cheerily, "Your witness, Counselors."

-56-

Proving the Lie

Solomon and Lord didn't want to mess with my paramedic, who detested Clark Calvert within ninety seconds of meeting him.

"No questions, Your Honor," Solomon said.

I called Detective Barrios to establish Calvert's false story about searching for Sofia on the day she disappeared. An old pro, he looked straight at the jury and told them exactly what I had said in my opening statement. Calvert claimed he'd gone to Bal Harbour Shops and checked out David Yurman, Bulgari, Balenciaga, Fendi, Gucci, Jimmy Choo, and a couple more pricey stores. He checked the restaurant Carpaccio, where she liked to lunch with friends, usually having three glasses of chardonnay and two bites of tuna tartare.

With Sofia nowhere to be found, Calvert told Barrios he'd driven to Haulover Beach, where she liked to sunbathe topless and occasionally nude. Then back down Collins Avenue to the Fontainebleau and its plethora of bars and restaurants. Still no Sofia.

"Did the defendant tell you what time he started on his search on June 3?" I asked.

"Between eleven and eleven thirty a.m.," Barrios answered.

"And when he returned?"

"Between nine and nine thirty p.m."

"Roughly ten hours?"

"Yes."

"What did you do to check out that story?"

"I reviewed recordings from the security system at the Calvert home. There's a camera that picks up cars leaving and entering the garage."

"And what did you find?"

"The Ferrari registered to Clark Calvert left the garage at eleven seventeen a.m. and returned at nine-oh-seven p.m."

"Consistent with what the defendant told you."

"At that point, yes."

"Then what did you do?"

"What cops do. I checked out his story."

That made me smile. Barrios was an old-timer. Sergeant Joe Friday on *Dragnet*. Just change the location. *"This is the city. Miami Beach, Florida. I work here. I'm a cop."*

"How did you check out the defendant's story?"

"I went to every store he told me he visited. I showed clerks his photo and asked if he'd been there, looking for his wife."

"Had anyone?"

"No one, which piqued my interest because several clerks knew Mrs. Calvert from her shopping trips. A few even knew Mr. Calvert, who sometimes accompanied her."

"Then what did you do?"

"I checked toll records on various expressways, plus SunPass and turnpike records for June 3."

"And what did you find?"

"SunPass records revealed that the defendant's Ferrari entered the turnpike and the Golden Glades interchange, heading north at eleven fifty-four a.m."

And where did the car exit?"

"There was no SunPass record after the entry. On that day or any other."

"What did you make of that, Detective?"

"Either the transmitter suddenly failed, or, more likely, it was discarded by an occupant of the car who realized his movements could be tracked."

"Objection!" Solomon bounded out of his chair and crossed the well of the courtroom in two steps. Quick feet. He'd played some baseball at the University of Miami, where he couldn't hit a lick, but he'd been a nifty base stealer. "Move to strike the answer as pure speculation, unsupported by any evidence."

"Granted in part, denied in part." Judge Gridley divided the baby in half in Solomonic fashion. King Solomon, not lawyer Solomon. "The jury shall disregard that last portion of the answer concerning what the occupant allegedly realized."

"Were you able to determine where the Ferrari exited the turnpike?"

Barrios summarized the rest. Turnpike cameras photograph license plates at every exit. He ran searches for the Ferrari's license plate, and bingo. The Ferrari took Exit 67 in Pompano Beach at 12:51 p.m. I spent a couple minutes with housekeeping details, entering the SunPass records and turnpike photos into evidence.

"Did you come into possession of other security videos showing the whereabouts of the defendant's car on June 3?"

"At twelve fifty-three p.m., the Ferrari entered the parking lot of a strip club called the Titty Trap on Hammondville Road just off Exit 67 of the turnpike. The car left the parking lot at one twenty-four p.m. Fourteen minutes later, at one thirty-eight p.m., it entered a secure area of Pompano Beach Airpark and was recorded leaving five hours and one minute later, at six thirty-nine p.m. Finally, at nine-oh-seven p.m., as I mentioned earlier, the Ferrari was back in Miami Beach, entering the garage at the Calvert home."

As Barrios spoke, a computer graphic appeared on a monitor in front of the jury box, creating a visual image of the timeline.

"In your interviews with the defendant, did he ever disclose anything about this?"

"To the contrary. He told me he was on Miami Beach all day and evening, looking for his wife."

"Whereas he was gone . . . ?"

"Nine hours and fifty minutes, all told."

At the defense table, Calvert looked away from the witness stand, scowling. It was not a charming look.

Barrios had set the table, proving Calvert lied about his whereabouts on the day Sofia disappeared. Now my job was to serve the meal.

-57-

The Facts, Ma'am

I asked Detective Barrios to describe his interviews with personnel at Pompano Beach Airpark. He told the jury that Calvert was well known there, a frequent weekend pilot, flying a borrowed Bellanca Citabria, tail number N72ZZ. The detective identified tower records from June 3, and I set about preparing the meat and potatoes of our case.

"What do the records reveal?"

"The aircraft was cleared for takeoff at two sixteen p.m. on June 3 with Calvert at the controls. He took off, flew to points unknown, and touched down on his return at five forty-seven p.m."

Again, the video monitor in front of the jury added to the timeline. Every juror had to wonder: *Where did he go, and what did he do for more than three hours on the day his wife disappeared?*

"Did he file a flight plan?" I asked.

"No."

"Did he tell anyone at the airport where he was going?"

"No one I talked to."

"Do you know where he went?"

"I only know the approximate distance he could have traveled. He would have been over the ocean a minute or two after takeoff, and assuming a cruising speed of 125 miles per hour for that aircraft, he could have easily reached Grand Bahama Island or even farther. Abaco or Nassau, if he had flown east, with more than sufficient time and fuel for the return."

"Lots of open water?"

"Hundreds of miles in three directions."

"A lot of territory to drop a body out of an aircraft."

"Objection, leading," Victoria said, never getting to her feet.

"Sustained," Judge Gridley said.

I nodded toward the bench, then turned back to the witness stand. My point had been made.

"During the ten hours the defendant had told you he was searching for Sofia on Miami Beach, in truth, he'd driven to Pompano Beach, spent half an hour at a strip club, driven to the airport, taken out his friend's single-engine plane, flown three hours and thirty-one minutes, and returned to the airport. Is that correct?"

It was a leading question, something forbidden on direct examination, but neither Solomon nor Lord objected. I shot a look at the defense table. Calvert was whispering to Victoria as she scribbled notes, nodding. She looked up and gave me a small smile I couldn't decipher.

"That's exactly what happened," Barrios said.

With a sparkle in my eyes, a smile on my face, and a song in my heart—Leonard Cohen's "Hallelujah"—I turned to Victoria. "Your witness, Ms. Lord."

Victoria Lord stood, walked into the well of the courtroom, and placed herself at a respectful distance from the witness stand. She wore a charcoal-gray pin-striped lady business suit with a tailored jacket and a skirt that stopped a bit below the knees. A white silk blouse with a bow. She was tall, pretty, and professional. And, I knew only too well, lethal on cross. But over a couple of decades, George Barrios had fended off the best, including me on occasion.

"Good afternoon, Detective," she said pleasantly.

"Counselor." Barrios nodded to her. The exchange was pretty much the equivalent of boxers touching gloves before they start swinging.

"Detective, what time did Dr. Calvert get on the turnpike for the drive back to Miami Beach?"

"I don't believe he took the turnpike."

"Because there are no photos showing Dr. Calvert's Ferrari on either a southbound entrance or an exit that day, correct?"

"Dr." Calvert. Victoria would use her client's title to imply honor and respect. I refer to him as the "defendant" to dehumanize the man. One of the many games lawyers play.

"Yes, ma'am," Barrios said.

"So how did he get home?"

"I assume he took I-95, where there are no cameras."

"You assume? Just as you assumed Dr. Calvert flew east over the ocean?"

Detective Barrios licked his lips. "I probably shouldn't have used the word *assume*," he said. "I logically concluded that if your client didn't take the turnpike, he took the expressway to get home. Likewise, I concluded he flew over the ocean if he intended to dispose of a body."

"But is that logical, Detective? Haven't you simply assumed that disposing of the body was the purpose of the flight, and then you worked backward from that conclusion to form the belief Dr. Calvert flew over open water?"

"That's where the facts led me, Ms. Lord. Facts are what I deal with."

Barrios in full Sergeant Joe Friday mode. *The facts*. Most people think the television character from *Dragnet* said, "Just the facts, ma'am." But he never did. Often, however, he said, "All we know are the facts, ma'am."

"Did anyone at the airport see Dr. Calvert carry a body into the aircraft?"

"No one I spoke to."

"Or see him with a large duffel bag or other luggage that could contain a body?"

"No one actually saw him enter the cockpit."

"What about video?"

"There are no cameras in the area where the Citabria was parked."

"Pity. Now, the body of water you're talking about, Detective. What's it called?"

"The Atlantic Ocean," he ventured.

"And more specifically, the body of water running parallel to the coastline?"

"The Florida Straits."

"Detective, do you have any idea how many sailboats and power-boats are in those waters on a Saturday afternoon in June?"

"No idea whatsoever."

"Would it surprise you to know that more than fifteen hundred boats would be in the Straits on any given Saturday?"

Barrios shrugged. "I'll take your word for it, Counselor."

"Would that be a smart way to dispose of a body, dropping it from a plane in broad daylight with boats in every direction?"

"In my thirty years investigating homicides, I've found criminals don't always do the smart thing."

Touché. But if she was wounded, Victoria didn't bleed. Without skipping a beat or mussing her silk blouse, she said, "Detective, let's get back to that assumption of yours that Dr. Calvert flew east over the ocean."

Barrios waited. There was no question, and he sure as hell wasn't going to say anything. Victoria continued, "In addition to their home on Miami Beach, do the Calverts own any other properties?"

"They have a vacation home in Frostproof."

"A little town between Tampa and Orlando?"

"That's right."

"Do you know the name of the development in Frostproof where their vacation home is located?"

Barrios scrunched his lips and squinted, as if trying to scratch out a memory. "I saw the name on a Polk County real-property list, but honestly, Ms. Lord, I can't remember."

"Aerofrost? Does that ring a bell, Detective?"

"Yes, that's it."

Aerofrost!

Barrios didn't see where she was going, but I did, and I wouldn't know Frostproof, Florida, from Bark, Arkansas.

"Why do you suppose the development is called Aerofrost?"

"No idea, Counselor."

"Are you unaware that it's a fly-in community, ninety homes adjacent to a thirty-five-hundred-foot paved runway?"

Oh, shit.

Barrios's mouth twitched. Just a slight involuntary motion. The detective sensed what was coming.

"Would you be surprised to learn that Dr. Calvert flew from Pompano Beach to his home at Aerofrost on June 3 to see if that's where Sofia had gone?"

"Objection! Argumentative and irrelevant," I sang out, mostly to buy Barrios some time. I was counting on the old fox to get his bearings and recover.

"Overruled," Judge Gridley declared. "The witness may answer."

"Pretty much nothing surprises me anymore, Counselor."

"And if the defense introduces security video showing Dr. Calvert entering the Aerofrost home that afternoon and going room to room, calling out Sofia's name, would that change your theory about flying east and dumping her body from a plane?"

One question too many, I thought. That's the problem with younger lawyers, always giving the nail an extra whack with the hammer. Victoria would have plenty of time on her half of the case to introduce her videos. No need to let my savvy witness opine about the weight of that evidence before she even had it stamped by the clerk.

"Not necessarily, Counselor. I'd conclude that your client flew up the coast, where he dumped the body offshore, then turned northwest and headed to his vacation home, where he could establish an alibi using those security cameras. He had time to do all of that and still get back to Pompano Beach a little before six o'clock."

Bravo, George! One old lion to another.

The ship of state, which is to say, the prosecution, may have sprung a leak, but my old pal Barrios plugged the hole with all the greasy rags he could find.

Still, the day closed with the score tied, not good for the state, which has the burden of proof. Though we had caught Calvert in a lie, we'd lost the motivation behind that lie. Our case was premised on Calvert hiding the plane flight from our view. Solomon and Lord would doubtless argue he was simply hiding the trip to the strip club out of embarrassment.

A little white lie, they would say. But the larger truth was that he had really searched for Sofia. No way he would do that, they'd argue, if he knew she was dead.

We were forced to argue that, as Barrios suggested, the flight trip to Frostproof was a charade. But suggesting it is one thing, proving it another.

The defense, of course, didn't have to prove a thing. It only had to cast the shadow of reasonable doubt over our case. My task was to continue tossing mud at Calvert, which meant spending a little more time talking about the Titty Trap.

-58-

Stab Me Again, Corky

When I was a young lawyer in the public defender's office, I once stood in front of the jury box and said, "Let me take you now to the scene of the crime."

Two jurors stood up, thinking we were about to board a bus.

So today, when I put Kirk "Corky" Corcoran on the stand, I did not begin by saying, "Let me take you now to the Titty Trap."

Instead, I asked direct questions, and he gave straight answers. Yes, he was the day manager of the strip club in Pompano Beach. He assured the jury that the Titty Trap was a legitimate business with no underage drinking, gambling, or prostitution. Fine. I like a man who takes pride in his work.

It took a few minutes to set the scene. I'd been fighting off a headache since breakfast, and now Beethoven's Fifth Symphony had taken up residence inside my skull, the kettledrums particularly prominent.

Corcoran seemed comfortable on the witness stand. He wore a black suit with a white shirt, open at the neck. The shirt could never have been buttoned, anyway. Corcoran had the neck of a water buffalo. Wiry, black hair curled out of his open collar. He leaned forward, overflowing the chair, his forearms leaning on the front rail of the witness stand, home to countless sweaty palms.

Yes, he knew both Clark Calvert and Sofia Calvert. Most men didn't bring their significant others to the club, so couples were memorable. Sofia had become pals with some of the dancers, paid for a couple to attend classes, maybe get their cosmetology licenses. Calvert was the quiet type. An observer. Didn't sit in the first row near the stage, even when all the seats were empty. Liked a table in the back of the room. Paid the two-drink minimum but drank only club soda.

"Did the defendant ever pay for lap dances?" I asked.

"He did. Sometimes Ms. Calvert would accompany him to the VIP room, and sometimes she stayed in the bar."

"And sometimes she didn't accompany him to the club, correct?"

"That's true."

"Let me take you now to June 3 of this year," I said, and no one looked around the courtroom for a time machine. "Did the defendant visit the Titty Trap?"

"He did."

"How can you be sure of that?"

"At your request, I looked up security videos from the parking lot. He got to the club in early afternoon, stayed a short while, and left."

"Was Ms. Calvert with him?"

He shook his head, his massive shoulders and the rest of him staying in place. "No. If she'd been with him, Dr. Calvert wouldn't have asked the question."

I wasn't sure I'd heard him correctly. My tinnitus had its own timpani section and had just switched from Beethoven to Max Weinberg hammering his drums in "Born to Run." Outside, the daily thunderstorm raged, wind gusts driving the rain horizontally against the courtroom windows.

"I'm sorry," I said. "Could the court reporter please read back Mr. Corcoran's answer."

The court reporter, a woman in her fifties with a pen jammed through her platinum beehive, lifted the folded pages from the stenograph machine and read aloud: "No. If she'd been with him, Dr. Calvert wouldn't have asked the question."

Everyone in the courtroom wanted to know, *What question?* And nobody wanted to know more than the big guy in the 46 XL, off-the-rack blue suit, standing there with his mouth open. Me.

But every schoolboy knows a lawyer risks being skinned alive by asking something without knowing the answer. That old saw assumes you're cross-examining an unfriendly witness. But Corcoran was my witness, called for the limited purpose of establishing Calvert's presence at the strip club instead of searching for his wife.

To take the risk or not?

In the large scheme of things, when a man is facing a slow, torturous death by brain disease, why the hell not roll the dice?

"What question did the defendant ask you, Mr. Corcoran?"

"Not just me. He asked Trouble and a couple other dancers."

Okay, spit it out already!

"Dr. Calvert said, 'Have you seen my wife? Has she been here today?'"

I stood still, my face locked in poker-playing mode. The jury would never be able to tell if I was holding four aces or a busted flush. I shot a look toward the defense table. Victoria was taking notes. Solomon was studying the jury. Calvert looked at me. He suppressed his snake's smile but raised one eyebrow just the tiniest bit.

I turned back to the witness. "And what was your answer, Mr. Corcoran?"

"I told him. We all told him no. We hadn't seen his wife since the last time she was at the Trap with him."

"Did you find it odd that the defendant would ask you about his wife's whereabouts?"

"I manage a strip club, Mr. Lassiter. I don't find anything odd. But Dr. Calvert told me they'd had a spat, and she'd left the house, as she sometimes does when they quarrel. So he was out looking for her."

Like Julius Caesar, my stab wounds seemed to be multiplying by the second. It was as if I had just said, *Et tu, Brute?* or rather, "Stab me again, Corky." I could sit down now, but I might as well ask one more question. If I didn't, Victoria would.

"Did the defendant say anything else to you before leaving the club?"

"He said he was going upstate and check out their vacation home. His wife loved it there, so maybe that's where she went for some peace and quiet. I think he mentioned he could get there in an hour or so by flying a private plane."

I could feel the blood gushing from all the wounds, the knife making a *slushing* sound with every entrance would, a *plopping* with every exit.

"Mr. Corcoran, you remember my visit to the strip club?"

"Of course."

"Did you ever mention your conversation with the defendant to me?"

"No, sir."

I was going to leave it at that. I wasn't going to ask the dangerous *why* question a second time, but Corky Corcoran went there without being asked.

"I would have told you, Mr. Lassiter, but you never asked me. I don't know why, but you never asked whether I spoke to Dr. Calvert."

Outside the windows, lightning crackled, and a thunderclap was so loud that the courtroom seemed to shudder. The lights flickered but stayed on. In a just world, the lightning would crash through a window and strike the witness, God smiting the heathen who bore false witness.

But is he lying?

I didn't know. Crazy as it sounds, I couldn't remember if I'd asked him the question. My mind was too fuzzy.

Are my brain cells dying at an alarming rate?

I had called Corcoran to bolster our case that Calvert had lied. But instead of being the concrete for the foundation of the house I was trying to build, the big guy became the sinkhole under the footings. A thought occurred to me. That Calvert intended us to catch him in the lie, wanted us to follow him to the strip club and the airpark and reach our conclusions that he could then destroy with his alibi.

Is he that smart? Did he bait the trap that I blundered into? Are my synapses so out of sync that I've lost my treasured ability to sense the other side's maneuvers before they do?

With those grim thoughts, I decided to live and fight another day. Or at least try to. "No further questions," I said.

-59-

Cloudy with a Chance of Shit Storms

Sweet jasmine filled the evening air. The afternoon thunderstorms had moved from the Everglades eastward over the city and then out to sea. They left behind a surprisingly cool evening, the pink bougainvillea glistening with moisture, the thorns of the twisted vines hidden in shadows. A pretty good metaphor for my philosophy that life is a gorgeous path through the woods, with unseen rattlesnakes waiting to sink their fangs into your flesh.

I sat on my back porch with Detective Barrios. We were in the Adirondack chairs, taking turns consoling each other and dulling our senses with alcohol and weed. I was using a vape pen, smoking the classic hybrid Blue Dream, heavy on the indica for relaxation and peacefulness. Maybe it would heal my brain cells, too. Who knows? Who cares? At the moment, I was swimming underwater in a warm, clear sea.

Barrios was drinking my best bourbon, Pappy Van Winkle. Aged twenty-three years, the elixir was a deep amber red, and you don't dilute it with ice. No, I don't spend twelve hundred bucks for a bottle of booze. This was a gift from a happy client.

Two words—*happy client*—that don't often fit together in my world.

"Damn sorry I screwed up, Jake."

"Could have happened to anyone, George."

"Not to me. Not ten years ago. Hell, not five."

"Forget it, George. The earth will keep spinning until some giant asteroid hits it and ushers in a new Ice Age. All the dinosaurs will die. That's you and me, pal."

"You're stoned, Jake."

"Nah, just reflective."

"A month ago, I checked property records statewide and found Calvert's house up in Frostproof." Barrios was unable to let it go. "But I didn't go far enough, or I would have seen it was a fly-in community. I wouldn't have stepped into quicksand."

"Hey, you came back, and you were right. Calvert's trip upstate doesn't rule out dumping the body first."

"Doesn't rule out . . . ?"

"I know. I know, George. That's not enough. We gotta prove it happened, not that it *might* have happened."

He took a sip of the Pappy, let it roll around his tongue, and swallowed. "Did you really not ask Corcoran if he talked to Calvert?"

"I'll tell you the sad truth." I rapped my knuckles on the side of my head. "I can't remember."

"Did you take notes?"

"I seldom do during the interview. If you write some things down and not others, the witness wonders why and double-thinks everything before saying it."

All evening my out-of-focus mind had been trying to call up the memory of my trip to the Titty Trap. Corcoran had answered my questions freely. Seemed forthcoming. Nothing devious. Volunteered that Sofia visited the club with Calvert. But did I ask him whether Calvert said anything to him that day? I still had no idea.

"You think Corcoran told the truth today?" Barrios said.

I sucked at the tip of my vape pen. A placidity had overtaken me, and I was in a state of drooping eyelids. "Dunno," I said sleepily.

"Even if he was telling the truth, why'd he sandbag you like that? Why no heads-up?"

"Hmm." I was letting Barrios carry both ends of the conversation.

I was vaguely aware of a cell phone chirping. Mine plays the Penn State fight song, but this was the iPhone's marimba ringtone.

After a moment, Barrios shook me by the shoulder.

"Lemme alone, George."

"Jake, did you hear my end of the conversation?"

"What? No. Are you hungry? How 'bout some chips and onion dip?"

"Listen up, Jake. I just had a call. A friend from the sheriff's department. They've been sitting on Billy Burnside's apartment ever since he failed to show up at work."

"What? You didn't tell me that."

"He quit his job, or more precisely, just stopped showing up. And I told you that."

"Really?"

"Yeah, but don't worry about it. You've been focused on the trial."

"For all the good it's doing."

"Burnside's missing. A deputy just had the apartment-building manager open his unit. Cleaned out. Burnside's gone. No forwarding address."

My dulled senses crackled to life. "He's my first witness tomorrow."

"Not anymore, Jake."

While I was still processing that information, my cell phone chimed and sang, "We're always true to you, dear old white and blue." Caller ID told me it was Samuel Merrick Buchanan. Divorce lawyer to the stars.

"Sam, I'm glad it's you. We'll need you in the courtroom at nine a.m. tomorrow, not eleven. A witness fell through."

"That's why I called. I've been hired to defend Calvert in the wrongful-death action Pepe Suarez filed today."

"What are you talking about?"

"Suarez filed papers to name himself administrator of Sofia's estate. Plus, he retained Stuart Grossman to sue Calvert for millions."

"And of all the lawyers in Miami . . ."

"Yeah, Calvert's retained me to defend the lawsuit. So obviously, I can't testify for you in the criminal case."

"It's not for me, Sam. It's for Sofia. It's for the people of the state of Florida. You have a moral obligation here."

"I don't see it that way. It would be clearly unethical for me to assist you. Good night, Jake."

The line clicked dead, and I looked at Barrios. He'd picked up the gist of the conversation and poured himself another three fingers of Pappy, then gestured with the bottle, asking me to join him. Yeah, I would like to add some whiskey to the weed. If ever I needed that combo, tonight was the night.

The jasmine-scented evening had just become fouled by a rank shit storm. I wondered what tomorrow would bring. Nothing short of a tsunami would surprise me.

-60-

Shrunk

Please state your name and occupation, sir," I said.

"Harold G. Freudenstein. Physician."

He did not appear to be stoned. I was not sure the same could be said for me. Waking up this morning with a crushing headache and a touch of vertigo, I stutter-stepped to the kitchen and had a breakfast of papaya, coffee, and Sour Diesel, the classic California strain of marijuana.

Though tasting a bit like motor oil, Sour Diesel, sativa, delivered a quick and powerful high. I usually go for the milder strains, the hybrids, or even pure indica, known as "in-de couch," because it will put you on your ass. But today I needed to be pain-free, with a sharp, focused mind, and the Diesel gave me the best chance. But there was also euphoria to contend with, which can have its downside. I didn't want to burst into laughter for no apparent reason or start talking with the speed of a tobacco auctioneer. Another side effect: loss of inhibitions. I would take care not to begin disrobing in the courtroom.

"Are you board certified in any specialties, Doctor?"

"Psychiatry."

I had the shrink run through his educational background. Undergrad at Duke, med school at the University of Miami, residency at Jackson Memorial Hospital, an impressive fellowship at Stanford, a stint as director of behavioral medicine at Mount Sinai Hospital on Miami Beach, and a bunch of boards and committees in his younger day. I omitted his more recent hippie-dippy Key Biscayne guru credentials.

"Have you published any scholarly articles, Dr. Freudenstein?"

"Many. I've written articles related to studies of intimate partner violence, bipolar disorder, brain activation during sexual arousal, irratio- nal beliefs in remitted depressives, socioeconomic factors in hyperactive sexual desire. I could go on."

"Please don't. Sorry. Please do!" I realized I was speaking both too quickly and too loudly. Perhaps one fewer puff of the Sour Diesel would have been better.

The shrink rattled off the names of papers he'd written around the time Sigmund Freud had dinner with Carl Jung, or so it seemed to me. Freudenstein had cleaned up well. He wore a seersucker suit with a white shirt and blue-and-white bow tie. His storm-gray ponytail was neatly tied into place. The only discordant note: the harsh fluorescent courtroom lights made his waxy, face-lifted complexion seem corpselike.

"Have you lectured at professional gatherings on any of these sub- jects?" I asked after he had finished running through his publications.

Solomon got to his feet. "In the interest of time, the defense will stipulate that Dr. Freudenstein is an expert for purposes of expressing medical opinions in the field of psychiatry."

"So stipulated," I agreed.

Of course, agreeing to the shrink's credentials would not keep Solomon and Lord from savaging him on cross-examination and again in closing arguments.

I laid the groundwork for the big reveal: Freudenstein's prophetic letter of doom. About three months before Sofia disappeared, the doc testified, she brought her husband to a counseling session. She had been a patient for two years, engaging in talk therapy for her anxiety and depression.

"After meeting with the Calverts, did you write a letter to both of them?" I nodded to the court clerk, and magically, a blowup of Freudenstein's letter appeared on a large screen.

"Ah, that," he said. "Yes, I wrote that."

"Would you read the second paragraph aloud?"

"Mrs. Calvert, it is my considered medical opinion that you are in danger of great bodily harm or death if you continue to reside with your husband. I urge you to immediately separate and refrain from all personal contact."

"Dr. Freudenstein, based on your professional training and decades of experience, you predicted that Dr. Calvert would harm and possibly kill his wife, did you not?"

He stared at the image of the letter on the screen but didn't immediately answer. I had no worries. The shrink made the prediction; the prediction came true; he had no choice but to confirm that. Seconds ticked by. It seemed even longer, my ability to judge time affected by the psychoactive weed.

Finally, he said, "I did. Yes, I did. Those are my words."

"And you diagnosed Dr. Calvert as a psycho-sociopath, did you not?"

"Yes. I told you that when we met."

"Did you further state that you had no doubt that Clark Calvert was fully capable of killing Sofia and of having no remorse for doing so?"

"I said those words, yes. Do you remember what you said in return?"

Damn right, I remember. My sativa-sharpened synapses are clicking at 120 miles per hour. But we're not going there.

"Dr. Freudenstein, I'm the one who asks the questions. So moving along—"

"You said to me, 'Don't you think such a quick diagnosis is, at the very least, premature and, at the worst, reckless and wrong?' And now I've had a chance to think about it . . ."

"Doctor, there's no question pending."

"I just want to explain my letter in light of further thought and reconsideration."

Reconsideration? No way! Further thoughts? Keep them to yourself!

"Please wait for a question, sir," I ordered him.

Solomon was on his feet. "Your Honor, Mr. Lassiter is arguing with his own witness, who ought to be able to explain himself."

"Very well. Doctor. What is it you want to say?" Judge Gridley said.

"Mr. Lassiter was right. I had insufficient information to make that diagnosis and to write that letter. As I look at it now, there was no reasonable basis upon which to make such definitive conclusions. I was reckless, and I regret it."

What the hell is happening? Was this even real? I'd been strolling down the sidewalk, and suddenly a piano had fallen out of a window and pulverized me.

"Hold on, Doc!" I ordered, trying to recover. "What about the house-tree-person test?"

Dr. Freudenstein dismissed the notion with a wave of the hand. "Diagnosing neuroses and psychoses from the way a person draws a tree. It's hocus-pocus, Counselor."

I stood there, gaping, my mind racing and my heart *ka-thumpety-thumping* in my ears. Louder and louder with each beat. If anyone in the courtroom was talking, I couldn't hear them. I've been sandbagged in court before and never had a physical reaction. Maybe it was the weed. Maybe my damaged brain cells. I couldn't get my mind or my heart to slow down.

I squeezed my eyes shut and saw a long-ago football field. But where? I could feel the cold and see diagonal slashes in the end zone, so it had to be Notre Dame. The Irish offense was in a huddle. And there

I was, number 58, a Penn State linebacker. Jeez, look at me. Young, healthy, strong.

The crowd noise was deafening. I saw the scoreboard. Penn State: 24, Notre Dame: 19. But the Irish had the ball first and goal on our six-yard-line with 1:28 to play in the game. Standing two steps onto the field, his tie flapping in the breeze, Joe Paterno was yelling at me and waving his arms toward the sideline. I shuffled in that direction as Notre Dame quarterback Steve Beuerlein barked the signals. He took the snap and pitched the ball to Tim Brown, a speedster who had already returned a kickoff for a touchdown that had been nullified by a penalty. How fast was he? He could hit the light switch and be in bed before the room got dark.

Brown planted a foot and cut upfield, headed my way. I lumbered toward him, knowing the tight end would be smacking me any second, blocking for the speedster, who would likely scoot around me, high-stepping toward the end zone and victory.

But there was no tight end!

Brown was in my sights. He juked, but I came straight on, ignoring the move, aiming for his belt buckle. I made a solid tackle for a three-yard loss. We would keep Notre Dame out of the end zone and win the game, defeat archrival Pitt the following week, and then upset Miami in the Fiesta Bowl for the national championship. I was one of the big lugs carrying Coach Paterno off the field that night. The high point of my life? Maybe.

Without my play, none of that might have happened. But my tackle was the result of fortuity, not fortitude. Luck, not skill. Notre Dame had only ten men on the field with no tight end to my side. Just how much of life is built on a foundation of chance? Probably far more than the rich and powerful would care to admit.

Where these images came from and why—just now—I had no idea. In the courtroom, I blinked, and the images were gone. I heard someone babbling, but who?

Oh, me!

"Doctor. Doc. Freudman. Schadman. Schadenfreudenstein. When? Why? What do you mean?"

"Mr. Lassiter," the judge said, "perhaps I should intervene here. Dr. Freudenstein, so that it is clear to the jury, are you repudiating state's exhibit seven, your letter to the Calverts?"

"I take back every word after 'Dear Dr. and Mrs. Calvert.' He looked toward the defense table. "I'd like to also apologize to Dr. Calvert for my lack of professionalism."

Calvert nodded his thank-you with a pleasant look.

"May I make a confession?" the shrink said.

"I wish someone would!" I fired back, my head spinning.

"When I realized I was too rash in reaching my conclusions, I asked myself why. And it was so apparent."

"How's that?" Judge Gridley asked.

"Some of the personality characteristics I found in Dr. Calvert—his brusqueness with his intellectual inferiors, his cocksureness, his abrasiveness—well, I recognize the same disagreeable traits in myself. And here's where the self-analysis came in. I realized I created Calvert the boogeyman, Calvert the psychotic, Calvert the enemy, to separate him from me. It's so simple, really."

"How much did he pay you, Dr. Fraud?" I yelled.

"Not a farthing, Mr. Lassiter. And I resent the insinuation."

"What a crock of shit!" I heard myself shout.

In the gallery, gasps, whispers, and laughter.

"Mr. Lassiter!" Judge Gridley raised his voice.

"What a load of horse manure!"

"You're flirting with contempt, sir!"

"Flirting, hell! I'm gonna take contempt to the motel and hump her from here to Hialeah."

"That's it, Mr. Lassiter. You are to remain silent. Do you understand?"

"I made the tackle, Judge. They can't take that away from me."

"What tackle?"

"There was no tight end to block, but that doesn't diminish my play, does it?"

"Mr. Lassiter, that's quite enough. We're going to take a ten-minute recess and calm down."

I pointed a finger at the witness stand, where Dr. Freudenstein looked at me with curiosity and a bit of wonderment, as if he'd found a chimpanzee lounging in his waiting room. "You quack! You fraud! You shamster! Quack! Quack! Quack! If it looks like a duck, swims like a duck, and quacks like a duck, it must be a fucking duck!"

Bang!

The judge's gavel crashed down, the echo a rifle shot.

"You're in direct contempt, Mr. Lassiter. The bailiff will remove the jury. Counsel, in my chambers, now!"

-61-

A Church, Not a Circus

Out of his robes, slouched in his high-backed, deep-cushioned chair, surrounded by unread law books and University of Florida gridiron memorabilia, Judge Gridley fired up a Camel with his Bull Gator cigarette lighter.

"Jake, what in the name of Tim Tebow just happened in there?"

"Don't know, Your Honor. One moment I was there, and then I was someplace else. Another time, another place."

"I got a third place for you. The stockade. Twenty-four hours to be served the day after the trial concludes. Plus, fifteen-hundred-bucks fine. You got anything else to say?"

"I apologize to the court and to Mr. Solomon and Ms. Lord for my conduct."

My two opponents nodded. Victoria looked at me with concern. Solomon, the cynical one of the pair, seemed to be appraising me.

"That's a good start," the judge said.

I wasn't sure what else was required, so I said, "Also to James Madison and Ben Franklin and Thomas Jefferson and all the Founding Fathers. They'd be pissed."

"Okay, that's enough, Jake. Now, tell me the truth. How's your mental state?"

"I can see clearly now, Your Honor."

"Good."

"The rain is gone."

"It didn't rain today, Jake. Wait! Isn't that a song?"

I had the good sense not to start singing. I remembered what Pincher told me. I could use my brain damage, or whatever it was, in court. For sympathy. To excuse bad behavior.

"It might be those experimental drugs messing me up," I said.

Not a total lie. I am taking experimental drugs, though Sour Diesel cannabis isn't one of them.

The judge tapped ashes into a coffee cup on his desk. "Oh my. I'm sorry. Heavy doses?"

"Right now, I couldn't pass the pee test Walmart gives its cashiers."

"Side effects, too, I suppose."

"They shake my nerves and they rattle my brain."

"Jake, are you jerking me off here?"

"Sorry, Your Honor. The drugs fog my mind and release my inhibitions."

Gridley exhaled smoke in the general direction of a poster of Ben Hill Griffin Stadium, packed with Gator lovers. "I hated like hell to hold you in contempt, Jake. But we were in open court with media present. I had no choice."

The judge sounded apologetic. Pincher was right. *I can play the sympathy card. Get a free pass and maybe a fruit basket with helium balloons, too.*

Victoria spoke up. "Your Honor, Jake's health comes first. Perhaps we should adjourn early today."

The judge stubbed out his cigarette in the coffee cup. "Or permanently. After that three-ring fire drill, the court would entertain a motion for mistrial from the defense."

"No way," Solomon said. "Let's try this to a verdict. Our client deserves that."

"My partner's right," Victoria said. "The state shouldn't get two bites at the apple."

"Can't say I blame you," the judge said. "You're way ahead." He turned to me. "Jake, you realize you haven't yet made out a prima facie case? If I were to rule today, the defense would get a directed verdict."

"If last year's Big Ten championship had been over at halftime, Wisconsin would have won. But Penn State took home the trophy."

"I take your point. But I gotta warn you. No more clowns piling out of a little car. My courtroom is not a circus. It's a church, a holy place. Got it?"

"Yes, sir. No elephants crapping in the pews."

"Exactly. Any more theatrics, any more expletives, any more disrespect for the court, it ain't gonna be Thomas Jefferson who's pissed at you."

"Understood, Judge."

"I'll dismiss with prejudice for prosecutorial misconduct and report you to the Florida Bar, experimental drugs or not."

So much for sympathy.

"Message received," I said.

"Well, then, shall we adjourn for the day, as Ms. Lord suggests?"

"Your Honor, I have an out-of-town witness who would love to get home tonight," I said. "Someone who will get the state's case back on track."

The judge looked toward Solomon and Lord. They each shrugged.

"Okay, let's hear what he has to say," the judge said.

"She," I said. "The state calls Ann Cavendish."

-62-

Star Witness

In the corridor, on the way into the courtroom, Pepe Suarez, his face florid, grabbed me. Physically grabbed me, his hand clenching the lapel of my suit coat.

"What the hell's going on?" he demanded.

"Take your hand off me, or I'll break every one of your manicured fingers." The marijuana high had mostly dissipated, and I was back to my normal, combative self.

He loosened his grip.

I smoothed the fabric of my coat and said, "I dunno."

"What the hell kind of answer is that? That jagoff shrink just sunk our case."

"*My* case. And it's not sunk yet."

I saw Solomon and Lord enter the courtroom. Waiting by the door were Detective Barrios and Ann Cavendish. The old cop wasn't letting our star witness out of his sight, not after what happened to Billy Burnside.

"I assume Calvert got to Freudenstein," I said. "Paid him off. Or threatened to sue him or go after his license."

"What's your strategy now, Lassiter?"

"Now? Now, I'm gonna destroy Clark Gordon Calvert. Ruin his reputation in twenty minutes. Make it easy for the jury to believe he could kill. Now, I'm gonna take my last best shot at winning the damn case."

***

Ann Cavendish wore a tailored navy-blue two-button jacket over a white blouse. Light-gray trousers. Sensible black pumps. An overall impression of a woman dressed for professional work. Her dark hair came to her shoulders in waves.

Her lower lip quivered as she swore to tell the truth, the whole truth, and nothing but the truth. Her voice trembled just saying her name and occupation.

She was nervous.

I gave her a warm smile and said gently, "I know this isn't easy for you, Ms. Cavendish."

"It's not. It's really not."

"I admire your courage."

Victoria was on her feet. "Really? Your Honor . . ."

"Mr. Lassiter. Please just ask questions and refrain from editorial comments."

"Of course, Your Honor," I said. "Ms. Cavendish, do you know the defendant, Clark Gordon Calvert?"

I pointed toward the defense table. Calvert was in whispered conversation with Solomon, but at the mention of his name, he swung toward the witness stand and stared at Ann Cavendish with those deep, dark eyes. She had difficulty even looking in that direction.

For several seconds, she neither moved her head nor answered.

"Ms. Cavendish," I said.

Finally, she glanced at Calvert. "Yes, I know him. That is, I knew him. In Boston."

As I had promised Pepe Suarez, it took about twenty minutes to tell the tale. Midwestern upbringing. Moved to Chicago, then Boston in early 2005. Worked as a medical sales rep, pitching hip- and knee-replacement gear to hospitals and orthopedic-surgery groups. Called on the defendant, who asked her out. First date, no problem, second date, no problem. Third date, she went to his apartment.

"What happened then?" I asked.

"We had some wine. Red, I believe."

"Then what?"

"He played the piano. Something classical. He's very good. I was impressed. I'd never met anyone quite like him. Accomplished in so many fields."

"What happened next?"

"We sat on the sofa and . . ."

"Yes?"

Her face took on a pinkish tone. "We made out. Kissed. He groped me a little bit, not offensively or anything. I pushed his hand away, and he stopped. We kissed some more, and he put one hand on my neck, just brushing the skin. But then he squeezed my neck with one hand. It wasn't so much painful as frightening. With the other hand, he gripped both my wrists so I couldn't move. He's incredibly strong. There was nothing I could do. Nothing!"

She stopped. Her eyes welled, and then tears flowed. "I'm sorry. I'm sorry."

"That's all right," the judge said. "Would you like a brief recess, Ms. Cavendish?"

She shook her head. "No, sir. I'd like to get this over with."

I took her through the rest of it quickly. She had passed out. When she came to, she was in his bed, naked, and he was inside her. She tried to fight him off then but couldn't. After he ejaculated, letting out a roar, he let her up. She gathered her clothes and fled into the night. The next day, her neck was bruised. She wore a turtleneck to work. Calvert called her, but she wouldn't answer. She spotted his car outside her apartment. She lived in fear of him, couldn't sleep, couldn't eat.

No, she didn't go to the hospital. Didn't call the police. Didn't even tell her friends.

"All the clichés are true," she said. "I was so ashamed. I blamed myself."

She fell into a deep depression. Missed work, bungled sales reports. She was fired and moved to Atlanta, vowing never to return to Boston.

"Thank you, Ms. Cavendish. On behalf of the state of Florida, thank you."

The jurors' eyes were all fixed on the witness, who had been both credible and an object of pathos. Our bleeding had been stopped, Ann Cavendish our tourniquet. And suddenly, our theory of the vicious sociopath hiding in surgeon's scrubs did not seem so far-fetched.

"Your witness," I said to Solomon and Lord.

Ann Cavendish exhaled a sigh, apparently grateful her ordeal was over, perhaps not realizing that it was just beginning.

-63-

Shock and Awe

Victoria Lord smiled at Ann Cavendish. If she smiled at me like that, I'd check for bruises. As Victoria approached the lectern, it occurred to me that the two women had something in common. They'd both slept with Calvert. But the similarities ended there. Victoria considered Calvert brilliant and, more important, innocent. Ann feared Calvert as a scheming rapist.

"Good afternoon, Ms. Cavendish," Victoria said.

The witness nodded her hello.

"Or should I say Ms. Smith?"

Ann Cavendish's mouth dropped open, but no words came out.

"You have been known as Jane Smith, have you not?"

"Yes . . . I . . . was . . . I was born with that name. I lawfully changed it."

My witness was rattled already. Her face seemed frozen, a stroke victim. We'd gone over this. I'd prepared her. A routine records search in Atlanta would have turned up the name change. No big deal.

"Why did you change your name?"

"To make sure your client couldn't find me."

"Is that true? Were you hiding from him? Or from creditors?"

Again, Ann Cavendish started to answer. His lips moved, but no words came out. Her eyes were not so much deer-in-the-headlights as deer-smashed-through-the-windshield.

"Did you understand the question?" Victoria pressed her.

"Objection," I sang out, trying to buy time for my jittery witness. "Counsel is badgering the witness."

The judge looked at me over his spectacles. "Mr. Lassiter, there's no such objection known to the rules of evidence."

"I know that, Your Honor. But I've seen it on *Law & Order*, so I thought I'd give it a whirl."

"Denied. The witness may answer."

Still, Ann Cavendish, aka Jane Smith, didn't say a word. Victoria shot me a sideways glance with just a hint of a smile. She could risk that, as all the jurors' eyes were fixed on my mute and paralyzed witness. I'd taught Victoria to cross-examine my way. Shock and awe. Sure, the book on cross-examination says to tread carefully and deliberately. Feign friendliness. Lead the witness down the path. Pin the witness down to one story. Set a trap and lower the boom.

Maybe I'm just impatient, but I like to score with the first punch. I played football in the days when you could horse-collar the runner, head-slap an offensive lineman, and clothesline the receiver who dared to run a slant. I liked to do all that, starting with a late and vicious hit on whatever speed demon chose to return the opening kickoff.

Yeah, I get the irony. I'm a guy who might have had his bell rung too many times, and here I'm singing about the joy of smashing an opponent's helmet with my padded forearm. Life is like that. We hold beliefs and take actions that are self-defeating.

Finally, the witness said, "I didn't have to hide from creditors. I declared bankruptcy. Lawfully."

"Lawfully. Just as you changed your name?" There was just a hint of sarcasm in Victoria's voice. Perhaps she picked that up from Solomon. I try to avoid it, often unsuccessfully.

"Yes, in the courts."

"When did you declare bankruptcy?"

"Eleven or twelve years ago."

"Hmm. Strange." Victoria pretended to be puzzled. "Where did you file your bankruptcy?"

"In court."

"Of course, but where?"

Victoria plucked a blue-backed legal document from her file. It could have been the bankruptcy petition or just a prop. The lawyer's trick of making the witness worry about what you're holding. I've done it with grocery lists.

"I think it might have been Chicago," the witness said.

Victoria wrinkled her lovely brow. "But weren't you living in Boston then? Isn't that when you dated Dr. Calvert, summer of 2005?"

Ann Cavendish's eyes darted to me for help. I had none. If you were scoring the fight at home, Victoria was ahead on points. The witness had not admitted anything of substance, but she seemed unnerved by the geography of her life. Chicago, Boston, Atlanta. When and where? This should be so simple. What was the problem?

"Yes, 2005, that's when he raped me. In Boston. That's where . . ." Her voice trailed off.

"Let's talk about Boston," Victoria said in an ominous tone. "You stated that Dr. Calvert had a condominium."

"Yes, a two bedroom, two bath. Stainless-steel appliances in the kitchen."

Victoria cocked her head and studied the witness. Yeah, it was an odd answer, though I couldn't quite say why.

"Where was Dr. Calvert's condo located?"

"In Allston. On Beacon." She fired off the answers quickly. "A red-brick building. Ten or twelve stories. His condo was on the top floor. Beautiful kitchen with stainless-steel appliances."

Repeating herself like a deranged android on *Westworld*.

Victoria smiled placidly at the witness but didn't ask a question.

She didn't have to. Ann Cavendish was now a motormouth. "The condo was very close to St. Elizabeth's, where Dr. Calvert was on staff. I suppose that's why he bought there. For the convenience."

And those stainless-steel appliances, I thought.

Victoria let the witness squirm in the silence for a few seconds. "Very good, Ms. Cavendish. A-plus answering questions I haven't asked."

I could have objected. Victoria was commenting on the witness's answer, but any objection would just have drawn attention to what was becoming obvious. Ann Cavendish was spitting out answers as if she had memorized them. Back in the war room, she had been relaxed and confident and credible. Now, under Victoria's attack, she was unraveling.

It started then, the noise in my skull. Slowly at first, a set of keys rattling inside the drum of a clothes dryer as it spun endless circles.

I noticed the courtroom door swing open. State Attorney Pincher walked in and resumed the position he had staked out earlier. Standing by the door, arms crossed. In the event of fire, earthquake, or legal disaster, he would be the first one out.

"And where did you live in summer 2005, Ms. Cavendish?" Victoria asked.

"I rented a one-bedroom apartment in Chestnut Hill off Boylston."

"Is that in Chicago?"

"No. No. Boylston is in Boston. I lived in Boston."

Again, Victoria looked puzzled. But I knew she was as confused as a safecracker who's got the combination in her vest pocket. She looked down at the blue-backed legal document she'd been holding and said, "In July 2005, still known as Jane W. Smith, you filed for bankruptcy in Chicago, swearing you were a resident of Cook County, Illinois, and that you were an actress, then unemployed, with substantial credit card debt. You are that Jane W. Smith, correct?"

Another long pause. *Easy question,* I thought. The jurors doubtless thought the same.

"Yes, but there may be a time mix-up. Date mix-up. Chicago. Boston. Here. There. It happens. When I met Dr. Calvert, I was a sales rep for surgical prostheses. Mostly hip for partial or total arthroplasty. Some cemented, some cementless. Cobalt chromium and titanium cobalt components. Knee prostheses, too."

The words were pouring out now. She seemed to believe that if she kept talking, she could halt the mortar barrage of damning questions. Inside my head, the dryer with the rattling keys had been replaced. Now, a Boeing 777 had fired up its giant engines, a discordant whine that quickly became a mechanical roar.

"You are an actress, are you not, Ms. Cavendish?"

"Part-time, yes. It's difficult to make a living at it."

"You have appeared in featured roles in regional theater, correct?"

"A few."

"A production of *The Belle of Amherst* in Macon, Georgia, correct?"

"Yes."

I thought I could see the light at the end of the tunnel, and unfortunately, it was an oncoming train. Solomon and Lord had apparently done more research into my witness's past than I had. But then, that was George Barrios's job. He was good, but aging. The same could be said of me. This was George's last case. Could it be mine, too?

"How many actors in that play?" Victoria asked. I could barely hear her over the jetliner inside my brain.

For the first time, Ann Cavendish smiled, albeit ruefully. "Just one. Me."

"You played the poet Emily Dickinson, and you had to memorize and recite several of her lengthy poems."

"Yes, I did."

"As well as all the rest of her dialogue?"

"It's a very talky play. That's all there is."

293

PAUL LEVINE

"And you also portrayed her sister, her brother, her father, her mentor, and others?"

"Fourteen characters in all," Ann Cavendish said.

"Wow, I could never do that," Victoria said, all friendly now.

Oh, you're good, Victoria. If you weren't whupping my ass, I'd take a moment to feel proud.

"It's one of the challenges of the stage," Ann Cavendish said.

"A courtroom is a little like a stage, a trial a little like a play, don't you think?"

"I guess."

"And 'all the world's a stage and all the men and women merely players. They have their exits and their entrances.' Would you agree?"

There was no more fear in Ann Cavendish's eyes. "That's from *As You Like It*," she said. "At a summer-stock production in Asheville, I played Rosalind."

"The spirited and clever young woman who disguises herself as a man. Shakespeare knew something about characters wearing masks, didn't he, Ms. Cavendish?"

The witness's head dropped just a bit, and she said softly, "I guess all of us wear masks, some more than others."

"Back to my earlier question," Victoria said. "Do you know the biggest difference between a play and a courtroom?"

"This is real," Ann Cavendish said.

Victoria nodded agreeably. "Yes, there's that. But also, onstage, if someone asks you a question, you know the answer. Everything is scripted, correct?"

"Yes, of course."

"If you tell a lie, it's only because the playwright instructed you to."

"I never thought of it that way, but yes."

"You don't have to answer truthfully, except to be true to the script. Isn't that right?"

"Yes."

"But here, what's the first thing you did when you walked in the courtroom today?"

Ann Cavendish looked toward me, then past me. I followed her gaze. Sitting in the front row of the gallery were Pepe Suarez and his goon, J. T. Wetherall. Was she looking at them? They were whispering to each other, an angry look scorching Suarez's face.

"I took an oath," the witness said.

"Not to recite someone else's story but your own?"

"Yes."

"The whole truth and nothing but the truth?"

"Yes."

"Did you honor your oath today?"

Ann Cavendish didn't answer. The business of swearing an oath always puzzled me. Honest people don't need to put their hands on a Bible to tell the truth, and dishonest people could swear on their mothers' lives and still tell whoppers.

With her question still pending, Victoria asked another. "Do you know what the penalty for perjury is?" She spoke so softly and gently that the words did not seem to be a threat so much as a clergyman's angst-ridden warning of damnation. Still, I couldn't sit here like a potted plant.

"Objection, argumentative," I said in measured tones.

"Sustained. Ms. Lord, let's confine your questioning to probative matters."

"Yes, Your Honor," Victoria said. "May I approach the witness?"

"Do you wish to show her a document?"

"No, sir. I just want to have a conversation with her. But not from behind a lectern. Just two women talking. I think the conversation might be extremely probative."

"Mr. Lassiter?" the judge said.

I shrugged. "Converse away, Ms. Lord."

PAUL LEVINE

Victoria left her file on the lectern. She moved to the corner of the witness stand nearest the jury box. Jurors would have a view of the back of her head while Ann Cavendish had to look straight at them to answer the questions.

With her elbow on the railing of the witness stand, her posture relaxed, Victoria spoke in a conversational tone. "Should we start over, Ms. Cavendish?"

"What do you mean?"

"Would you like to recant anything you've said today?"

The witness looked at me. What could I do? She's the one who built a castle out of sand. There was no way I could stop the incoming tide.

At last she said, "I don't know what to do."

"Let me help you out." Victoria had dropped her courtroom voice. Now she spoke in a tone you'd use to give advice to a troubled friend. Girlfriend to girlfriend. "You never lived in Boston, did you?"

Tears welled in Ann Cavendish's eyes. Real tears. Not stage tears.

"No," she whispered. "I never lived there."

"And you never dated Clark Calvert?"

"I did not." Sobbing now.

"And therefore he never choked you?"

"He never did."

"And obviously, he did not rape you?"

"That's correct. I'm sorry."

What the hell! What the hell, Jane Smith, Ann Cavendish, the Belle of Bullshit?

My mind wandered. Years ago, I was offered a job coaching prep-school football in Vermont. Autumn leaves. Alumni picnics. Skinny rich kids tossing a ball. Why the hell didn't I take the job?

"Thank you, Ms. Cavendish." Victoria spoke softly, compassionately. She had ripped my case to shreds, but oh so elegantly that I could not help but admire the work.

I respect artistry, even when I'm the piece of stone being sculpted.

"I must ask you one more question," Victoria said. "If I don't, Judge Gridley surely will."

Ann Cavendish nodded. Victoria had become her friend, guiding her through these alligator-infested waters.

"How did you come to be in this courtroom today?"

The witness looked at me, and a bolt of fear shot up my spine.

I didn't bribe you. Or if I did, I don't remember. No. No. I didn't. You were a name on a slip of paper. I was suckered.

Don't lie! Not now.

Her head swiveled past me toward the gallery. Her eyes stopped at the first row where Pepe Suarez and J. T. Wetherall squirmed in their seats, or so it seemed to me.

"That man," Ann Cavendish said. "The large man with the bad teeth."

J. T. Wetherall. Dirty cop turned bagman.

"He came to see me at a rehearsal in Atlanta," she continued. "Said he was a private investigator. He had all these facts about Dr. Calvert. Where he lived in Boston, where he worked, the bad things he'd done. He told me Calvert had killed his wife. I'd be doing a public service. All I had to do was be an actress in court. And he paid me thirty thousand dollars in cash."

A wave of murmurs swept over the courtroom like a thirty-foot tsunami striking the beach. Tears spilling, Ann Cavendish turned to the judge and said, "I'm sorry. I'm so sorry."

Judge Gridley looked toward Orville Limegrover, his uniformed bailiff, who was sleeping peacefully in his chair. "Orville! Up and at 'em. Remove the jury!" Limegrover stirred and rounded up the jurors, guiding them back into their little room.

"Now let's see who's gonna be ejected and who's gonna stay in the game," the judge said.

I turned toward the gallery, spotted Pincher still standing by the door. "C'mon down, Sugar Ray. Suit up and take over! The quarterback job is yours."

Pincher didn't move.

"It doesn't work that way, Mr. Lassiter," Judge Gridley said. "May I assume you were not behind the hiring of this perjurious witness?"

"You assume correctly, Judge. I'd have hired a better actress."

I considered what to do next. There was nothing to lose. I was inside a barrel, hurtling down the river, about to go over Niagara Falls. Meanwhile, the jet engines inside my head made the Falls seem like a whispering stream.

I walked slowly toward the swinging gate that separated the gallery from the well of the courtroom. In the first row, Suarez and Wetherall saw me coming. They each got to their feet and waited. Neither knew who I was going to slug first.

-64-

Disorder in the Court

I didn't shove the swinging gate open. I kicked it like a cop bursting through the flimsy door of a cheap motel. The gate had a rusty hinge. It had been opened countless times by sleazy lawyers, lying witnesses, and the occasional innocent defendant. This time, the hinge tore out of the wood, and the door smacked J. T. Wetherall in both knees with a satisfying *cra-ck*.

Wetherall reflexively bent forward, both hands dropping toward his knees. It wasn't fair. I had a clean shot and took it. A left uppercut that had a lot of hip in it. I hit him squarely on the nose, and I could hear the cartilage pop, even over the ferocious roar in my brain. Both his hands shot to his broken nose, which spurted blood. I curled a short right hook into his solar plexus. He exhaled a loud *oomph* and toppled into his seat.

Next to him, his boss, Pepe Suarez, wanted no part of me. He was crawling over his seat, trying to get into the second row. I grabbed the back of his shirt collar and whipped him backward, whiplashing his neck.

Judge Gridley didn't throw a flag, didn't call horse-collaring. He was, however, banging his gavel, shouting, "Order! Order! Bailiff, restore order!"

Limegrover, a retired parking-lot security guard, stood in the center aisle of the gallery, attempting to get my attention by waving at me and shouting, "Jake, please! Please!"

I still had Suarez by the scruff of his neck and shouted at him. "You bastard! You can pay off all the politicians you like, but you can't buy the justice system."

The newsmen and newswomen surrounded me. The television camera at the end of the front row had swung around, and I was about three feet from the lens. My close-up, ready or not.

Suarez tried to say something, but I had balled his shirt collar into my fist, and he was choking on his words. "Flu-ck you, Lash-i-ter."

"Let him go, Jake!"

I turned. Ray Pincher stood in the aisle, glaring at me. "Let him go," he repeated. "We need to talk. In private."

Now the reporters began firing questions.

"Talk about what?"

"Is this a conspiracy?"

"Are you running for governor, Mr. Pincher?"

I ignored them all and focused on Pincher. "Did you know about this, Ray? Were you part of this?"

"Shut your stupid lawyer mouth. You know better than that."

I pushed Suarez to the floor. "You're going to jail, shitbird!" I turned my attention back to the State Attorney. "Ray, you gonna captain this sinking ship yourself or give the wheel to another sucker?"

"I'll tell you one last time, Jake. Shut up. Let's go talk to the judge in chambers."

I could barely hear him over the jet engines.

"Mr. Lassiter!" the judge called out. "Kindly resume your position at the prosecution table so that I may resolve this matter and schedule further proceedings in accordance with what just occurred."

"Whatever you do is fine with me, Judge. I'm retiring."

"Whoa, Nellie!" Judge Gridley called out. "You can't just hang up your jock in the middle of the game. It isn't done."

"Going home now, Judge. It's been a pleasure. Seriously. You're fair and honest, and I apologize for this goat fuck. Maybe I should have seen this coming, but I didn't. Maybe this is the way I find out that I just don't have it anymore."

I took a step toward the aisle, and Pincher blocked my path. "You're embarrassing me, Jake."

"Me? What about your buddy there?" I gestured toward Suarez, who had crawled into a chair in the second row and straightened his collar, trying to regain some semblance of self-respect.

"Get back to your table and play this out. That's an order."

I laughed. "Go screw yourself, Ray. That's a suggestion."

Around us, cameras clicked and reporters buzzed. Pincher's chances of being our next governor were somewhere between laughable and nil.

"I don't know if you took part in the bribery and perjury, Ray," I said. "But that doesn't mean you're clean. You walk so close to the line, your shadow's in foul territory." I turned to the reporters. "Sugar Ray Pincher's campaign slogan is 'Elect a Fighter.' From his Golden Glove days. Sounds better than 'Elect a Crook.' From his three terms in office."

I saw a blur from the corner of my eye. In the next trillionth of a second, I realized it was Pincher's fist. Twenty years ago, my fast-twitch muscle fibers would have reacted with lightning speed. I would have bobbed or weaved or ducked. Maybe blocked the punch. But now my brain sent smoke signals in slow motion to my muscles.

As I would later learn from endless television news replays, it was a left hook. A gorgeous, well-timed, powerful blow. Pincher was on his toes, his torso twisted slightly to the left, his left arm cocked at ninety degrees. He pivoted on his left foot, his body unwinding with startling speed. Head down and chin still, he uncorked the punch, which landed like a sledgehammer on the point of my chin.

I was aware of stumbling backward, toppling ass-over-elbows across the bar and into the well of the courtroom, my feet comically in the air over my head. As I fell, I heard music. A drum-and-bugle corps banging away with a military march. Horns blaring, cannons firing, thunder echoing.

And then darkness fell.

-65-

Cosmic Questions

No one likes hospitals.

The smell. The noise. The fear.

Even if I'm visiting, I'm aware that one day I'll be the one in the bed. Likely, it will be where I draw my last breath, hooked to tubes, monitors flashing, buzzers singing the tune of my last exit from Shakespeare's stage.

Today, I was not visiting.

I was the occupant of a dandy room at Baptist Hospital, complete with a peaceful view of the lake and its waterbirds. I was pondering my life. How much sand was left in the hourglass?

I asked myself cosmic questions about the meaning of it all. We know that nearly fourteen billion years ago, all matter and energy in the universe was compacted into an infinitely dense mass so tiny as to be invisible. Then *whoosh*, the Big Bang, the galaxies, the stars, the planets, and eventually the cosmically laughable and insignificant human race. Which makes me—makes all of us—as trivial as a speck of asteroid dust.

My thoughts were interrupted by voices in my room. They sounded worried.

I say "sounded" because I kept my eyes closed, pretending to be asleep, so I could hear them talk among themselves.

"The last thing Jake needed was another concussion," Melissa said.

"Will this worsen his condition?" Victoria asked.

"She means, will it kill him quicker," Solomon added, never one to add sugar to his coffee.

"It won't help," Melissa said, "but I'm not sure that a new concussion will have any immediate impact. My concerns are the tau proteins already formed."

"Bummer," Solomon said.

"Jake told us about the experimental treatments. Is he responding?" Victoria said.

Silence. C'mon, Melissa. I just dropped in to see what condition my condition was in.

"There is a new report," Melissa said in her neutral doctorly tone. "But I think I need to tell Jake first."

Maybe it's my imagination, but she sounds a little grim.

I cracked my eyes open just enough to see Solomon reaching for a box of chocolates. Presumably, *my* chocolates. The box was on a table with several flower arrangements, a bottle of Perrier-Jouët, and a few fruit baskets, each with a bottle of wine.

"I hope Jake doesn't turn into a drooling idiot or die before the wedding," Solomon continued. "What will I do for a best man?"

"Rent one!" I exploded.

"It lives." Solomon burst into laughter. "I knew you were awake, you big galoot. I was punking you."

Melissa, in a white lab coat, her russet hair pulled back, came to my bedside and stroked my cheek. I hoped she didn't do that with every patient. "How do you feel, Jake?"

"Not terrible, surprisingly." That was true. Okay, a penny-ante headache for a guy who's used to high-stakes pain. And my vision was in soft focus, like morning fog on the California coast. "Melissa, why am I here?"

"Do you remember Ray Pincher striking you?"

"Pincher? I thought I'd stepped in front of a bus."

"You were unconscious. Concussion protocol for someone with your condition requires forty-eight hours observation."

"Your condition?" Brain damage to some undefinable degree. A route that cannot be mapped like a ship on the high seas . . . unless it's the Titanic.

"Only forty-eight hours?" I took her hand. "I'll stay longer if you're gonna be here."

Melissa leaned over and kissed me on the lips.

"Oh, get a room, you two!" Solomon was munching on chocolate-covered nuts.

"This *is* our room. And stay out of my chocolates, unless you gave them to me."

Victoria said, "They're from Pincher."

"What about the rest of the stuff? I didn't know I had that many friends."

"You don't!" Solomon said. "Everything is from Pincher."

"He's very contrite," Victoria added. "He wants to apologize in person."

"I'd like to go four rounds in the ring with him. He can apologize then."

"No, Jake!" Melissa pointed an index finger at me. "No boxing. No contact sports of any kind."

"*Any* kind?" I gave her my crooked smile.

"There he goes again," Solomon said. "Getting KO'd make you horny, pal?"

"Solomon, why don't you go downstairs and donate blood?"

On the loudspeaker, a Dr. Prystowsky and a Dr. Emery were being summoned to ICU. *There are lots of patients,* I reminded myself, *in far worse condition than yours truly.*

"We thought you might want to know what happened in court after you checked out," Solomon said.

Court! State vs. Calvert. I had nearly forgotten.

"I'm a little fuzzy. Did I get held in contempt?"

"Couple of times. But Judge Gridley has bigger catfish to fry. He dismissed the case against Calvert."

"Mistrial, you mean?"

"Nope. Dismissal with prejudice for prosecutorial misconduct."

A sound came from my throat—*aargh*—like a death rattle.

"Not to worry, Jake," Solomon said. "The witness's perjury is imputed to the state, but not to you personally. After you took a nap, the judge questioned Cavendish, who said Wetherall ordered her not to mention anything to you about the falsity of her testimony because you wouldn't play along. She saved your ass, buddy."

"What's going to happen to her?"

"Pincher's giving her immunity. She's flipping on Wetherall, who's almost certain to flip on Suarez."

"No governor's mansion for Ray Pincher. He must be pissed."

"Not at all," Victoria said. "He's gonna prosecute Suarez himself. Thinks taking on his biggest financial backer will get him votes. 'Sugar Ray Can't Be Bought' is his new campaign slogan."

"And your client?"

"Says he's going to take some time off. Charitable work in a third-world country."

"Is he an innocent man who was exonerated? Or a guilty man who got away with murder?" I asked.

"Above my pay grade, pal," Solomon said. "Vic says he's innocent. Me? I don't know."

"Your client paid off Freudenstein to tank my case."

Solomon shrugged. "Probably. But that doesn't mean he's guilty."

"What about the missing Billy Burnside? Did Calvert get to him, too?"

"He swears he didn't, but who knows? You know what I tell clients, Jake?"

"Don't write a check that bounces."

"I tell them, 'Lie to your spouse. Lie to your priest. Lie to the IRS. But always tell your lawyer the truth.' Not that it does any good. Calvert? Your guess is as good as mine."

"I think I need some of that booze," I told my pals, gesturing toward the gifts.

"You need rest," Melissa said.

On cue, Solomon and Victoria said their good-byes and reminded me not to be late for their wedding rehearsal dinner on Friday night.

When they were gone, Melissa said, "They love you. You know that, right?"

"Aw, they're good kids. Gonna be great lawyers when they grow up."

On the loudspeaker, there was a Code Blue on the second floor. Someone in dire need of resuscitation. Another reminder of the fragility of life and the need to be thankful for every breath we take.

"So what's new? With my brain?"

"You were listening, weren't you?"

"If your medical advice is not to buy any green bananas, I'd like to hear it."

Melissa sat on the edge of my bed and took my hand. "Actually, your newest MRI is quite interesting. It's the first one since we started you on the new recipe."

"More gin, less vermouth."

"I don't want to oversell this, Jake, but we're seeing something remarkable. The strands of misshapen tau proteins are shrinking. Whether they'll disappear or return and eventually harden into tangles, we don't know. We'll monitor further changes, but for now, Infusion X-7 is our best chance yet for defeating the disease before it fully takes hold."

"Wow!"

"Yes, wow."

I spent a quiet moment pondering where I'd been, where I am, where I might be going. So much to ponder.

"What are you thinking about, Jake?"

I straightened to a sitting position. "This hand I've been dealt . . ."

"Yes?"

"It's no bum deal. It's a great deal! A great life!"

"I'm so happy to hear you say that," Melissa said.

"Lately, I've been thinking about the big picture, trying to figure what's important in life."

"Which is . . . ?"

"Us, of course. I've been reluctant to move forward with you. Not because of any doubts or reservations about us, but because, well, of my condition."

"I know that, Jake. We've discussed this. I know you're concerned about me, should anything happen to you."

"Exactly. I don't want you to be a young widow."

She smiled sadly at that bittersweet notion. Love, marriage, death.

"But lying in a hospital bed, I was thinking. We're all dying. The patients. The doctors. The nurses. The visitors. The cafeteria workers. Everybody. It's a question of when, not if. So isn't the answer to the great human dilemma that we have to make the most of every day, of every minute, of every breath, of every step we take?"

She didn't answer, unless a kiss on the lips is an answer. I closed my eyes and kissed her back. In my mind, I saw a sailboat on smooth seas with a steady breeze on a spring day. There we were, the two of us, the sail crackling in the wind. I saw happiness on earth, joy in the quotidian moments with the woman I loved.

So just say it!

When our lips parted, I said, "I love you, Melissa."

"I love you, too, Jake."

"Then, why don't we . . . I mean, will you . . ."

"Go on, Jake."

"Melissa, will you marry me?"

-66-

The Isles of Hidden Loot

Tomorrow night we will gather in a big white tent on the grounds of Vizcaya Gardens. Potted birds-of-paradise will line the interior. There will be an ice sculpture of Lady Justice, and the proceedings will be officiated by both a rabbi and a Protestant minister. Victoria will wear white and look regal. Solomon will be nervous and gabby.

Tonight, at the rehearsal dinner, Melissa will wear a rather daring cobalt-blue off-the-shoulder cocktail dress with tiered ruffles front and back. Her shoes will be white Manolo Blahnik satin pumps with some crystal beaded doodads on the front. The four-inch heels could be used as a deadly weapon.

Oh, I left something out.

Melissa said yes!

Actually, she said, "Hell yes!"

Tonight she'd be wearing her new engagement ring. Fernando, at Richard's Gems and Jewelry downtown, called it a "French set band with surprise diamonds." My own description would be shiny and expensive. We hadn't told Solomon and Lord about our engagement. Later, after stone crabs and Key lime pie in the private dining room at Joe's on South Beach, we'll deliver the news.

Call it a reenactment. In the hospital room, I didn't have a ring. And my presentation, frankly, was pretty amateur. Tonight I'll drop to one knee like a quarterback in the victory formation and do everything again, this time with the ring. Hopefully, Melissa will give the same answer.

At the moment, she was in the shower, and I was practicing my toasts in the living room. Wedding toasts are dicey. One good rule is not to mention the bride's or groom's earlier lovers or recent debauchery. No problem there. Solomon and Lord had met cute, if that's what you call it when a cockatoo craps on a woman's business suit. It was a case involving bird smuggling, with Solomon defending and Lord prosecuting during her brief stint in the State Attorney's office. Solomon insisted on calling a bird to testify. Lord lost her cool, and the rest is an often-told tale of bird poop, contempt, and Solomon falling hard for his opponent.

"Victoria, you had Steve the second you told him to get lost," I planned to say.

I was rehearsing when I heard a pounding on my front door. I opened it to find Ray Pincher, briefcase in hand.

"How you feeling, Jake?"

I'm so damn tired of that question.

"Great, Ray. You have more champagne and pistachios for me?"

He walked inside, eyeing me suspiciously, as if I might be hiding a baseball bat behind my back. "Have you forgiven me, Jake?"

"I'm not sure."

"I didn't want to hit you. It was Suarez I was furious with. He rigged the system. But you were standing there, wreaking havoc in the courtroom, talking trash about me, and I just lost it."

"Okay. If that's yet another apology, I accept. Let's move on."

"Gonna offer me a drink?"

We moved into the kitchen. I poured a generous Jack Daniel's on ice for Pincher and a thimble for me so I could deliver my toast while sober.

"I got a call from a friend at Homeland Security," Pincher said. "Some bells started ringing in their money-laundering division. Suspicious bank wire transfers. He looked into it, saw the party involved, and thought I might be interested. Sent me this."

Pincher opened his briefcase, pulled out a laptop, and clicked on a video. Security footage. A bank-teller window. A petite young woman in big sunglasses stood at the window, filling out a form. Her dark hair fell to her shoulders. A man in a polo shirt was standing next to the woman, but his face wasn't visible. The teller's right hand pointed to one side, and the woman looked in that direction.

"The teller is saying that a bank officer will be needed to complete the transaction. Plus, they'll need to fingerprint the woman to confirm her identity."

"So?"

"Don't you recognize the woman?"

Pincher froze the screen.

"She's got a nice suntan and a lot of hair." I looked closer.

A luxurious pelt and a smooth, tan hide.

That's what Calvert said in appraising his wife's looks.

"Is that Sofia Calvert?"

"Bingo!"

"She's alive."

"And rich. This was taken three days ago, her thirtieth birthday."

"The day her spendthrift trust ripened. Is that the bank in the Caymans where Pepe stashed the money?"

"You got it. Forty million bucks, most of which is Pepe's, if you ignore the fact he's hiding it from the IRS."

"Did she get the dough?"

"The whole forty mil."

I let out a long, low whistle. "Jeez . . ."

"Yeah," Pincher said. "Ain't it something?"

I heard the shower turn off in the bathroom. Melissa would be ready in fifteen minutes. Fully dressed, with makeup and jewelry on. No muss, no fuss. I liked that—and everything else—about her.

"Did your friend at Homeland Security trace the money she withdrew?" I asked.

"Tried. It was wired from the Cayman Islands to a bank on the Isle of Man, and from there to a bank on the Cook Islands. After that, he doesn't know. Cook Islands won't cooperate with our government."

"All those islands. Why not just call them the Isles of Hidden Loot? As for Pepe Suarez, serves the bastard right."

"Jake, you always say that rough justice is better than none."

"This is more like poetic justice, Ray."

"You won't get an argument from me. Pepe was about to file a petition in the Cayman courts to have Sofia declared dead so the money would revert to him. Now he doesn't get a buck, and I'll put his ass in jail."

I thought about it. "Sofia planned all of this. Is that what you're saying?"

Pincher shrugged. "What do you think?"

"It's possible. She was scared her father was gonna have Wetherall snatch her if she didn't give him his money. Maybe kill her. My guess is she taunted Calvert into choking her. Sets up the argument and her disappearance. She really did storm out of the house that morning. Calvert really did go to Frostproof looking for her. Unbeknownst to him, she'd enlisted Freudenstein and Burnside to frame him for murder. My theory, anyway."

"Kill two birds. Father and husband."

"And give herself time to reach her birthday and grab the money. Her father, thinking she was dead, gave her breathing room."

"By the way, Jake, that cat of Sofia's that Calvert strangled."

"Yeah. Escapar."

"For what it's worth, in Spanish, *escapar* means 'escape.'"

312

I reached for the Jack Daniel's. "I need another drink.",

"Me, too."

I poured, and we sat in silence a moment.

From the bedroom, I heard Melissa's sweet voice. "I'll be ready in a couple minutes, darling."

"Take your time, hon. Ray and I are out here drinking whiskey and solving mysteries."

I sipped and said, "Where do you suppose Sofia is?"

Pincher thought about it a moment. "I'm guessing with Mr. Polo Shirt in the video. Unfortunately, his face doesn't show up on any of the footage, so we don't have an ID."

"You don't need his face. You've got his arms."

Pincher gave me a look.

"His right forearm is heavily muscled," I said, "much larger than his left. What you've got there, Ray, is a tennis pro."

-67-
Body Heat

Raiatea Island, French Polynesia . . .

The beach was white crystalline sugar. The water was turquoise, the waves quiet whispers. The sun bore down, bounced off the sand, and baked the air.

"It's hot," Billy Burnside said.

"Yes," Sofia Calvert said. "Very hot."

Sofia wore a white thong and was topless, her small breasts golden from weeks in the sun. He wore Speedos, sweat trickling down his chest. The two lovers were stretched out on cushioned chaises, holding hands across the small divide. A uniformed servant delivered icy drinks. No fruity cocktails or coconuts filled with rum for them. Gin and tonics, icy steel in the throat, a quick buzz in the brain. It was only 11:00 a.m.

Soon it would be time for lunch. *The biggest issue of the day,* Sofia thought. Whether to have Papeete Tahitian prawns or oka popo raw-fish stew. And whether to dine on the beach or the outdoor pavilion adjacent to the kitchen. She would have to inform the cook soon. *So many decisions,* she thought, smiling to herself.

Her house was separated from the beach by only blooming bougain-villea—a riot of pinks, purples, and yellows. The house was a sprawling affair, seven separate high-roofed tropical pavilions. Two on each end were open-air, no walls at all. The five enclosed pavilions were linked by stone paths and flanked by outdoor gardens with waterfalls and stone sculptures of Polynesian gods. Inside, the walls were warm woods and the floors brushed travertine marble, cool on bare feet. The house had cost Sofia $4.5 million, barely a dent in her accounts.

"Do you want to hit some balls after lunch?" Billy asked.

"Golf or tennis?"

She would do either one. Billy was easy to be with, so she chose to be likewise. She'd never been that way with Clark, but therapy with Dr. Freudenstein had helped her change. He'd been a huge help in her personal life, not to mention writing that nutso letter for $20,000. And then recanting, as planned, so Clark wouldn't have to go to prison.

"Tennis," Billy said. "We oughta work on your backhand."

"After it cools off."

"I gotta tell Manu to water the clay court," Billy said. "He doesn't understand clay needs way more maintenance than a hard court."

"You do that, honey." Her voice sleepy.

They were silent a moment, listening to the soft splash of waves at the shoreline. Billy said, "Got a question for you, sweetie."

"Hmm?"

"Do you ever think of him?"

"Who? My father or my husband?"

"Your husband."

"Not really." Nothing to be gained telling Billy too much. He was sweet but simple. Perfect, really, if you knew his limits. Whereas Clark, bless his dastardly heart, was as twisty as a corkscrew. But he came through for her when it counted. Her mind drifted to the night she nearly died.

***

Sofia regained consciousness, coughing, hacking, sputtering . . . and cursing.

"Ath-hole! Fucking ath-hole!" She sat upright in the bed, put her hand to her neck, and greedily sucked in painful breaths.

"Thank God!" Calvert said. "I thought for a minute you were gone."

"Fuck you, Clark, you maniac!" She tried to swallow but couldn't. Her voice was scratchy, each word a serrated knife. "I want a divorce."

He winced and his eyes blinked. She'd taken him by surprise.

"You're screwing that tennis pro, aren't you?" he said.

She didn't answer. What could she say that he didn't already know?

"Aren't you!" he demanded.

"I've seen a lawyer."

"What! Who?"

"Sam Buchanan."

"That shark! You want to clean me out, is that it?"

She pulled the bedsheet to her neck. "Only half. I figure that's close to ten million."

Clark's dark eyes burned like hot coals, and for a moment, she feared he might strangle her, this time with finality. But his shoulders slumped, and he sat on the edge of the bed, staring into space. After a moment, he said, "Which would you rather have, years of bitter litigation, after which you get half of what's left of my money, or an easy forty million in a few months?"

"You're talking about the trust? It's only six million. The rest is my father's."

"And every cent in your name."

"You want me to steal his money?"

"Money he's hiding from the IRS. God, how I'd love to see you fleece the bastard."

"How?"

"Pepe took a helluva risk putting dirty money in your name. He has no recourse if you swipe it."

She shook her head. "He'd kill me."

"Not if you're already dead. Or if he thinks you are."

Intrigued, she thought about it a moment. "You want me to go missing?"

"I could orchestrate it."

"How? I take a swim off Haulover Beach and not come back? Then what, you pick me up in our boat and drop me off in Bimini? He'll never fall for that."

"It's a little more complicated. Pepe has to believe I killed you."

"Why would he?"

"He's predisposed to think the worst of me. If you go missing, he'll point the finger at me. When I let the cops catch me in lies about your disappearance, when your tennis-pro paramour says you're terrified I'll kill you and dump your body in the Glades, when Sam Buchanan tells investigators you wanted a divorce, when you bribe that quack shrink to start yakking that I'm a psychopath, even I might think I killed you."

He laughed. That little snorting bark of superiority that she usually found so irritating. But now she smiled along with him. Sticking it to her father appealed to them both in equal measure. Clark loved the gamesmanship, moving the pieces on the chessboard. Winning!

Her desires were simpler. She loved the money. She'd recently watched a piece on one of the travel channels about French Polynesia. A faraway paradise called Raiatea Island. Even the name appealed to her.

"What if they prosecute you?" she asked.

"Without a body, unlikely. Anyway, the day you empty the trust account, it will be clear you're very much alive and very, very rich."

They laughed in tandem.

"I think I still love you a little," Sofia said. "I just don't want to be married."

"That's okay, sweetheart. Neither do I."

***

"I almost wish your hubby could see us, that prick," Billy said, wiping sweat off his Ray-Bans with a beach towel.

"Clark's not that bad."

"Jeez, he almost killed you."

"He didn't mean to. The game just got out of hand."

"You're too nice, Sofe. Way too nice."

"You're nice, too, honey. But you're not gonna be tonight."

"Whadaya mean?"

"In bed."

"Yeah?"

"I want you to choke me," Sofia said.

ABOUT THE AUTHOR

The author of twenty-two novels, Paul Levine won the John D. MacDonald fiction award and was nominated for the Edgar, Macavity, International Thriller, Shamus, and James Thurber prizes. A former trial lawyer, he also wrote twenty-one episodes of the CBS military drama *JAG* and cocreated the Supreme Court drama *First Monday* starring James Garner and Joe Mantegna. The critically acclaimed international bestseller *To Speak for the Dead* was his first novel and introduced readers to linebacker turned lawyer Jake Lassiter. He is also the author of the Solomon & Lord series featuring bickering law partners Steve Solomon and Victoria Lord. Levine has also written several stand-alone thrillers, including *Illegal, Ballistic, Impact,* and *Paydirt.* A graduate of Penn State University and the University of Miami Law School, he divides his time between Miami and Santa Barbara, California. For more information, visit Paul Levine's Amazon Author Page at www.amazon.com/Paul-Levine/e/B000APPYKG/.